*New York Times* and *USA Today* bestselling author

# HEIDI MCLAUGHLIN

*Fall in love one book at a time.*

FIGHTING FOR OUR FOREVER
HEIDI MCLAUGHLIN
© 2018

COVER DESIGN: Okay Creations.
EDITING: My Brothers Editor
Ultra Editing Co.
Traci Blackwood
Models: Blake Sevani | Madison Rae
Photography: RPLUSMPHOTO

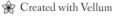 Created with Vellum

# FIGHTING FOR OUR FOREVER

THE BEAUMONT SERIES - NEXT GENERATION

## JAMIE

I don't know how many times I've wiped the bar down, scrubbed water stains that I know won't come off, restocked the already stocked bottles of beer, washed, dried and polished pint glasses, and watched the minute hand on the clock move painfully slowly. This is what a night at Bailey's Bar and Grill looks like when there's a huge concert happening in the big city; Bailey, North Carolina becomes a ghost town. Its population of seven hundred dispersed into caravans of buses, cars, and trucks, traveling south into Wilmington for a night of debauchery. Okay, maybe not a full night of corruption, but definitely a little wickedness. When we small town folks get out in the wild, we let our hair down. Sometimes a little too much. Sure as shit, a few of my friends will be arrested tonight, likely for public drunkenness or trying to start a fight because someone looked at them wrong. Not me though, this is one concert I was okay with missing.

The door opens with a loud bang taking my attention away from the slow-moving clock. My part-time boyfriend, Logan, is standing there with his hand on the door. He's not supposed to be here. He was roped into going to the afore-mentioned concert with my two best friends, Dhara and Fletcher, but here he is looking pissed and with a quick tilt of my head, I see that it's raining. However, that doesn't explain why he's here. He takes two steps in before Dhara and Fletcher come storming past him.

"Shouldn't you be at the concert?" I ask the three of them as they sit at the bar. Each of them sighs dramatically, except Dhara. She takes everything to the extreme and puts her head down on the bar top.

"*Someone* forgot the tickets," Logan says as I slide a pint of his favorite ale toward him. Dhara cries, Logan shakes his head and Fletcher mumbles something about how he's waited years for this concert.

"Well, I'm sorry I made a mistake," Dhara says through sobs. She's now staring at Fletch, who's refusing to look at her.

"Hey, I thought they were in your purse? You've been carrying them around for months."

She looks at me. Her mascara has smeared onto her cheeks, her eyes are bloodshot, and her nose looks like Rudolph's. "They are, but I swapped purses before we left and forgot to pull them out of the inside pocket."

"Oh." I know my mouth forms into a little O. I've been told I do this often when I don't agree with what someone has said or have nothing concrete to add to the conversation. I glance at the guys. Fletcher's clearly pissed while Logan is staring at his empty glass.

"Oh? That's all you have to say to her?" Fletcher barks out. "For months we've been waiting –"

"You don't think I know that, Fletch? I've been waiting to see Liam Page for years. Years! And this was my one chance. The one and only time 4225 West comes to Wilmington and I forgot the tickets. How do you think I feel? I am in love with that rock God!"

Fletcher rolls his eyes. Dhara's right, she's been in love with Liam Page since forever. The sad fact is, she still has posters of him up on her bedroom walls, which probably explains why she doesn't have a steady boyfriend. Although, I shouldn't criticize. Even though Logan and I have been seeing each other for about a year or so, it's an every other weekend kind of thing. He wants to get serious. I don't. He wants to be a father figure to my daughter. I'm afraid he's going to run. The last person I was in love with ran. He ran so damn fast and far that I could barely catch him when I had to. So yeah, I'm okay with an every other weekend arrangement.

"Look, mistakes happen. There will be another show." All three of them look at me and suddenly I feel about two feet tall. Clearly, this wasn't the right thing to say.

"Do you know how much those tickets cost me?" Dhara asks. I nod because we've had many conversations about it.

"Do you know what it's like to drive hours, listening to every song from this band, to stand in line for a couple more hours in the pouring rain, only to get to the front and have her..." Logan points directly at Dhara, who starts crying again, "...rummage frantically through her purse? She could've done that at any time while we were standing there, on the drive over or when I asked her if she had the tickets. There was time to go back, but no, she was *so* confident that she had them — adamant, really — and told me to not worry."

"Eat a Snickers man, she made a mistake," Fletch says, coming to Dhara's rescue. I know he's pissed, but I also know that he's in love with her and has been since high school. She doesn't see it. He's her best friend. Her go to

3

when life is... well, *anything*: Happy or sad, she tells him everything, and he listens, never passing judgement. Sometimes I feel sorry for him, but he won't tell her how he feels. He's afraid to ruin what they have.

"I did, and I'm sorry. No one wanted to see them more than I did. I'll make it up to you, Logan." When the tickets went on sale, she automatically bought three. Normally, I would've gone but the opening act... I'm not a fan. I waited until the last minute before I told her I couldn't go and begged Logan to take the extra ticket to the sold-out show.

Logan shakes his head and sighs. I pull the tap after placing a clean pint glass on the tray and hand him another beer. He'll stay with me tonight because my daughter, Evelyn, is with my parents. Logan and Evelyn know each other, and we do what's considered "family things" together. When we're out, people refer to him as her father and he doesn't bat an eyelash. I'm the one who will lay awake at night, running scenarios through my head, plotting out how Logan is going to leave one day.

Honestly, I'm not sure how or why he puts up with me. I'm honest with him about my past... to a point. He knows I was hurt, and deeply. He doesn't know by whom, yet often suspects it's Evelyn's father. I've never had the courage to correct Logan or tell him about my past. Those are days I want to keep buried forever.

After an hour, the activity in the bar starts to pick up. Normally, we have a band playing. We alternate between country and rock, giving everyone something to listen to. Tonight though, it's quiet and when the jukebox isn't playing, there's a lull. You can hear people talking, telling their friends about their day or as is the case tonight, complaining about missing the concert.

"I can't believe our seats are empty right now," Dhara

sighs. I finally gave her and Fletcher something to drink and ordered them up some food. The three of them seem content to sit at the bar while I work. At least they aren't trying to kill each other, and for the most part, Dhara's tears have stopped.

That is until her favorite song comes on and her tears start flowing again. She's on the dance floor, swaying. People are watching, some are pointing. My best friend is having a colossal meltdown over a missed concert. Fletcher finally goes to her, bringing her back to the bar.

"Dhara, it's only a concert. There will be others," I say to her.

"But, I'm in love with the lead singer."

"Dhara, singers are just..." I stop myself from finishing my statement. It's pointless to remind her because her head is in the clouds right now. In a few days, after reality is done slapping her in the face, she'll realize how over dramatic she was during this whole thing and hopefully learn a lesson. What that lesson is, I'm not sure. But knowing her, she'll find a way to turn this into something positive.

"Singers are what?" Logan asks.

"Nothing," I say quickly.

Fletcher leans forward so he can see down the bar. "Jamie prefers drummers," he says, winking at me. It takes everything in me to not pummel his face into the wooden top. He's an ass.

"Is that so?"

"Yep, something about them banging harder."

My hand comes to my face just as my eyes close. Of all the things to say, he has to be crass. I finally look at him and tell him to shut the fuck up before I go to the other end of the bar and help some new customers. I stay down there as long as possible. I'm far too angry to deal with Fletcher and know Logan will have something to say. He'll want to know more, ask if he should take drum lessons or pretend to play imaginary drums with a knife and fork all because of Fletcher's big stupid mouth.

When two a.m. rolls around, I breathe a sigh of relief. The cook out back turns the music up loud just as I lock the door to the bar. Fletch is taking Dhara home and will probably end up crashing on her couch just in case she needs him in the middle of the night, and Logan is waiting for me in the parking lot. If he didn't live so far away, I'd tell him to go home, that it's been a long night and I just want to sleep. However, he would be hurt and that's the last thing I want to do.

Thankfully, the small crowd means that clean-up is easy. I kept the bar fairly stocked through the night and made sure my dirty glasses didn't stack up. With the bottles taken to recycle, the floor mopped, the only thing left to do is turn out the lights. I tell the guys out back that I'm leaving, and one offers to walk me out. I decline, knowing Logan is waiting.

Outside, he's leaning against his car with his eyes held steady on the bar. He makes me feel safe, secure. I know that when I'm with him, his training as a Marine is never far from his mind. Six months ago, he was injured, hurt in a training accident. It's been nice having him around more, but that'll end when he returns to active duty.

He stands tall when I approach. He's just over six feet with dirty blond hair and green eyes. Even though he's no longer required to, he keeps his hair short. Logan goes to the passenger side of his car and opens the door for me. He waits until I'm situated before closing it and walking to the other side.

"I found a playlist that you might like." He presses his

phone a few times and a cacophony of drummers beat through the speakers. Fletcher will die tomorrow. I will torture the shit out of him, pulling each and every finger nail off with pliers. He shouldn't have said anything, and I don't have the heart to tell Logan that I don't want to listen.

Instead, I find myself tapping along and remembering a time when I used to sit on a milk crate, watching my friend's garage band. The drummer was... well he was trouble. The kind of trouble that you never forget. The kind that you want... you *crave*... despite your mama's warnings against it. I found that kind of trouble before. That was the only time I had ever been truly in love and vowed to never love again. The pain far outweighed any happiness and I definitely learned my lesson. It's a hard pill to swallow knowing you'll always be a second or third priority in their lives, and that's if you're lucky. The drums always come first, followed closely by the band. You're technically just background noise, offering undying support and a place for them to lay their head at night. Nothing more.

And always so much less.

AJAY

There needs to be a handbook on how to cope with tour life. Something to guide starving artists on the ins and outs of road survival and how to deal with the lack of home cooked meals, decent showers, and a good-night's sleep, which are a few of my gripes. Not to mention a shortage of clean clothes. I miss the comforts of my lonely apartment. The ability to sleep, do my laundry whenever I please, go to the bathroom without hearing my friends talk about why it's taking me so long, making something that isn't Ramen noodles or filled with grease are high on my priority list. Not that I'm any kind of an actual chef, but I do like to take care of myself. For the most part, my place is quiet with the exception of when my neighbors have a party, but I'll take that over the big rigs traveling down the highway going fifteen to twenty over the speed limit, shaking the bus as they go by and blaring their horns in some sort of solidarity to their comrades on the other side of the road. Of course, this is how things are until Sinful Distraction hits it big.

Right now, we're opening for 4[...] never been so grateful in my entire l[...] The rush I get every time I step ont[...] able. The thundering vibration from [...] name, over and over, sends chills dow[...] I pull my drumsticks out, and the w[...] fingers, I'm transported. Nothing else exists except me, my kit, and the people surrounding me. We become one. And for an hour we play our hearts out to a mostly full venue. I wouldn't change anything right now other than the fact that I'd really love to fly on 4225 West's private jet and stay in their fancy hotels instead of living on this damn bus.

For the most part, our stops are somewhat close. After our performance, the tour company makes sure our dressing room is stocked full of food. Often, we're taking anything left over with us because most of the time the food is decent. We relax a bit, eat as much as we can, chat with a few of the roadies and some of the fans who managed to get backstage passes, and watch our biggest supporters perform. The tour is a family affair with 4225 West's family tagging along. Quinn's mother hovers over us, making sure we're not drinking too much, insisting we take our vitamins, and giving death glares to any women who try and get close. Keane's daughter is also on tour with us, however she's traveling with Liam's daughter by plane. I don't know how she got so lucky, but there are times when I want to point out that Harrison's my mentor and I need some quality time with him. Still, when it comes time to leave, my steps are slow, and I feel like a geriatric when I have to climb the steps to the bus.

Maybe it's because the décor never changes. The wood paneling starts to become muted in color, the shine it had

boarded the first time is long gone. The chairs
ll lost their comfort from the constant sitting we do in
m, becoming lumpy and misshapen. Our shower is small,
and the water is often cold. Elle made a schedule for us to
follow but honestly most of us wait until we get to the
venue, hoping we have a chance to sneak into the locker
rooms. Our sleeping quarters aren't much better, although
I've always wanted to sleep on a bunk bed. Now that I have,
I can cross it off my "never want to do this again" bucket list.
Keane is my roommate and for the most part, things are
great. He's quiet, doesn't snore and really keeps to himself. I
know he worries about his daughter, but I'd gladly take her
place if given the chance. That girl is living the life right
now with the Page entourage.

There are a few people standing outside when we exit
the building. This still shocks me, especially considering
who we opened for. Like why wouldn't they be inside experiencing that show instead of waiting for us? Elle tells us to
embrace it, to give the fans what they want, which are
stinky hugs and selfies for their social media. The fans form
two lines on either side of the door. Some have signs, while
others have their phones out likely taking pictures as we
walk toward them. Names are called and declarations of
love are made, something Liam Page warned us about ahead
of time. His motto is to thank them and never return the
sentiment. He said what we feel for them isn't what they're
feeling for us. We are grateful, humbled and in debt to
them, and they see us as a fantasy, someone they long to be
or be with. He says the line needs to be clear from the
beginning.

Oh, and we're never ever to get involved with a fan.
That's something JD Davis pounds into our heads before
every show. According to Liam, JD used to be the worst of

the worst when it came to fan hook-ups, and we're to heed the word of the famous Brit. Not that we could do anything if we wanted. Elle is fierce and no one gets past her. She's like a shark and can sense when someone is "up to no good", as she calls it. So even if we, with the exception of Quinn, wanted to find some adult entertainment while on the road, Elle would slam that door shut so fast it would make our heads spin. She's strict but with good reason. Quinn said once that his dad and the band went through some shit with their former manager, most of it public if I wanted to search through the confines of the internet, and that was the main reason Elle chose the business. He said his sister would make sure nothing ever happened to any of us. Thing is, I believe him.

After posing for a handful of pictures and signing just as many autographs, we're finally on the bus. The door is shut making the outside voices muffled. Hendrix and I kneel on the sofa, looking out the window. We can see the fans, but they can't see us. A few are jumping up and down, trying to get our attention, while others linger in a group, and some walk away knowing we're about to hit the road. The rumble of the engine changes everyone's mood. Dana goes off to the room she shares with Elle. Hendrix watches her like a puppy dog yearning for attention. Keane disappears into our room to video chat with this daughter. Quinn reclines in the chairs and puts his headphones on. He and Elle are used to living on the road. Me, I continue to stare out of the window imagining what the scenery looks like. Are the trees still the greenest I've ever seen them? Is the ocean still as warm as I remember? Are my friends still working on the docks or have they finally left our small town in hopes of pursuing their dreams? That's what I did, and I never looked back. Probably not the wisest decision I ever made but there was nothing left for me. I was broken, shattered. If I hadn't fled, I would probably be in jail right about now.

Still, I watch the darkness drift by as we head down the highway. The bus is quiet, minus the lull from the motor and the faint music I can hear from the driver's radio. The headlights flash on a road sign, telling us which town we're approaching. Instantly, I'm overcome with emotion and dread, fear and longing. My body hurts and I feel like I'm going to be sick. My hometown of Bailey is fifty miles away, much closer than I anticipated on this leg of the tour. I don't want to see the signs as we get closer because I know I'll smash my forehead against the glass hoping to see something that looks familiar, so I get up and head to the bathroom. The small confined space is stifling, the air reeking of floral air freshener. I gag and pull my shirt over my nose but quickly change my mind because I haven't showered yet and definitely do not smell the greatest right now.

When I feel the motor coach stop, relief washes over me. If luck is on my side, we've pulled over for the night and I can shower, and maybe get a decent night's sleep. Even as I open the door and look out the small window, I know we haven't stopped at a campsite, but along the side of the road. I come out of the bathroom to find Elle standing in the middle of our makeshift living room talking to a man in uniform. Something tells me to turn away, to go back into the bathroom or go hide out in my room, but I don't. I step further into the living area and make eye contact with the man who tried to shoot me years ago.

Sheriff Foster, the man who can and will terrify you in your sleep is standing in front of Elle with his eyes trained on me and his hand on his gun. I swallow hard as Elle turns slightly. She has a piece of paper in her hands and she looks... sorry. I'm not sure what her expression means, but it's not one I've seen before.

"And you're sure this matter can't be taken care of with some community service? We're on a time schedule here."

"Ma'am, as I said, this matter must be dealt with immediately," the Sheriff's booming voice echoes through the bus. By now, everyone's awake, and no one is saying anything. Sheriff Foster steps toward me and I lose all ability to think. I'm a grown ass adult and this man scares the shit right out of me.

"Sheriff Foster," I say as kindly as possible. "Missed you at the show tonight. I had tickets set out for you and everything." My voice cracks at the end. He won't find humor in my statement. He won't even crack a smile.

He comes toward me, each step slow and methodical. He's going to kill me and hang my body in the center of town in front of everyone. It's what I deserve especially after what I did, and something tells me that saying "I'm sorry" isn't going to cut it.

"Ajay Ballard, I have a warrant for your arrest." He pulls out his handcuffs and motions for me to turn around. I suppose that this isn't a good time for me to tell him that his daughter and I used them once even though those are the words sitting on the edge of my tongue.

Instead, I'm a complete and utter fool when I ask, "For what?" as snottily as possible.

He chuckles and his round belly jiggles slightly. I try not to laugh but the years haven't been good to his midsection. "Turn around asshole."

"Not until you tell me what you're arresting me for this time."

"This time?" Elle barks out. "Do you have a record that I should know about?"

"No, ma'am."

"He will once Judge Harvey is done with him."

Harvey. Harvey. My mouth drops open as it all comes back to me. My girl, Whiskey, and me, drunk as hell, decided to teepee the judge's house one night. Only I got cold feet and couldn't go through with it. Whiskey did though, and decorated that house like a Christmas tree, eggs included.

"Wasn't me," I tell him, smug as can be.

"Warrant says otherwise." He holds up the piece of paper. I reach for it, but he pulls it away. "Not so fast. Turn around and put your hands on the wall."

"What? No. I didn't do anything wrong."

Wrong choice of words as he moves so fast that I'm pushed against the side of the bus. His forearm is pushing down on my neck and his leg is between my thighs while his weight presses against me. He reads me my rights and tells me I'm under arrest for resisting arrest and for the outstanding warrant.

The cuffs are tighter than they should be, and I have a feeling he's taking perverse pleasure in escorting me off the bus in front of my band. Elle's already on the phone, to whom, I don't know but she doesn't sound happy. If I lose my gig, I'm going to sue Sheriff Foster. Not that he has much money and the last I remember, his house wasn't much, but it'll be mine by the time I'm done with him.

He puts me in the back of the car, making sure I've hit my head a few times while he jostled me in. In the front, he gets on the radio and tells them he's out of service and returning to Prineville with a prisoner.

"I'm not your prisoner. These are trumped up charges."

Foster ignores me and continues to talk. "Roger that. I'm in route with one." He turns on his lights and sirens, all for show, and starts down the road. The bus is following, but unable to keep up. Hopefully Elle knows where she's going because I don't have a cell phone and I don't have her number memorized. In fact, I don't have anyone to call.

Truth is, I don't really have anyone who cares.

This isn't how I thought I'd come back to Bailey. Honestly, I never really imagined stepping foot back into town after I left years ago, let alone coming back in handcuffs. Bailey's as small as small gets, at least from what I remember. A few houses, some farmland, a gas station, grocery store, a few restaurants and bars, a bank or two and that's about it. We went to school in the next town over which is where the run-down police station is, and it happens to look exactly the same as the day I bailed. As the door slams shut behind us, a familiar face pops up. The old man smiles, and I shake my head. I'm not surprised to find the same deputy behind the desk as Sheriff Foster pushes me through toward the interview room. Unfortunately, I've been here many times before. Stupid teenage stuff mostly, but being as he's Whiskey's dad, nothing ever happened to me. There were times, though, when the Sheriff read me the riot act, held up his baton and threatened to dismember me and feed my limbs to the wolves if I didn't get my act together. Something tells me he's about to make good on his threat.

"Looks like you have a live one there... or many," Deputy Pate says as he leans to the side. Behind me the door slams shut again and the energy in the small reception area changes. I look over my shoulder at my bandmates. Elle's still on the phone and has decided to stay in the corner to speak to whomever is on the line with her. Hendrix's head is bopping to whatever he's listening to. Quinn looks tired as fuck as he slouches down in an uncomfortable chair, and Dana's standing in front of me with her hands on my cheeks. She's our mother hen, always making sure we are okay. I know she does it because not only are we her family, but also because she wants the band to succeed and not become one of the industry's statistics. The rate of overdoses among our peers is astronomical and something we talk about often, finding other outlets for our energy.

"Only the important one," Foster barks out as he yanks my arm toward him.

"Don't worry, Ajay. Elle's on with our lawyer now. You won't be here long," Dana yells, although it's only for show. We are only a few feet away from her and if I remember correctly, the acoustics in here suck. You can hear everyone talking despite being behind blocks of concrete.

The interview room is nothing like what you see on television. Missing is the two-way mirror and the window letting some natural light in. What there is, though, is a table that looks like it's been through some sort of struggle with gouges of wood missing, teeth marks and the everlasting symbol of eternal love: Two people's initials inside of a heart. Mine and Whiskey's are on the side of Foster's house — at least they were when I left.

Foster takes me to one of the two chairs and parks my ass down on the hard surface. Finally, he uncuffs me. My wrists hurt. There's a red gash where my skin has rubbed raw against the metal. I flex and rub them, praying there won't be any lasting effects from the angle they were in for the past hour or so. It's bad enough that Elle is going to rip me for this little detour, I don't want to think what she's doing to do if I can't play in our next show because my wrists hurt. He pulls the chair out across from me, scraping its aluminum legs against the worn-out linoleum tile. The sound radiates and sends chills down my spine.

We sit across from each other. The smart ass in me wants to smile, ask him how things are going, but I bite my tongue. The last thing I need is for my mouth to write a check my ass can't cash. I don't care that I know the law man sitting across from me, the fact is, he's the law and I need to behave myself. When he came onto the tour bus, I thought he was joking. Even when he put me in the back of his car, I thought he was doing it just to be an asshole. Looking at him now, I know he's serious. But it makes me wonder why. All we did, Whiskey and I, was teepee a house, and it was really more her than me. I just drove the getaway truck.

The door opens and Pate comes in. In one hand, he has a folder and the other is resting on his gun, as if he's trying to scare me. As far as I remember the guy can't shoot worth a lick and is the biggest push over in the county. Whiskey and I used to joke that if we were to get caught being dumb, we wanted Pate to respond, and when he did, she would just bat her eyelashes and he'd let us walk. Too bad he wasn't the one to come on board the bus, but I have no doubt that wasn't ever going to be the plan.

Foster takes the folder and sets it calmly down on the table. "That's all, Pate," he says, looking directly at me. No, that's not all. *Don't leave, Pate*! My silent plea is met with the shutting of the door.

"In case you're wondering, this folder is full of crimes you've committed over the years."

The brown dossier is thick, much thicker than it should be. I was a punk ass kid, but I wasn't a criminal. I never stole anything or did any serious damage, except for the one time a bunch of us played baseball with some mailboxes. We fixed those, though, and no charges were pressed. Oh, and there was a little drag racing incident but that was swept under the rug.

Foster folds his hands and rests them on top of the stack papers. "I've waited a long time to finally haul you in."

"I've been here before," I point out. I can't tell if he appreciates the reminder or not. I probably shouldn't have reminded him but there are times like this when my mouth works faster than the logical side of my brain.

"This time is different. There isn't someone in your corner, crying in my ear to let you go. You know, I never understood what she saw in you."

"Whiskey?" I say her name with a hint of flavor. After I adjust in my seat, I lean toward him a bit. "I could tell ya, but—"

Foster slams his hand down onto the table. "You think I'm joking around with you? You think I'm going to let you get away with what you did?" He stands, pushing the chair out as he does. "You listen good," he says with his hands pressed into the table. "I don't give a rat's ass about your fancy California lawyers or how much money you have in the bank. Your ass is mine." He stalks toward the door, shaking his head.

"You can't keep me here."

He chuckles. "I can, and I will. Your name means nothing around these parts anymore. Judge Harvey is sitting on Monday, he's who you'll see."

"Isn't that a conflict of interest being as you're charging me with decorating his house."

"Is that what you free loving hippies call putting toilet paper all over someone's house?"

"I ain't no hippy," I tell him. "About time you turn off your old cop shows and step into the real world."

He laughs again and shakes his head while mumbling my name. "I'll tell your little girlfriend she can come see you now before I take you to your holding cell for the night."

I should correct him about Elle being my girlfriend, but that all seems so trivial in the big picture. The more pressing matter is the fact that he is putting me in a holding cell. "Sheriff, you can't be serious. Surely, I can come back Monday and see Judge Harvey?"

He looks to the ceiling and I follow his gaze, wondering if the answer to my plight is up there even though I know it's not. "And risk you running? Not a chance, Ballard." Foster walks out, leaving me to my thoughts. Rumors in small towns travel fast making it only a matter of minutes until Whiskey knows I'm here. I can't imagine she'll come and see me, as I probably wouldn't go see her either. Everything we needed to say to each other, we did years ago. She hates me, and I'm okay with that. I left because I needed to find myself. I needed to get a damn job so I could support a wife and any children we were going to have. Being in a small town really prevents growth and lacks opportunity, and I was never going to make it big by playing in random garages for street parties. Being paid in a six-pack or case of beer doesn't equate to putting food on the table.

The door opens again and Elle steps through. Her long hair is piled into a messy bun and she's changed from her sweats into work clothes. She looks pissed. I don't blame her. This stop really puts a wrench in our tour. She pulls the chair out, much slower, and apparently mindful of the awful sound it could make. She sits down and clasps her hands together.

"I've spoken to our attorney; he'll be here in the morning. I've also left a message for my dad. Because this is their tour, it's their call on what will happen."

"What does that mean?"

"A few things really. The band could decide to postpone a few stops while we sort this out."

"Or? I feel like there's a huge 'or' floating in the air."

She sets her hands down on the table. "Or the band could decide to replace you as their opening act."

"But your dad—" She shakes her head and I stop talking.

"This is business, and they've already done us a solid by having the band open up for them. I won't ask my dad or uncles for any favors. It'll be a decision they make with their manager."

I nod because there isn't anything I can say right now.

"Ajay, do you have a record?"

Shaking my head, I meet her gaze. "No. I was a rough kid, did some stupid shit, but I've never been arrested. The Sheriff..." I pause and think about what I'm going to say. "We have a history and I may have broken his daughter's heart."

"It'd probably be better if you had a record. Scorned law enforcement are not our friends."

"Sorry," I mumble. Look at that, I can't even break the law right — or whatever it actually is that I've done.

Elle takes a deep breath. "He won't let you out without seeing a judge and being that it's the middle of the morning on Sunday, you'll have to stay here until Monday. We're going to find a place to sleep or at least park the bus. I'll see

21

about bringing you some food or something after we all get some sleep." She reaches across the table and sets her hand on mine. Her grip is reaffirming, but I'm still scared shitless. Not about spending the night in a cell, but of losing my job. I worked my ass off for it and if something happens, it'll destroy me.

Foster doesn't return. Instead, it's some kid I went to high school with by the name of Eddie Mahon. He squares his shoulder when we make eye contact. "Stand up," he says gruffly. I do as he says, which it seems isn't good enough for him. He kicks my chair away from me and it goes flying into the wall. "Let's go."

I'm surprised he doesn't put me back into cuffs, not that I'd be able to break away from the death grip he has on my arm even if I tried. Out in the hall, things are quiet with the exception of the dispatch radio going off. I'm hoping that Foster wasn't too nasty to Elle, but knowing him, he probably tried to charm her. The old man can't even charm a snake.

The Prineville County jail is nothing more than three holding cells which consists of two cots each and no urinals. Lovely, I get to raise my hand like an elementary student and ask to use the facilities.

Mahon puts me in the middle cell, directly across from an open-spaced office. He pulls the door shut as soon as I'm over the threshold. "Lucky for you, I'll be right over there if you need me."

I don't say anything. I don't even acknowledge him. Sitting down on the cot, I sigh and cover my face with my hands. I can only hope and pray that once all this blows over, Elle doesn't kick me in the nuts and send me packing.

## 4

## JAMIE

*B*y noon on Sunday, Bailey's has a fairly steady crowd — almost everything else in town is closed, not opening until dinner or people realize that going home to cook after church isn't always what they want to do. Sundays are the only time minors are allowed in Bailey's as well, and part of me thinks that the teens beg their parents to come here. I know I used to. The thrill of being in a bar, underage, added an odd bit of excitement to my life. The teen boys seem to enjoy shooting a game of pool or throwing a round of darts while the girls hog the juke box, playing all of their favorite songs and dancing in large groups. It's days like today that are my favorite, mostly because my daughter will come in later with my parents and seeing her can change my outlook instantly.

Dhara, who just walked in, looks worse for the wear. She takes one look at me and plops down into a booth, not her usual spot at the bar. She barely looks at me as I approach the table. "Did you sleep at all last night?" She shakes her head.

"I'm so angry with myself."

"It's just a concert, D. It's not like you were going backstage to meet the band."

"I know, but I can't help the way I feel. Like something's missing."

"It's called food. What can I get you?" I set a drink napkin down on the table and wait for her to tell me what she wants. She has the menu memorized and doesn't need to look it over.

"Steak and cheese, and a Diet Coke. No onions or mushrooms. Extra mayo."

"Chips or fries."

"Fries with a side of mayo."

"Got it. So, you want an order of mayo with a few sides?" I wink at her, but she doesn't find my humor funny, returning my gesture with a scowl, which coming from her red blotchy face is a bit comical. Still, I don't stay and poke the bear. She's liable to become whiney or throw a fit. I love Dhara, but her emotions are all over the place, and I blame Fletcher for that. If the two of them would just get together, do their thing, and get it out of their system or run off and get married, she wouldn't be such a scatterbrain when he's around.

I tend to a few other customers at the bar before I put Dhara's order in. When I notice Fletcher come in, I put his usual order in as well. It's a shot in the dark, but he's so calm about everything I don't think he'll mind. Still, I plan to ask him when I take a Coke over to him. If all else fails, I'll eat his cheeseburger and feel good about it.

"Brought you a Coke," I say, setting the glass down in front of him and doing the same for Dhara. "Also ordered your fave, unless you want something different?"

"Nah, I'm good. Logan around?"

I hear my name called from the bar and glance over my

shoulder to find our short order cook setting a couple of plates under the heat lamp. Focusing back on Fletcher, I answer him. "No, he had to get back to base. Might be able to come down next weekend though."

"Ooh, two weekends in a row. Better watch out, you might get serious," Dhara jokes.

"Hardy har har." I stick my tongue out at her and head back to the bar to pick up my order. By the time I return with Fletcher and Dhara's food, they're deep into a conversation about the concert. Not wanting to keep beating a dead horse, I set their plates down and head to my next table.

Most Sundays I have a hostess or another waitress on staff but with the concert last night, everyone asked for the day off. Being that Bailey's is part of the community, and good help is sometimes hard to find, those who asked, received. Never mind the fact that we could be busy. The cook, table busser and I just roll with it.

The dining area is full when a group of out of towners walk in. They look around and are about to leave when I tell them they can sit at the bar. The group of four look tired, haggard, like they had an incredibly rough night. My guess is that they partied a bit too hard last night at the concert and are slowly making their way back home. Placing menus down in front of each of them, I ask, "Coffee?"

They all barely nod at me, making discernible audible mumbles.

I give them a few minutes to look over the menu after I pour each of them their coffee. A couple of them add cream, while the other two drink it black. "Do you know what you want?"

"What's good?" The lone female of the group asks.

"Just about everything," I tell her. I'm biased though.

"We pride ourselves on good food and heaping quantities." There's nothing worse than walking into a new place, ordering food, and getting a skimpy plate. When I go out to eat, I want food.

While she's thinking things over, I look at the guy who is farthest from me. He looks familiar but I can't remember where I know him from. He orders our plated special of two eggs, hash browns, bacon, and toast. His friend orders hash and eggs. The lady settles on pancakes, and the girl next to her asks for a burger. Odd but not uncommon. The woman slaps him on the arm, and I hear her say, "You're ridiculous," before turning away.

As their order cooks, I cash out people who are ready to leave, refill sodas, coffees, teas and waters and chat for a few minutes. Dhara and Fletcher seem to have given up on the missed concert and are going on about their upcoming week at work. Dhara works at the hospital and Fletcher works for the State as an attorney in Bailey. He's only a year out of law school and thankfully the worst crimes he has to prosecute are petty misdemeanors. I'd be scared if he had to face a murderer because he's too nice and gentle for the ugliness that his job could bring him. We all knew he would return home after he graduated from college. Well, I did. Dhara was certain he would leave for someplace like Raleigh or Charlotte, but I knew better. He's far too in love with her to stay away. He looks at her the same way... well the way someone should look when they're smitten.

"Do you need anything else?" I ask them. Dhara's head is turned, staring toward the bar. I follow her gaze but don't see anything amiss. "D?"

"Jamie, do you know they are?" she whispers.

I look again and slowly shake my head. "Paying customers?"

"Dhara..." Fletcher's voice comes as a warning and now I'm officially curious.

"What's going on?"

Dhara stares at Fletcher who shakes his head slowly. I lean down, my hands grip the end of the table and I look back and forth between my friends. "What the hell is going on?" Her shoulders fall and she finally opens her mouth to speak.

"The people at the bar are the members of Sinful Distraction," she mumbles quietly. First off, I don't believe her. She's sitting in her booth, not making a scene. She's not fixing her hair, her make-up or doing anything else to prepare for a selfie. Second, no... they wouldn't come into my bar.

"D, I know you're upset about the concert, but you really need to get over it. I'm sure the band is on their way to their next stop, doing some meet and greet, or whatever it is bands do these days. Okay? Just stop."

She reaches for my hand, but I pull away. "I have to work." I leave them at the table and head to the back to calm my breathing. Everything about this weekend has been messed up. I don't want to be that friend, the one that tells her friends they can't listen to a certain group or like a certain movie, but right now that's what I want to say because *this* group... I put my hand on my forehead and tell myself to stop thinking about my past. What's done is done. Life happened, I moved on. I worked hard to overcome a troubling time in my life, to make something of myself, and the things Dhara's saying, well it's just a rabbit hole of hell waiting for me that I'm not willing to travel down.

Taking a deep breath, I center myself, and give myself a mental pep talk. *Ignore Dhara and her incessant crap about missing the concert and who may or may not be in the bar right now.* I push open the wooden door and step back out into my reality, a packed establishment where groups of parents are happily conversing while their children are playing amongst themselves. Life is good.

The cook calls my name and I go to the window to pick up the plates of food. Easiest delivery of the day so far as I just have to turn around. I set some condiments onto the bar for the group to use and refill their coffee mugs. One asks for a Sprite and another asks for some ice water. Easy peasy.

And that's how I expect the rest of their encounter to go, that is until I see Dhara approaching. Everything in me wants to think she's coming to see to me, to pay her bill, but deep down I know better. She's a celebrity hound, lives her life for posting pictures of her with famous people. One time, she vacationed in Hollywood and spent her week looking for movie stars. I love her but it's a bit much.

"Dhara," I warn as she gets closer, but her eyes are set on the group at the bar.

Her hand reaches out and she taps one of the men on his shoulder. He's definitely cute, seems a bit shy. He turns toward her. "Are you Quinn James?"

"I am," he says.

"And you're the members of Sinful Distraction, right?" She asks. "Dana, Hendrix and Keane." *Please say no. Please say no, although I shouldn't care, right?*

They all nod, and my heart hits the floor. *He* chose not to come here. *He* chose not to see me. Honestly, it's for the best. I have things to say to him that his friends might not like to hear. I tune out of their conversation as my mind starts running a mile a minute. Too many thoughts are mixing with the pang my heart is feeling. The fact that he's not here should be a blessing.

My eyes are steadily watching the door, and when it

swings open, I hold my breath. This is the longest ten to fifteen seconds of my life, waiting to see who's coming in. I can hear my heart beating in my ears, my palms are sweating, and my eyes are starting to water.

"Jamie," Dhara says next to me. "I'm sorry."

I shake away the cobwebs and look at my best friend. "Are you?" I ask. "Are you really?"

"You needed to know—"

"Know what? That *he's* in town and wouldn't come in?"

She takes a step back. I know my words sting, but so do her actions. "You could've waited until they were leaving to ask them who they were, instead, you just... you don't get it, Dhara. I *didn't* need to know."

I leave her standing there and retreat to the back, and into the alley where I bend over and gasp for air. For years, I haven't thought about the life I had before my daughter came. I haven't thought about high school and everything that happened. I worked hard to erase the bad girl image I had to become a decent member of the community. And while I know it's not Dhara's fault, I'm blaming her. I didn't need to know who those people were at the bar, and I don't need to spend the rest of my day wondering why *he* didn't come in with them.

Except, that's exactly what I'm going to end up doing.

## 5

## AJAY

*B*eing in a band on tour means our sleep pattern is all messed up. It's not odd for us to sit down at four or five in the morning to eat dinner or go to sleep around noon. Once we're off tour, we crash hard for days at a time, hoping to ease back into the normality of everyday life. There was a time when I would stay awake for days, practicing on my kit, trying to hone my craft. However, those days went by the wayside when my big break came, and I started to value sleep. Say what you will but going to bed at nine or ten o'clock at night is good for you... trying to stay awake in a jail cell is *not*.

I'm exhausted, having been kept awake by the blaring television, the constant chatter of the guard talking on the phone, and the noise from the video game that he's playing. And just when I'm about to doze off, Eddie starts talking to me. Talking about shit that is of no consequence to me, my life or this trumped charge that has me sitting in a cell. But he yammers on like he knows I'm trying to get some shut eye, going on and on about Bailey, how the town has changed since I left, how he's married but doesn't have any kids yet, and how the town historian is trying to pin an unsolved murder on some serial killer from the west coast. "Big happenings in Bailey since you left. You're not the only famous one to come out of here ya know," he says, as if the jab he's taking is supposed to hurt. It doesn't. I did what I did to survive... there isn't a single doubt in my mind that if I'd stayed here, I'd be behind bars permanently. I was going nowhere fast. I am thankful, though, that he doesn't bring up Whiskey. As far as I'm concerned, she's off limits to everyone. I may give the Sheriff shit about his daughter, but that's between the two of us and no one else.

"That pretty little thing that visited, she your wife?"

I say nothing.

"She sure seemed to fancy you. Maybe she's a groupie you're trying to con into paying your bail."

"I can pay for my own bail," I say quietly, hoping he can't really hear me over his obnoxious game and the television.

"I bet you can," he replies, making me wish I would've kept my mouth shut. "You and your big, fancy money. My wife follows your group. She doesn't say much about you, though. Not too many people talk about you between Prineville and Bailey."

*Thank God.*

"Although sometimes the boys like to get a bit rowdy when the wives go gaga over one of your music videos and we have to remind them that you're a nobody, that you still piss standing up."

Thankfully he stops talking, giving me a chance to close my eyes. I have no idea what time it is, except that it's morning so the sun's coming up, and I'll finally see the judge today. My internal clock is all messed up. I know I arrived early Sunday morning and have been served three meals but haven't had a guard change. Good old Eddie here has been on since he slid the door shut on me, which sucks for him.

"You still piss standing up, right pretty boy? Or are you all 'sissified' from living in California?"

Do I answer or ignore?

I ignore because nothing good comes from answering men who are determined to be pricks. He's macho and thinks because he wears a uniform, he can act like this, and I'm going to let him. The sound of something hitting the bars of my cell causes me to lift my head. Eddie's pacing back and forth in front, dragging his baton along the metal.

"It seems that you've lost your manners since you left Bailey."

"Nope, just gained a bunch of sense." I cross my arms and lay my head on them.

"Sense about what, pretty boy?"

"About answering dumb ass questions."

"I'm the law, you have to answer me."

"Not without my lawyer present."

"All right then, wise ass, I'm a fan. If you don't answer, I'll have my wife post it all over her *Facespace*."

*Facebook, you idiot.* "When my manager shows up, you can ask her your questions and if she says so, I'll answer them."

"She? What do women know about music?"

*A lot more than you think.* I sigh. "Eddie, it's like you've never left the area. Women are more than capable to manage bands, write and produce music, direct movies, run Fortune 500 companies."

"Never heard of that company."

"No, I can't imagine you have." How can someone be so dense as to the world outside of their small town?

The door opens and the Sheriff's voice bellows out my name. "Ballard, your attorney is here. Let's go."

I have never been so thankful in my entire life as I am now to see Sheriff Foster. As much as the man despises me, I'd rather be in his presence than Eddie's. I'm not sure how much more of his stupid I can take.

Foster doesn't handcuff me, and for that I'm also thankful. My wrists are still pretty raw and sore. He leads me by my elbow back into the precinct and into the small interview room. There, Elle and some guy I've never met are sitting at the table, both staring at me. Foster shoves me in and slams the door.

"Did you sleep?" Elle asks.

"I tried, but the guard kept the television blaring. And when he wasn't watching TV, he was playing some game on his phone with the volume turned as high as it could go and talking to himself all night."

The lawyer scribbles something down on his yellow notepad before looking up at me and extending his hand. "Saul Russo, Jr. My father has represented 4225 West for many years and I'm happy to do the same for Sinful Distraction."

"Thanks," I mumble.

"Can you tell me about the night in question, as much as you can remember?" I nod and dive head first into my past and that night in particular. If this were another time in my life, I'd probably take the blame for Whiskey, but right now I have too much to lose. Saul continues to ask questions about growing up in Bailey, my relationship with Sheriff Foster, more questions about Whiskey, and about the night I just spent in jail. When he's finished, Elle hands me a garment bag and tells me that my suit is in there — one that

I didn't know I owned — along with the toiletries I need to clean up.

When Foster returns, he leads me to the bathroom and tells me not to even think about trying to escape through the window or he'll make sure my pretty little girlfriend pays. I don't correct him. It's better that he thinks Elle's my girlfriend because then at least he won't think about Whiskey and me together. It's best that he thinks I've moved on.

The suit Elle brought for me fits like a glove. Elle is like the Jack of all trades. There isn't anything she can't do and if she happens upon an issue out of her control, she has a back pocket full of resources. She was meant to be in show business. After Sinful Distraction first came on the scene, she and Quinn were accused of using their fathers' connections to garner some attention for us when in fact, Elle had done all the legwork. 4225 West did help but not in the sense the media portrayed. Our music is good, great even. I may be biased but I know how hard we work, how much time Dana and Quinn put into the songs, and their efforts shouldn't be discounted as favors from Harrison James.

Foster pounds on the door, yelling that my time is up. I tug my white dress shirt down a bit, closer to my wrist, to hide the tattoos I have. I need to make the best first impression, even though the cards are already stacked against me. If Judge Harvey can see that I'm not the same person I was when I was seventeen, maybe he'll throw this whole thing out. As much as I want to remain positive, I have a feeling that whatever the judge can throw at me, he will. Saul Jr. is about to earn his money.

As soon as I open the door, Foster is at attention. He motions for me to step in front of him. "I'm not going to cuff you."

"I appreciate that."

Instead, he grabs a hold of my bicep and squeezes it as hard as he can. After Harrison took me under his wing, one of the pieces of advice he gave me was to stay strong and healthy. He introduced me to his brother-in-law Xander, who put together a workout regimen for me and the band. With being on tour, it's hard to get a good workout in, but we always try. Elle has made sure the bus has a few weights, mostly five and ten pound dumbbells, ankle weights, and yoga mats to help us out.

The sun is bright, and the air is warm. I tilt my face toward the sky, close my eyes and breathe in deeply. "After today, this will be your last time seeing the sun for a while."

Shaking my head, I turn and look over my shoulder at Foster. "At best, I'll get a night, maybe a couple in jail, even though I didn't do anything wrong."

Foster laughs. "We have a hungry new State attorney who's trying to send a message to all you punks. You're looking at a year minimum," he says without a hint of laughter. I know him well enough to know he's serious. He believes I'm going to get a year in the clink. I wasn't scared after meeting with my lawyer, but I am now.

The ride over to the courthouse takes a whole three minutes. It took longer to park than it did to get here... we probably would've saved on emissions had we just walked. That's not Foster's style though. He loves the fanfare, the pomp and circumstance of people stopping and staring. I'm willing to bet the guy would love to bellow out, "dead man walking" if given half the chance. Not in Prineville or Bailey though. These are the two dullest towns in America.

Inside the courtroom, Saul is at the table waiting for me. He smiles and holds the swinging door open so I can pass through. Foster stands off to the side, hands clasped in front of him, and the court reporter is setting up her odd little machine. The door opens behind me, but I turn around to take a look at this legal eagle that is hell bent on ruining my life. Instead, I wait until he or she comes into view. Once he does, I study him hard as he puts his briefcase down and memories flood my mind. The last time I saw this kid, he was a pimply, lanky, clinger who followed Whiskey and I everywhere because of her best friend, Dhara. We weren't friends then. In fact, I couldn't stand him.

What does regret feel like? That's what I'm asking myself right now because I'm sure as shit scared of what's about to happen. The breakfast I didn't eat is threatening to come up as Judge Harvey enters the courtroom. The bailiff tells us what to do: Stand, sit, turn your head and cough as I squeeze the life out of your nuts. Okay, maybe not that dramatic, but that's how I feel right now.

"Mr. Oakes, the floor is yours."

He stands, scooting the chair back with his legs as he does, buttoning his jacket and stepping out from behind the table. "Your Honor, Mr. Ballard was picked up early Sunday morning for an outstanding warrant for trespassing and vandalism, issued by yourself on November the thirtieth, two-thousand-ten. Sheriff Foster apprehended the suspect as the vehicle he was traveling in crossed the county border. Mr. Ballard resisted arrest, although only temporary."

"Mr. Ballard, how do you plead?"

I stand and face the man of the house Whiskey teepeed. "Not guilty."

He scoffs. "Mr. Ballard, are you sure that's the plea you want to enter?"

This time Saul stands and clears his throat. "Your Honor, with all due respect, my client's plea is what it is and should not be questioned."

Judge Harvey points his gavel at Saul; his eyes are menacing, and I feel my life starting to slip away. "Mr. Oakes, what's the State's request?"

"Remand, Your Honor. Mr. Ballard has proven that he's a flight risk."

"I agree," Harvey says, sighing as if he's sad for me when this is nothing but a joke.

"Your Honor, my client was not aware of the outstanding warrant. He has been a pillar of the community where he lives, volunteering his time at the local high school, teaching music. Keeping him locked up over a misdemeanor is unethical, and there isn't a previous case tried in the United States that will support a decision of this nature."

"I will decide how things go in my county, Mr. Russo."

"Judge, can you please tell me when the incident occurred?" Russo asks. He looks pissed.

Harvey looks at Fletcher, who is flipping pages back and forth in his book. "Mr. Oakes?"

"Um... the incident occurred in July of the same year."

"Your Honor, according to my records, Mr. Ballard was in Nashville, Tennessee when this warrant was issued, and therefore had no knowledge of its existence. I'd also like to add that if the incident he's being charged with took place in July, charges should've been brought forth immediately. This is a small town and from what I understand, your house was and continues to be an easy target, and to this date, you have not brought charges against any of the other unruly teenagers." Saul pauses and stares down the judge. "I request my client be released, without bond, and that the charges be dropped."

"Mr. Oakes?"

"The States position has not changed."

"And neither has mine. We'll move this to trial. However, Mr. Ballard you are free, but you cannot leave the county. You will surrender your passport with the clerk on your way out." He slams down his gavel while Saul's yelling at him, citing different laws. His words are falling on deaf ears as Harvey disappears behind the door.

"Small town bullshit," Saul says to Fletcher who is doing his best to ignore him.

I turn to Elle, who has been sitting behind me. She doesn't look happy. In fact, she's downright pissed.

"I'm sorry," I tell her, but she doesn't respond.

## 6

# JAIME

$\mathcal{E}$velyn sits down in front of me, and hands me her brush. "I'd like a ponytail with a braid." She smiles a toothless smile at me through the mirror. Last week she lost her first tooth and has told the entire town about the tooth fairy coming to see her, but only after she cleaned her room. I may have gone on about how even fairies need to land in clean spaces, so they don't step on baby dolls or Legos. While Legos can be fun, in the middle of the night when your child is crying and you need to get to them, stepping on one unleashes a string of curse words no one should ever hear.

"What kind?" I ask her. "Do you want me to braid your ponytail or do you want me to French braid your hair half way?"

She places her finger on her temple, tapping her face. This is her thinking face. I wish I could say she learned it from me, but I copy her now. "I think two braids that start here," she points to the spot on her scalp, "and two ponies here." She finishes by touching the back of her neck.

"You got it, princess." Evelyn is my one constant, my

reason for turning my life around. When I found out I was pregnant with her, my life was circling the drain. The moment I peed on that stupid little stick, I was torn. I wanted the little bean growing inside of me, but I also couldn't take care of myself.

"Mommy, where did you learn to braid?"

"Mommies know everything," I tell her. Someday, when she's older, I'll introduce her to the world of YouTube. I swear I could kiss every single YouTuber and their DIY videos out there. They have saved me a million times over, especially when she comes home with notes from her teacher that it's wacky hair week and the designs should be as crazy as the child wants. My child and her imagination always exceed my abilities.

"And what about Daddies?"

My hand slips a bit when she says the D word. "Daddies know a lot too."

"What does my daddy know?"

"Hmm, let's see..." I pause and step back to make sure her braid is even with the first one I did before securing her hair with a rubber band. "Daddies know almost everything Mommies do."

Evelyn sighs. "I wonder what my daddy knows."

*Me too, kiddo. Me too.*

I lean down and kiss the top of her head. We make eye contact through the mirror and both of us grin, although she can't see my smile, my eyes light up just the same. "I love you, baby girl."

"Love you too, Mommy." She gets down from my stool and runs out of my room. From down the hall she yells, "Do you think I could drive today? I've been working on my skills with Grandpa."

Sitting on the edge of my bed, I hang my head. My dad

is the worst, in the best way. When I told him I was pregnant, I thought for sure he was going to launch a State by
State manhunt rather than respecting my wishes that her
father be left alone. My dad stepped up and took on a
fatherly roll with Evelyn, and it's only been as of late that
she talks about her father, thanks to kindergarten.

"So, can I?"

My little priss is standing in my doorway, with her backpack on and her hand on her hip. I shake my head.

"Why not? Grandpa says I'm good to go."

"Maybe in his field, with him helping, but you're not
driving my car."

"When?" she asks.

"When you're sixteen and have passed Driver's Ed
class."

Evelyn throws her hands up and stalks down the hall. I
want to laugh because I love her antics. I love how dramatic
and expressive she is. When she's out of sight, I cover my
mouth and try to stifle the giggles. She makes my world
complete, bringing joy when I'm upset, and always knowing
what to say to change my day around.

On the way to school, she sings along to the radio. I
know I should sensor what she hears, but I don't. If that
makes me a bad Mom, so be it. I'd rather let her listen and
discuss with her what things mean than hide behind some
veiled curtain. From the day she was born, I vowed to be as
honest as I can with her, and when she asks where her
father is, I tell her the truth... I don't know.

During the week, I work days at the bar, working
around Evelyn's school schedule. The flexibility is nice
because when the opportunity arises it affords me the time
to be a room mother. I know there will be a day when she
doesn't want me there handing out snacks and helping with

school parties. For now, I'm going to soak it up while maintaining that cool Mom edge.

By the time I run my banking errands, it's shortly after ten when I pull into the parking lot. Another hour and the bar will open, serving lunch before switching over for dinner at five. That's when I'll pass the reins to the evening staff and head home to cook dinner. Thankfully, my mom is retired and picks Evelyn up from school and gets her started on her homework. My parents have been lifesavers when it comes to kicking ass as a single parent. If it weren't for them, I don't know how I'd survive.

After I unlock the door, I flick the lights on and pull the chairs off the tables. It's a bit backwards, but so is life. The line cook has been here for two hours already, preparing food and making sure the grills are heated to the right temperature. I used to come in at nine, but it didn't make much sense. If the night crew does their job, opening is a breeze.

The other waitress on today is Mary. She'll take most of the dining room, leaving me to handle the bar and a couple of the tables nearby. She's a college student working to pay her way through night school, it's the least I can do for her. For the most part, the lunch crowd is steady. We have a lot of regulars, who don't always venture far from their normal eating habits. A couple of years ago, we did a huge social media push to put Bailey's Bar and Grill on the map, hoping to increase tourism business. Even got the State to add us to the signs along the highway so people knew where to find us. I think, for the most part, it's paid off, but we can't be sure unless we ask each new person where they're from or how they heard of us.

"I just had a total hottie sit down at seven, but I have to pee and fix my hair. Can you get his drink order?" Mary asks. She's a good waitress and hates to keep people waiting, especially guys. She tells me that she's waiting for Mr. Right and swears she'll meet him here. I don't believe in that hokie crap, at least not anymore.

As I approach the table, the guy in a dark suit is staring down at the table. From the slump of his shoulders, he looks dejected. "Your wait..." my words fall short as a familiar pair of rich brown eyes look at me. My heart is on the floor. My stomach bobs up and down in my throat. I can't swallow, can't think, can't see clearly because if I could, my mind would comprehend who's in front of me. My mouth opens to say something, anything, but words fail.

*The bar is packed. People are standing shoulder to shoulder trying to dance, while I struggle to weave in and out of them in an attempt to get to the stage. This is my last night in Nashville, my last shot at trying to find Ajay.*

*I finally find an opening and shoot through the gap. The stage is within view, but I can't see who's drumming. I pray that it isn't him just as much as I hope it is. He swore he'd be gone weeks, not months. I want him to come home. It's time for him to come home and be the husband he promised he would be. It takes a lot of shoving, a bit of feet stepping, but I'm at the stage. From the side it doesn't look like Ajay. For one, he has a tattoo on his arm and the Ajay I know and love would never ink his body like this.*

*When the band finishes, the singer tells the crowd everyone's name. Ajay Ballard on drums. It's loud in here, but I'm sure that's what he said. I don't hesitate and step onto the platform, heading right toward him. I'm within arm's reach when someone grabs me and tells me that I have to leave.*

*"Ajay," I yell as loud as I can, but he doesn't hear me. I scream his name as I thrash against the man who is holding me back. "Let me go, he's my husband!"*

"That's what they all say, sweetheart."

Finally, he looks in my direction and his face pales, but he doesn't move to help me or tell this goon that I'm his wife. "Ajay!" I call his name again and that seems to spur him into action. He comes forward and tells the bouncer that I'm with him. He finally lets go, but by the look on Ajay's face, he doesn't look happy.

"What are you doing here, Whiskey?"

I feel my eyes bug out at his question. "Um, I'm sorry that I came all this way to track down my husband."

Ajay places his hand on my waist and directs me toward a dark hallway, through a door, down another hallway and finally outside to an alley.

"What's going on?" I ask him.

He steps away and puts his hands into his pockets. His head shakes slowly, back and forth. "Jamie..." The tone in his voice tells me all I need to know. My marriage is over.

I reach into my bag, now thankful that my father forced me to see an attorney. I refused to believe Ajay would do this to me, to us. Not with our history. Not after we... not ever. I hand the papers to him. "Sign these."

"What are they?"

"Divorce papers."

He looks at me and doesn't say anything as he pulls a pen out of his back pocket. He scribbles his name on the three marked pages and hands them back to me without a single word. I wait for him to say something, but he doesn't. He stares at the ground for the longest time before pushes off the wall and kisses me on the cheek. "This is for the best, Whiskey girl. I love you," he says as he leaves me standing in the alley. The only noise I can make out is the slamming of the door behind me.

Someone brushes against me, muttering that they're

sorry. I look for the voice to find a beautiful brunette now sitting across the table. Ajay immediately turns his attention toward her, and a small smile plays on his lips. I realize I can stand here and think about how much I hate him, or I can do my job.

"What can I get you to drink?" I ask in a sugary sweet, fake as fuck voice.

"Whiskey," he says.

"You're not drinking," his babe of a girlfriend or wife says.

Ajay shakes his head. "That's her name," he points at me, but I scoff.

"Sorry, my name's Jamie. I'll send your waitress over in a minute to get your order."

It's been years, far too many to count, since I've heard him call me by my nickname, a name he gave me to tease me because my parents named me Jameson, after my dad. There were times when I longed to hear him say my name, desperate times when I would drive to Nashville on a bender hoping to find him, just to hear his voice say my name the way he used to when we were together. It took years of therapy to get over my obsession with him, and now here he is, in my bar calling me that name once again.

I tell Mary that her table wasn't ready and head to the back to call Dhara. She picks up on the first ring and asks me what's wrong and whether Evelyn is okay. "He's here, D."

"Who?"

"Who? Who, really? Ajay, that's who! And he brought his wife or girlfriend in. Why would he do that?"

She jostles her phone and clears her throat. "Sweetie, listen. Fletcher called me this morning. Your father arrested Ajay early Sunday morning on an outstanding warrant.

That's why his band was in yesterday. Fletcher is the prose-cuting attorney on this, and Harvey is trying to throw the book at Ajay."

My mouth goes dry. "Arrested for what?"

"For some prank on Harvey's house."

I end the call and press my dad's name on my phone. My call goes to voicemail. "Dad, next time you arrest my ex-husband, maybe you want to give me a heads up so I'm a little better prepared to deal with the sight of him as he's sitting in my damn bar!" I press end again and lean my head against the wall. That's when the tears start flowing... tears that I haven't cried in a long-time stream down my face in frustration, longing and pure heartache.

## 7

## AJAY

Of all my dumb luck I would pick the one place where Whiskey works. Not that I had many options to choose from but still, why did I have to run into her here? Why not the park or the bank or when I'm walking down the street and she's walking toward me looking like she doesn't have a care in the world? Why did I have to see her at all? Why couldn't she be someplace else? Why couldn't I? The pain, regret, confusion, anger, and the need to fucking pull her in my arms and tell her how sorry I am for what I did is overwhelming. And she's standing here, watching me like I'm supposed to say something profound and I've got nothing. I can't even get the words "hi" or "hello" to go from my brain to my lips. I only want to say her name and when I move my mouth to form the letters, I'm reminded of what she feels like when she's under me, how much passion she has and how she used to make love to me with every part of her being. Then I'm back to the beginning, trying to say "hi" because that seems like the logical thing to say.

Whiskey jerks her head up as Elle steps by her and

places a black duffel bag on the table which I slide onto my seat. My clothes. Elle doesn't have to tell me I'm not leaving with her; I know I can't, but having the proof in front of my face really hurts. I don't understand why Foster is being like this. I mean I *do*... it's revenge... but *come on*. He's going to ruin my career. I glance at Elle and simultaneously want to strangle her for showing up at the wrong time and hug her for making this incredibly awkward moment less uncomfortable.

"What can I get you to drink?" Whiskey's voice lacks the confidence I know she has. Me being here is upsetting her, that much I can tell by the way her lips pucker. I know she's biting the inside of her cheek right now. What I don't know is whether she's about to scream or cry. I want to get up and leave, to find some motel on the edge of town and drink myself into a stupor so I can forget having seen her and put all of today behind me.

"Whiskey," her name finally comes tumbling out of my mouth.

"You're not drinking," Elle snaps.

I shake my head and point to the one time love of my life. "That's her name."

"Sorry, my name's Jamie. I'll send your waitress over in a minute to get your order." Whiskey storms off, giving me an opportunity to watch her until she disappears behind a door. She looks the same, except for the time lapse that comes with aging. Her breasts are fuller, and she has curves. Curves I've never seen on her. My Whiskey girl grew up and I wasn't here to see her transform from a teenager into a fully-fledged, smoking hot woman.

"Who names their daughter Whiskey?" Elle asks as she looks at the menu.

"Her name's actually Jameson, named after her dad. Sheriff Jameson Foster."

Elle drops her menu and slowly turns to look over her shoulder and back at me. "That's the Sheriff's daughter?"

I don't say anything.

Elle reaches across the table and smacks me upside my head. I deserve it. "What is wrong with you? Didn't your father ever teach you not to mess around with the Sheriff's daughter?"

I crack half a smile. Aside from everyone in Bailey who knows me, Quinn is the only person I've told about my parents. It's not something I like talking about. The only people who ever made me feel like I belong were the Fosters, and I turned my back on them without another thought. I avoid answering Elle's question. My life story is for another time and any other place.

"Did you ever perform here? I like the ambience." There's a dance floor, currently covered by tables. In the side room, there used to be an arcade and dart machines. Bailey's used to hold some serious dart competitions when I lived here. Makes me wonder if they still do or if things have changed.

"No, I was too young or not good enough. I tried a couple of times, but the guys who played here just shooed me away. Our prom was here though, the house band played. It was quite the party," I laugh. Nothing like having a dry prom in a bar. Good thing for Whiskey and me, I always had the right provisions.

"Small towns, I get it," she says. "Our prom was held in our gym."

"Who'd you go with?"

"Ben. Noah came home and took Peyton. We had a good time." She studies the menu instead of looking at me. I

49

like her boyfriend, Ben. He seems like a good guy and completely in love with Elle, which seems to make her happy.

"What's good here?" she asks.

Shrugging, I pull the menu from the condiment stand and look it over. "It's been a while since I've eaten here."

"I suppose pub food is all the same," she sighs. I'm waiting for her to deliver the blow, to give me the kiss off. I figure this is my last meal for a bit so I might as well enjoy it. When the waitress appears, I'm saddened to see that it's not Whiskey even though I knew it wouldn't be. Honestly, I was hoping she'd come back and poison me, put me out of my misery.

"Hi y'all, I'm Mary and I'll be your waitress. Can I start you off with something to drink?"

"We'll have waters, please," Elle says for the both us. Mary looks from me to her and back to me with a bit of confusion on her face. I know for a fact not many women order for men around these parts, and I have a feeling if things were a bit different Elle wouldn't have taken it upon herself to speak for me either.

"We have a full bar and ten—"

"We're okay, but thanks," Elle says, smiling at Mary. She nods and heads toward the bar. I can't take my eyes off her, even though I'm not really staring at her. I'm waiting for Whiskey to reappear so I can see her, so I can refresh every memory of her. She's always been my weakness. The one person who knew every single secret, never judged me for where I came from, and who could bring me to my knees with one look. One, single solitary look that could reduce me to mush.

"Ex of yours?"

"Wife," I say without thinking.

Elle's eyes are sharp and boring into me when I look to see why she didn't respond.

"You're *married*? Anything else you want to tell me while I'm sitting here? I really don't like surprises, Ajay, and ever since we left Wilmington you've inadvertently dropped a few on all of us."

Mary comes toward us with two glasses of water, setting each one in front of us. "Are you ready to order?"

"I'm going to have the turkey club," Elle requests.

"Fries or chips?"

"Is it possible for me to get a side salad?"

Mary nods. "Of course." She lists the dressings and Elle chooses Italian.

"And for you?" Mary directs her question to me.

"I'll have the same thing." I'm not hungry, at least not anymore. I'm tempted to head to the back and talk to Whiskey. There are words that need to be said, but I know they won't come out so I don't bother. When she asked me what was going on years ago, all I could do was shake my head so she handed me the papers and I signed because I needed her to have a better life. Following a wannabe rock star around from bar to bar was no life for her. It wasn't the life I wanted her to have. She deserved someone better than me.

Elle sighs heavily grabbing my attention. "Wife?"

"Ex, but yeah. High school sweetheart. We were stupid and young. Didn't last."

"Looked like she was pissed off when I sat down."

"I was a jerk to her in the end."

"And she's the person who actually committed the vandalism that you're being charged with?"

I nod.

"Well, this will be easy. I'll have Saul subpoena her and this mess will all be over."

"No," I tell her adamantly.

"What do you mean, no? Ajay, we have a tour to get back to and right now you can't leave the damn county."

"I know and I'm sorry. If I could change—"

"You can. It's simple." Her phone dings, taking the focus off me. While she's answering whatever message she received, I'm back to watching the bar, waiting for any sight of Whiskey. I tell myself that if she comes out, I'm going to talk to her. I'm going to apologize and tell her that I'll be out of town as soon as possible. I'm going to tell her that I didn't mean to interrupt her life and that once I'm gone, she'll never have to see me again.

"Okay, let's talk about the tour. My dad said he would cover for you this week, so we don't have to cancel our shows. I think it's important to the band that they continue to get the exposure from the tour. Our sales are up, and we have four songs in the top one-hundred... bad press in this case isn't going to help us."

Hearing that Harrison James is going to take my place hurts. I think I would be okay with some nobody sitting behind my kit, but Harrison is a different story. I'm embarrassed by this, but I'm appreciative. I don't want the band to suffer because of my misfortune. It's not their fault I made some bad decisions along the way.

She looks at me, but before I can say anything, Mary arrives with our food and two fresh waters. I haven't even touched mine yet, but she takes it away anyway. I pick at my food, and with one taste I know I'm not going to be able to eat. I lean forward and rest my elbows on the table.

"Am I out of the band?"

"What? No. This is a hiccup, Ajay. We've all done

stupid shit in our lives, unfortunately you just pissed off the wrong person and it caught up with you. Had we known, we could've directed the bus around the county to avoid this. This really just seems like a set-up."

I laugh and push the pickle spear around on my plate. "Some people hold grudges, I guess."

"Right, well it is what it is. I'm assuming you'll stay at your parents?"

My parents... I don't even remember what they look like, that's how long it's been. If it wasn't for my grandma, I would've ended up in the system. When she died, the Fosters opened their door for me, as well as a few of my other friends. I couch surfed so I wouldn't wear out my welcome.

"Yeah," I lie. I don't have a place to stay. The motel on the county line is a possibility if it's still there. I can be the guy sitting in the 1970's metal and nylon weaved chair, sipping on a Bud Light while wearing my t-shirt and boxers, making me every motel cliché out there. Maybe I'll go back to jail and hang out with my buddy, Eddie, because that sounds better than any of my other options right now.

Elle continues to eat while answering emails and texts. She takes another call while we sit there, and never once asks why I haven't touched my food. When Mary checks to see if we need anything else, I tell her no, and she's back moments later with our check and a box for my food.

"Need a ride to your parents?"

"It's not far from here, I'll walk." Technically that's not a lie. The house I used to live in is about a block away. Not sure who lives there now, not since my grandma died.

"You gonna need a car?"

I shake my head. "Nah, it's only a few days and I'm sure

I can call Sheriff Foster if I need a ride someplace." I laugh but she scowls.

"Not funny. I'll call you later and see how things are going." She gives me air kisses, drops money on the table for the bill, and leaves.

Nope, it's not, but the alternative of telling her about my life is worse. Elle pays for the check and tells me she'll check in tomorrow. She leaves me sitting in the booth to drown my sorrows in my untouched water and boxed food.

## 8

## JAMIE

*I*t's a rare occasion for me to call out sick. Normally, I can manage with a sniffle, a cough or whatnot. Nothing really keeps me down since I get my flu shot like clockwork... nothing except for the sight of Ajay Ballard. Telling the staff that I'm taking the rest of the day off not only stunned them, but left a few scratching their heads, wondering how they're going to manage without me.

Coping, it's what we do when we hit a bump in the road. We ride the wave and move on, waiting for the next obstacle to step in front of us. We hope that we're better prepared or can handle the challenge. Preparation for whatever life throws your way is key. It's one thing to *know* your ex is back in town and planning on stopping by your work, but it's something else entirely when you're taken by surprise. No preparation means you stumble to find your words. Words that have been festering in your mind for years, things you always thought you'd say to him when you saw him again. I always thought that when Ajay and I crossed paths again, I'd punch him in the face, and maybe even spit on him. Okay, the spitting is a bit much, but in my mind I'm a mafia princess and that seems like the right thing to do to an enemy because that's what Ajay is to me, the enemy. He's from the other side, the wrong side. The side that wasn't raised right or with respect for others. The side that I completely fell in love with the first time I met him. Thinking that and remembering how I used to feel makes me want to go back to Bailey's and punch him in the face for good measure. Just so he knows I mean business.

Would he care? Probably not. Maybe? I don't know. He seemed like he wanted to say something but didn't or couldn't. Was he tongued tied because his perfect girlfriend — or *wife* — was sitting across from him? She was very matter of fact, telling him that he wasn't drinking. I found that comical. She has his balls in a vise and I want to applaud her, but I'd be afraid the real me would show up and I can't have that. The wall I have up is there for a reason and needs to stay there. At least for my own sanity.

My house is quiet as I stand in the dimly lit living room. The voices inside my head are screaming. One telling me to go find Ajay and talk to him, find out why he left the way he did. The other part of me is saying, "Who cares? What's done is done. The past is the past and we should move on." I could be the bigger person, strike up a conversation and ask him how things are. Ask about his new family and whether he has... *No*, I don't want to know. I don't want to him to know that I still care about him. He doesn't deserve my thoughts or the tears that are leaking from my eyes.

Even though Ajay has never been to my house, it feels like he's everywhere. I can see him sitting on my couch with his arm causally draped over the back cushion with his right ankle resting on his other knee. He's wearing a hat and a flannel. His jeans are worn in and he tells me that he needs to buy a couple of new pairs and wants to know if I want to go for a ride. I say "yes", because I've always told him yes, and then Evelyn walks in and Ajay's pissed. No, he's not angry. He's hurt because she's not his and because I was with someone else.

*He* has to be okay with that.

*He* left me.

*He* chose a different life.

I don't even know why I'm thinking about him meeting Evelyn. There's no need and I can't imagine we will ever be in the same spot as him. Besides, once his legal issue is taken care of, I'll never have to see him again.

I finally move from my spot by the door and into my dining room where I sit down with a heavy sigh. Pulling my phone from my pocket, Fletcher's name is the third down my list. I press his number and wait for his secretary to answer. Fletcher's that guy, the one who won't answer his cell phone while at work because he's afraid of giving off a bad impression. I know other lawyers that he works with get irritated with him, but I respect him for sticking to his guns. Nothing worse than being on your personal phone while your work phone is ringing.

"Prineville County."

"Hi, LouAnn it's Jamie.

"Oh honey, you just missed your father. Do you want me to see if I can get him on the radio?"

The benefit, or maybe it's a drawback, of living in a small town is that there's one person who knows everything and for us that's LouAnn Jerrish. She's worked for the county since she graduated high school some eons ago and is the main operator. Chances are, if you call to talk to the police, a district attorney or need some information, you'll get her.

"No, ma'am, I'm calling for Fletcher. Is he free?"

"One moment, sugar." She puts me on hold. Normally, I don't mind the elevator music that plays while I have to wait, but today, it's just prolonging the inevitable.

"Fletcher Oakes," he says into the phone.

"How long did you know?"

He sighs. "Hey, Jamie."

"Don't 'hey, Jamie' me, Fletch. How long?"

He pauses, likely wondering how he's going to get out of this. "Let me call you back." He hangs up and before I can even register frustration about it, my cell phone rings. "Tell me about your day," he says.

"Fletcher, I don't have time for this."

"Well you need to humor me until I'm outside and across the street."

"Oh," I say as I realize what he's doing. "Today shitty. Everything started off great though. Evelyn was happy until I told her she couldn't drive to school." He laughs. He's a damn good uncle to my girl but right now I want to strangle him. "I closed last night so opening was easy until..."

"Until Ajay Ballard walked back into your life?"

"Fletcher, how long?"

"This morning, when I arrived at work. There was a file on my desk and an emergency hearing."

"Why? What did he do?"

"That's just it, Jamie. He didn't do anything that I've ever prosecuted before, but Harvey and your dad are pissed. Harvey has me looking at case law for misdemeanors that allow for jail time. I'm completely stumped here, and your dad, he didn't want him out of jail."

I understand why my dad is angry. I do. My parents endured the hell I put them through after Ajay left. The endless nights of tears, the drinking, and not wanting to live.

They experienced firsthand the heartbreak I suffered. As angry as I am at Ajay, it's not enough to try and ruin his life. "When did my dad arrest him?"

"Early Sunday morning, right after their tour bus crossed into the county."

I close my eyes and repeat in my head that I don't care, that this isn't my problem. "What are you going to do? I don't want him here, Fletch."

He clears his throat. "I think for once you might get your wish. His lawyer is a shark and knows what Harvey is doing is unprecedented. I've never had a judge so knee deep into a case before either. He's called me a half dozen times, and your dad's even been by to see me. Right now, I have to do what my boss says, otherwise I'd never send this to court. It's wasting time and money."

"None of this makes sense." Mostly because Ajay didn't do anything except drive the getaway truck. I did the damage.

"Fletcher, for me, *please* make this all go away."

"I'm trying," he says before telling me he has to go. My friend cares about his friends, sometimes too much. I decide that I'm going to get Evelyn from school and send a text to my mom. I don't want to see my dad right now, not until I've calmed down a bit.

I opt to walk to Evelyn's school. It was my school as well and where I met Ajay. We must've been in the fourth grade or maybe it was the fifth. He was the kid everyone picked on because of his clothes. He rarely had money for lunch and one day I shared with him. When my mom would pack my lunch, I asked for extra. Same when we would go shopping for clothes. After a while she caught on and suggested I invite my friend over for dinner. I did. He didn't have parents and lived with his grandma who was aging and couldn't take care of him. When she died, he would stay at our house or his friends', but he fought to stay out of the system.

We were rough and tumble kids, always coming to my mom with banged up knees. We spent our time riding ATV's, climbing trees, jumping off rocks into the river. If my parents were hoping that Ajay would follow me by getting good grades, they were sadly mistaken. Instead, I turned into him because he didn't have a care in the world and that was exhilarating. Except he did care, he just didn't know how to show people. As we got older, things changed, and our friendship went from best friends to lovers. Suddenly, he wasn't allowed in the house when my parents weren't home, but that didn't stop us one bit.

Evelyn's tiny voice brings me back to the present.

"What are you doing, Mommy?"

"I just want to look at you for a minute," I tell her as I move a few lose strands away from her face. She has deep blue eyes like her father, but the rest of her is me. I don't know how many times I wished she were Ajay's. Even though he left, I would've had a part of him to hold onto, something that would've eventually brought him back. Knowing he was so close, and yet had no intentions of stopping, hurts. I get it, but the pain is still there.

"You're my angel, do you know that?" I ask her.

She nods and reaches for my hand. "Where's Grandma?"

"Well, I got off early and thought what a better way to spend this beautiful afternoon than with my girl."

"That's because you love me the most." She looks at me and smiles.

"That's right, I do. I was thinking we could go to the park, maybe get some ice cream."

Evelyn jumps up and down, never letting go of my hand, telling me that going to the park is a great idea but having ice cream is even better. We walk hand in hand until we get to the park. She tells me that it would be best for us to have ice cream after she's played because she doesn't want a tummy ache. I let her lead the way and she shows me where I can sit, then promptly heads to the slide. Last year, she was afraid of it, fearing that she would fall off the side or slip on a rung as she climbed the ladder. Between Fletcher and Logan, they helped her conquer her fear. A little too much if you ask me, probably because she reminds me how I used to be: A dare devil in a dress.

"Watch me!" she yells from the top when it's her turn. Evelyn grabs the bar and swings herself out before landing on the slide. My heart lurches and I feel sick to my stomach, but she's laughing and so are the other kids. "I'm going to do it again," she says as she runs by.

*Please don't.* "Okay, be careful," I say, wishing I could tell her to bring it down a notch, but I never will.

Someone walks in front of me, shielding me from Evelyn. I have to lean to the side to watch her, while wondering why people are so inconsiderate. Whoever it is, sits next to me, which I don't care about until they start speaking to me.

"Ajay's in town," Jolene Johnson-Johnson says as she sits down next to me. We aren't friends. Never have been. She used to chase after Ajay like she had something to offer him that I wasn't already giving him. She's the only woman I know who would hyphenate her last name even though it technically didn't change when she married Lee Johnson, the guitar player from Ajay's garage band.

"Wow, news travels fast."

"He stopped by to see Lee this afternoon, offered him a

spot in that band of his. Lee turned him down of course, with the baby and all just being born."

"Isn't your son like four?" I look at her in her made up, over exaggerated style. Her hair is curled, twisted, pinned, and sprayed with so much Aqua Net it's like a fly trap, and her leopard print dress is far too much for the town of Bailey to handle. Jolene has always wanted to be this generation's Dolly Parton and even went as far as to stuff her bra until she married Lee and his family's money gave her the rack she always dreamed of.

I scrunch my face at her and turn my attention back to my daughter. I could tell her that I think... no, I *know* she's lying about Ajay asking Lee anything, but it would be a waste of time and effort.

"I suppose Ajay's gonna stick around once he finds out about Evelyn."

"And why would that be, Jolene?"

She shrugs. "Most people talk. Ajay has a right to know his kin."

I sigh as loudly as possible. I stand, grab our things and look at her over my shoulder. "You're about as useless as a screen door on a submarine, Jolene. Y'all need to mind your p's and q's and stay out of my business."

Ruining Evelyn's trip to the park isn't something I'm willing to let happen so I move to the other side of the jungle gym. The sun's in my eyes here, but I'd rather go blind than to have to listen to Jolene Johnson-Johnson lie about things when she has no idea what she's talking about.

## 9

## AJAY

*I* don't know how long I waited outside of Bailey's for Whiskey to come out, hoping she'd follow me outside to yell at me, but she never came. Must've been an hour or two, maybe even three before I decided that I better see if the Inn down the street had any rooms available before I hoofed it to the edge of town. What I should've done was take Elle up on her offer to get me car, but being as I can't leave the county, everything I need is close by. And I wasn't joking about calling Sheriff Foster for a ride. I will because I know it'll piss him off. He won't tell me no either, that much I'm sure of.

Inside the Inn, I'm met with the soft smile of Mrs. Buxley. "I heard you were back in town."

"Yes, ma'am, just for the week. Trying to clear up a matter with Judge Harvey."

She waves off his name. "That old coot needs to retire and make way for the young'uns."

"Wouldn't hear me complaining." If he wasn't a sitting judge, I might not be in this position right now.

"I hear you on the radio every now and again, playing those drums."

I smile shyly at her. "Thank you, Mrs. B. Can you tell me if you have a room available? I'm looking to stay the full week."

"Let me see what I have." She thumbs though what looks like an old, outdated reservation system, pulling cards and matching them to the calendar on her counter. "Looks like room 4a is available. Would that work?"

"Sure will."

She hands me a form to fill out and in turn, I hand her my credit card, hoping she takes plastic. If not, I'll have to call Elle and tell her I need cash. There's no way the bank here is going to give me anything other than the two-hundred daily limit on my debit card.

Mrs. Buxley hands my card back to me and holds the key, letting it dangle from her hand. "You know, this room has a view of Bailey's."

"Okay," I say, unsure where she's going with this.

"Miss Jameson works Monday and Tuesday during the day. She arrives between nine and ten. Friday and Saturday nights, arriving around five."

"And on Sundays?" I ask.

"I don't know, but I know she's not in church."

"Why you are telling me this, Mrs. B?"

She shrugs. "Sometimes true love needs a little push in the right direction."

I take the key and thank her for the information. I don't believe in that true love thing. Love is messy. It hurts. It causes you to bleed and do stupid things like leave your girl behind. The room I'm staying in has one full-size bed, a decent size television and a very small kitchen with a small table by the window. However, the bathroom is a nice size with a soaking tub. The bonus of the room is the balcony.

Pulling the sliding glass door open, I step outside and place my hands on the ledge. Main Street in Bailey is bustling. Cars are parked along both sides of the road and people are out walking. Sure enough, the bar and grill's within eye sight and I can see who's coming and going. With nothing but time on my hands, I can sit here and people watch. I can try to recall faces that I've long forgotten and pull up old stories from the recesses of my mind. I can try to sit here and think about any and everyone except for Whiskey, but I know that won't happen. Not now. Not since I've seen her. It would almost be better to know she wasn't living here or working across the street. And now that I know what days she'll be there, I have every excuse it the world to stay in my room, yet I know that won't happen. I'm going to be there every time she is because I'm sick it the head and madly in love with that woman, although, I'll never tell her. She has a life and doesn't need the likes of me coming in and disrupting things for her.

As much as I want to stand here and watch my former hometown move along with the day, a hot shower sounds more appealing. The duffel bag Elle packed for me has most of my essentials. I strip out of my suit and hang it up, preserving the almost wrinkle free garment for my next court hearing. I'm tempted to take a bath but am eager to get the filth of the jail off me and don't want to wait for the water to fill up. Besides, the last one I had, Whiskey was with me and for some reason it doesn't seem right to take one without her.

She'd be shocked to find out I've only casually dated about three women over the past five years. It took me close to two years to stop having dreams about Whiskey. Dreams that would turn into nightmares, nightmares into panic attacks. I often wondered if she ever figured out that the person calling and hanging up in the middle of the night was me or if her father figured it was some punk kid from town harassing him. I waited for her to answer, to whisper my name in the darkness, but she never did. I don't know what I would've done if she had. *Come back, probably.*

The water pressure is a god send, pounding down on my neck and shoulders. I rotate my head back and forth, loosening up my muscles. They're tight and in traction from the lack of sleep or better yet, quality of bedding. As much as I complain about the tour bus, I'd gladly take a rocky night of swaying on the road over what I just went through.

When the water turns cold, I finally shut it off and step out, wrapping a towel around my waist. The alarm on my phone is going off, reminding me it's time for rehearsal. Not tonight or tomorrow night. Fans of Sinful Distraction are going to find Harrison behind my kit, playing our songs and wowing the crowd while I sit here and have a pity party for myself. If I were a betting man, I'd place a Vegas style wager on how long it takes social media to speculate why I'm not there. Drugs will be the foregone conclusion, followed by exhaustion. It won't take them long to figure out that I've been arrested, if they haven't already. I'm not sure Sheriff Foster or Judge Harvey is smart enough to alert the media, nor do they probably care. Doing so does give the town of Bailey a tourism boost though. People, mostly teens and the younger generation, will come to town looking for me. They won't have to look hard, no one here is going to keep my secret except for maybe Mrs. B. I left all those years ago without a word, except to Whiskey. I'd be back in a few weeks. I was just going to go to Nash-ville and make some money, hopefully enough to get us to

Los Angeles. Boy, did my plan go array as soon as I got there.

*Bar after bar, I look for notices of house bands needing a drummer. Bar after bar, I'm rejected or told to come back later, but later is an indefinite time. These managers have no idea, they expect the house band to be on their game each and every night and don't care for the likes of me hanging out, praying that someone isn't showing up for work tonight.*

*I'm desperate. My time's running out. Two weeks is what I told Whiskey, and I'm down to three days. I need to find work. I need to make something of myself and this is my only skill. Sure, I could become a dishwasher but what kind of life is that for my wife? It's not. She shouldn't have to work to support me, it should be the other way around. What she should've done was tell me no when I asked her to marry me, but the baby... I still believe we were doing the right thing by getting married, even if her parents didn't think so.*

*There are only a few more bars to try before I have no choice but to give up. The place is empty except for one single guy sitting at the bar nursing a drink. The bartender is stocking his shelves, probably preparing for the nightly onslaught of people that plan to come in tonight.*

*"Excuse me, I was wondering if your house band needs a drummer tonight. I know it's a longshot—"*

*"Don't have a house band," he says without looking at me. "The groups that play here are booked by booking managers. You'd have to ask them, but..." he finally turns, looks at me and shakes his head. "Let me guess, small town garage band drummer looking to make it big?"*

*I shake my head slightly. "Just looking for a chance."*

*The man at the bar looks at me. "What can you play?"*

*"Anything," I tell him. "I can read music and have a photographic memory. It's really the only thing I have going*

*for myself right now. And I can play. I'm not great, but I'm good. I can follow lead and I'm a hard worker."*

*The man turns and holds out his hand. "Mitchell Mooney. I manage—"*

*"I've heard of you, Sir. You're one of the most sought-after managers for new bands trying to break into the industry. I'm pleased to meet you."*

*"What's your name, son?*

*"Ajay Ballard. I'm from Bailey, North Carolina."*

*"You got a family or are you free to be at my beck and call?"*

*"Free, Sir. Nothing holding me back."*

*He hands me his card after he writes something on the back. "Meet me here, five thirty. Rehearsal starts at six after I've fed ya."*

*I take it and read it over, committing the address to memory. It's not lost on me that he mentioned food. I haven't had a real meal in weeks, not since Whiskey cooked me some fried chicken. "I'll be there."*

*He nods and turns back toward the bar. I could stand there, but I don't want the man to think I'm a creeper. Instead, I say "thank you" to the bartender for not throwing me out and rush out of there. I don't know what possessed Mr. Mooney to give me his card but there's no way I'm going to let him down.*

My phone rings and Harrison's face stares back at me. I clear my head of the night when everything changed for me and accept his call. "Hello?"

"Ajay, heard you're in some trouble."

"Nothing that shouldn't be taken care by the end of the week."

"Do you need me to come to town, straighten some folks out for you?" Harrison laughs. Since joining Sinful Distraction, he and I have grown closer. So have Quinn and I. They've showed me what it's like to have a family. I always knew I was welcomed at the Foster's, but with the James's, it's different. At Christmas, I had a stocking hung from their mantle, one that Ms. Katelyn had made especially for me. I don't remember having a single Christmas with my parents or even my grandma for that matter.

"Maybe," I tell him because right now I could use a friend. "I'm hoping things blow over."

"If not, I'll be there. Katelyn's worried about you and doesn't like that you're alone so don't be alarmed if my fiery wife shows up in town looking lost."

I have to fight the lump in my throat from overtaking my emotions. "I appreciate that. I'll be on the lookout for her. She won't have a hard time finding me, small town and all that."

"Don't worry about tonight's show; I have you covered. JD has promised to make sure Twitter knows you have the flu or something. I don't know what means."

A laugh escapes me. JD and his Twitter — it should be outlawed. "Thanks, Harrison. I appreciate everything."

"You're family. There isn't anything we don't do for family. I'll see you in a few days, son." He hangs up, leaving that last word lingering in the air.

## 10

## JAIME

When Evelyn and I arrive home, she sets up at the dining room table to do her homework which is nothing more than writing letters and numbers. For some reason, I'm anxious and pacing between the dining and living rooms, expecting a surprise knock at my door. As much as I know Ajay won't show up at my house, I can't help but think he's out there watching me. Not in a creepy way or that he wants to hurt me, but because he wants to talk, and I have nothing to say. Except, I do. I just want to know why I wasn't good enough for him. But I'm afraid of the answer. I'm afraid that whatever he'll tell me I'll believe, and I'd rather find out that he met someone else who could offer him the world when all I could offer him was me. I realize now that I *was* enough, but back then I didn't and feeling inadequate took a toll on my psyche.

This is all my dad's fault. If he would've just left Ajay alone, I wouldn't feel like I'm crawling out of my skin. I wouldn't feel the need to cry, scream, or to punch holes in the wall to let out my frustration. If my dad had just let the past stay where it was, my heart wouldn't be in my throat right now.

"Mommy, can you help me?"

Evelyn's sweet little voice brings a smile to my face and pulls me away from the window. I don't know what I'm looking for. I don't have any idea what kind of car he would drive. When we were together, he used my truck. He never had anything to his name, other than me. I pull the chair out next my daughter and ask her to show me where she needs help. She shows me that she can't make an eight, so I show her the way I was taught by making two ovals, almost like a headless snowman.

"I've never seen snow," she says.

"Be thankful. It's cold and wet."

"Like the beach?"

"Only the wet part. We don't go to the beach when it's cold, silly girl."

She shrugs. "Can we go this weekend?"

I play with one of her braids and smile. "How about next weekend? I have to fix the schedule at work."

She nods and continues to work on her numbers. I sit there and watch her, wondering how I got so lucky when she came into my life. When I found out I was pregnant, I was adamant that I was going to give the baby up for adoption. I wasn't done partying. I wasn't done being wild. I didn't want the responsibility of another human to fall on my shoulders. It wasn't until I started looking at prospective parents and no one seemed good enough for her. No one could love her the way that I already did. Being a single parent hasn't been easy, but it's been the most rewarding job of my life. To see her smile, to know her, it's a blessing that I'll never look past.

HEIDI MCLAUGHLIN

"What do you want for dinner?" I ask as I head into the kitchen.

"I'm not hungry."

I walk around the half wall that separates the dining room from the kitchen and watch her focus on her worksheet. "Because we had ice cream, right?"

"Mhm. My tummy's full."

"Fair enough. Do you want to watch a movie when you're done?"

She glances up from her paper and smiles that sweet toothless grin. "I like it when you get off work early, Mommy."

I go to her and press my lips to her head. "Me too." I suppose I should thank my father or Ajay for that, but I won't. Neither of them needs the satisfaction of knowing my crappy day turned out fantastic.

As soon as Evelyn's done with her homework, I give her a quick bath. We brush our hair and teeth in unison, making a game out of it before snuggling together on the couch. Tonight's movie of choice is *Toy Story*, which makes me cry every single time. An hour into it, and after repeating most of the words and belting out a song or two, my baby girl is fast asleep in the crook of my arm. I stay like this, relishing in the closeness and the moment. I'm in no hurry to move even though I can hear my phone vibrating on the table. Whoever is calling or texting can wait. Right now, I need to hold my daughter. I need to tell myself that everything's going to be okay, that Ajay isn't here to screw up my life, that whatever he's doing, it's his thing and not mine. What we had, our short-lived marriage, is a thing of the past and there's nothing that can change that. His actions today, by not speaking to me, is a clear indication that he's moved on... just as I have.

When the movie ends, I shut off the TV and rouse Evelyn. She's cranky but going to bed without a bathroom stop is just asking for trouble that neither of us want to deal with in the middle of the night.

"I love you," I say to her as I get her tucked in.

"I love you more, Mommy." She places her hands on my cheeks and pulls me forward. "You're the best Mommy in the whole wide world."

Her words bring tears to my eyes. It's times like this, when I'm doubting myself, that she knows just what to say. I'm not the best, but I try. I struggle and drown a lot, but I try just for her. "You're the best daughter a Mommy could ever ask for." I close the gap between us and give her the butterfly kisses that she loves so much, we rub our noses together and finally a kiss goodnight. "See you in the morning."

"Not if I see you first," she tells me before rolling over.

Sleep is going to evade me tonight. I know this as I pull the covers back on my bed. My mind is racing, wondering about Ajay, and I hate myself for it. He should be an afterthought, a moment that was missed and never thought of again, but he's at the forefront of my mind when I should be thinking about anyone or anything but him.

I reach for my phone to call Logan, only to remember I left it on the table. Because of Evelyn, my house has night-lights all over, letting off enough of a glow to guide me through each room. I pick it up and tap the screen to look at the missed calls and messages. Most are from Dhara, a few from Fletcher and one from my dad. None of whom I want to talk to. On my way back to my room, I press Logan's name and wait for him to answer.

"Hey, I'm just walking in the door."

"Long day?" I ask him.

"Something like that. Had some kids mess up and I had to deal the bureaucratic paperwork, and then one of their mothers called. Why is it that parents think they have a say in how the military treats their kids?"

"Probably because parents are meddlesome and coddle their children."

Logan sighs. "I think you're onto something. I have duty this weekend so I can't come down, but I'll be down next weekend. There's a fair in Wilmington if we want to take Evelyn."

"I think she would like that. I'll change my schedule around on Saturday, so we aren't pressed for time. She asked about going to the beach too."

"We can probably manage that."

Thoughts about having more with Logan run through my mind. I know it's because I saw Ajay today. Logan and I are comfortable with what we have. It's a weekend thing, a couple of times a month. If I don't speak to him every day, no big deal. What we have works for us.

We talk for a few more minutes, and while I'm tempted to tell him about what my father has done, I don't. Having an overzealous father is definitely a turn off to many men, even a macho Marine. After we hang up, my thoughts get the best of me and I find myself rummaging through my closet until I unearth a box. I pull it out and sit it on my bed. The writing is faded but the words are still clear in my mind, "never ever open this box." Maybe I should heed my own advice and put it back where it was.

But I don't. I pull, tug, and pick at the tape until it rips from the box. It's only then that I hesitate before lifting the lid. Some of the contents I remember. Old photographs. The little cards that you get when someone gives you flowers. Notes we wrote back and forth. Things I saved because

I thought they were important at the time, that I didn't want to let go. As angry as I was, as hurt as I still am, Ajay was my first love. We experienced something together that only we can share the heartache in.

Taking a deep breath, I settle myself on my bed, open the flaps of the box and wait for the tears to come as I pull memories out piece by piece. Each picture that I take out of the box brings a smile to face. My thumb brushes over Ajay's face. We were young and so in love. And so incredibly stupid. I continue to dig through the box and pull out his high school diploma. I set it aside, knowing full well I'm going to be the bigger person and make sure he gets it. I don't have much in life, but I have mine and it means something. The last thing I take out of there is a sealed envelope. Looking at it doesn't spark any type of recollection. I turn it over in my hand, seeking a name or anything to give me a clue but there's nothing. Opening it carefully, I pull out the document and unfold it.

It takes me a moment to realize that I'm reading my divorce decree. Jameson Foster vs. Ajay Ballard – Dissolution of Marriage. I flip the pages, reading the legal jargon that still to this day doesn't make sense. Our divorce was simple. We had no assets and we weren't married very long. The one thing we had between us was gone. The lawyer called this divorce a piece of cake and had the nerve to ask me if understood the pun. I probably would've had I had wedding cake, but we were married in front of Judge Harvey on my eighteenth birthday.

"Happy birthday to me," I say out loud.

When I come to Ajay's signature, my finger brushes over his name. He signed it so fast, without any hesitation. He told me this was for the best, but I didn't believe him then. Now, I do. We lead two completely different lives, and I'm not sure I could've been the wife he needed me to be at the time. I didn't want to share him with the world, but it's what he wanted. He yearned to make his own money, to make a name for himself. To prove to his absentee parents that he could be something that they weren't.

Noticeably missing from the page where he signed is my signature. In fact, it's not on any of the pages proceeding. I pull the box forward, looking for another copy. There's nothing. In sheer panic, I tip it over and shake it, thinking maybe it's stuck to the underside. Still nothing. Getting out of bed, I tear through my closet until I find the box with all of Evelyn's baby stuff. I look inside, hoping to find something buried within because the reality of the situation is bearing down on me. There's no way I didn't sign! As I sit on the floor with mementos spread all around me, I try to recall when I signed these damn papers. It would've been a milestone for me, a moment I wouldn't want to forget. I would've celebrated on the anniversary of my divorce, yet I haven't.

I haven't because it never happened. That's the only conclusion that I can come up with. I didn't sign the papers, nor did I take them to the court to have them filed. I did nothing except ask Ajay to give me a divorce... one I apparently couldn't even grant him.

## 11

## AJAY

*T*here are so many stories about famous people coming back to their home towns. You even hear about soldiers coming back from war and the whole town, as they should, comes out and celebrates. We're shown stories of politicians being honored in parades, activists being given the keys to their cities, and statues being erected in honor of a celebrity because their town is proud of them. Not the Town of Bailey. No, the Town of Bailey arrests you on trumped up charges that shouldn't even make it past an assistant district attorney. This, according to Saul, is what he plans to say to Judge Harvey today. I don't know if this is a smart tactic or not. Someone like Harvey, who is holding a grudge, may not take too kindly to the comparison. I don't deserve to have the red carpet rolled out for me. I certainly haven't given back to the community and I probably should. I could donate to the music department at school, help them buy new instruments. I could volunteer to teach a music class or tutor a student — all things I do in California. The reason I don't, or haven't, are simple — I never wanted to come back and interrupt Whiskey's life. Even a donation would draw attention, word would spread, and I didn't want that for her. Yet, I think my lack of community involvement here will end up biting me in the ass.

Saul paces my room as he talks to himself while I stand on the balcony watching traffic move at a snail's pace down Main Street. I've spent many hours standing here, taking in life around me. It's so different here versus Los Angeles. Everyone is in a rush out there, moving at the speed of light, and here, they seem to slow down. People in Bailey stop to talk to you on the street, they care about what's going on around them. Not that I've spoken to anyone but Mrs. B. She grew concerned when she hadn't seen me leave my room and started bringing food to me. For that, I'm thankful because just the thought of running into Whiskey physically hurts. Seeing her from afar is doing enough damage to last me another lifetime. I wish Mrs. B hadn't told me her schedule, yet I'm thankful that she did. Even the smallest glimpse reminds me why I left... so she could have a better life. For years, I struggled, barely making enough money to put a roof over my head and eat one meal a day. Everything changed when I took what I had left and entered the *Battle of the Drums* contest. Winning the competition and subsequently meeting Harrison James changed my life.

Down on the street, a black Escalade pulls up to the curb and the doors open. I recognize Katelyn first, followed by Elle. I'm assuming Harrison has gotten out of the driver's side. I step back inside of my room where Saul is still talking to himself. "I'll be right back," I tell him as I leave. The entrance isn't far from my room, but still down a flight of stairs, which I head down as fast as I can and come to a halt when I see my band family in the entryway. As soon as

Katelyn sees me, I'm in her arms and she's telling me that everything will be okay. I wish I had her confidence, but I don't. Harrison and I hug quickly, and Elle doesn't say much. Not uncommon as our relationship is a bit different from what I have with her parents. She's my boss and I respect that.

"Saul's upstairs, talking to himself."

Harrison laughs. "He's good like that. His father could carry on conversations with himself and never miss a beat."

"Good to know," I sigh. I motion for them to follow me, but Saul appears on the steps before we can head to my room.

"Perfect. I'm glad you're all here," he says as he comes into our fold.

"Did you arrange this?" I ask.

He looks at me oddly.

"Mom wanted to be here," Elle says. "I would've been here regardless. Dad followed because I took his plane." She acts like it's no big deal, commandeering a jet.

Katelyn comes to my side and wraps her arm around mine. "We're family, and family always supports family."

"Thank you," I tell her and the rest of them. Saul claps his hands and tells us all it's time to leave. As I walk by Mrs. B, I let her know that I'll be back later. Hopefully, it's only to get my stuff, but with Harvey, I can't be so sure.

Harrison and Saul sit up front while Katelyn, Elle and I pile into the back. There's third row seating, but none of us care to use it. Katelyn sits in the middle and holds both mine and Elle's hands. I'm in complete awe of the relationship she has with her daughters. Sure, they're adult women with one already married and the other traveling the country with a band, and yet they still hold hands with their mom. I wish I had a relationship like that... or one at all with my mother... although I don't know what I'd say to her after all this time. She left me when I was six to fend for myself.

It doesn't take us long to get to the courthouse. During the short ride there, Saul continued to talk to himself, practicing his summations on Harrison, who deemed this trial business nothing but bullshit. I happen to agree with him but saying as much in court won't get me very far, especially with the likes of Judge Harvey.

After Harrison parks, the five of us walk up the courthouse steps and go through the metal detector. One of the guards asks for Harrison's autograph, to which he replies, "Depends on my mood after this trial." I think the guard was taken aback, but the man is one pissed off dude right now. With his hand on my shoulder and Katelyn's arm wrapped in mine, we follow Saul down the somewhat busy hall. I think everyone is here to bear witness to the fact that I'm here, and not really conducting any actual business.

When I see Whiskey standing at the counter, I freeze. I would know her anywhere by the shape of her neck when her hair is pulled up. I spent many hours memorizing every inch of her skin there. "What's wrong?" Katelyn asks.

"Nothing, I just need a minute." I walk away and toward the love of my life. She sees me coming and quickly wipes at her cheeks. "Why are you crying?" I ask her, as if I have a right to know. Without hesitation, I reach out and touch her arm, as if there isn't a huge divide between us.

She looks from me to her arm and adjusts the way she's standing so I have no choice but to let her go. "Go away, Ajay." She steps to the side to get away from me.

"Whiskey?"

She stops, turns, and looks at me with tear-streaked eyes. Whiskey opens her mouth to say something, but then thinks twice. She walks away while shaking her head, disappearing into the women's rest room. If we weren't in a courthouse filled with people, I'd follow her in. It wouldn't be the first time I've done something like that with her.

"Ajay, we need to go," Elle's behind me and unfortunately reminding me of what I have to do now. I glance at the door one more time before following Elle into the courtroom. Harrison and Katelyn are already sitting in the front and Elle joins them while I take the seat next to Saul.

Fletcher Oakes is the next to arrive. He's followed by Sheriff Foster. I'm slightly upset that I haven't been able to take a jab or two at him in the last few days. I fully expected him to stop by my room a few times to try and arrest me for drinking a beer. Sadly, he's disappointed me there.

The bailiff tells us to rise, which we do, waiting for Judge Harvey to take his seat. He reads his script, reminding the people — all my people — that we're here to hear the case of the State of North Carolina versus Ajay Ballard on the charge of vandalism. "Mr. Oakes, please present your case." As Fletcher stands, I stare out the frosted glass window, not needing to hear any of this.

*"Whiskey, this is a bad idea. What if he wakes up?"*

*She giggles. I kiss her to keep her quiet.*

*"Come on, Whiskey, let's go home."*

*She pushes away from me. "Don't be such a stick in the mud, Ajay. Come on, it'll be fun. It's like a rite of passage to teepee Harvey's house." Whiskey goes to the truck and fills her arms with toilet paper. She's spent months collecting and hiding them where her parents wouldn't find them, all for this moment.*

*Whiskey throws roll after roll, laughing as she does. I refuse to help her. I don't want to get caught up in this mess.*

If she gets busted, her parents will do whatever they can to help her. The only person I've got is her.

Roll after roll is thrown over the shrubs, trees, the car parked in the driveway, and the house. Once she runs out, she runs back to the truck and grabs more, all while I stand there, pleading with her. "Whiskey, that's enough, come on."

"No," she snaps. "Harvey deserves this."

I step back and put my hands up in the air. "Have at it, sunshine!" She takes my words to heart and continues to decorate the good Judge's house. And just when I think she's finished; she goes back to her truck and pulls out a cartoon of eggs.

"Seriously, Whiskey?"

"What, I can't make it easy for him."

"What'd he ever do to you, huh?"

She starts hurling eggs at his house, ignoring my question. They crack and splat down the wood siding. This man is going to have to get up at the crack of dawn and clean this up before the sun heats up.

"Whiskey?"

"What, Ajay? You want to know what this bastard did?"

"Yeah, I do, because if we're going to get busted, I at least need a reason."

"He won't touch us because if he does, I'll tell his pretty little wife that he fancies my mama and told my mama that if she wants to keep her job, she'll fancy him back."

"Does your dad know?"

"Yeah, he does, but Harvey is a piece of shit and my daddy doesn't want to lose his job, so I'm going to take care of it for him."

I shut up and let her get her aggression out on the house. I know Mrs. Foster loves the Sheriff, so I'm not worried about *her cheating on him. But the Sheriff, he might not appreciate the Judge if he were to find out.*

*When the sprinklers come on, she screams and runs toward the truck. I hop in just as she slams the door.*

*"Drive, Ajay!"*

*I do as she's ordered, burning rubber as I try to get away from the house. I look over at my girl; her hair is wild, but there's a damn smile on her face and that's all that matters.*

"Mr. Ballard, you've entered a plea of not guilty. Do you still stand by your plea?"

"Jameson Foster did this," I blurt out, forgetting where I am. There's a gasp in the galley, and I turn to find Whiskey sitting in the back, turning red. *Fuck, my life.*

"Order in the court," Harvey slams his gavel down.

Saul stands. "Your Honor, if we could take a short recess—"

"Proceedings just started and now you want to take a short recess. What kind of fool do you take me for?"

"Your Honor, the State requests a recess to go over this new information."

"Fine, fifteen minutes." He slams the gavel down again and heads to his chamber. As soon as he's up, I rush to the back of the room and drop to my knees.

"Whiskey, I'm sorry. I was thinking about that night and your name... it just came out. I remember what you said about Harvey. I need you to tell him the truth."

"Why should I?" her glare burns a hole right through me.

"You shouldn't," I tell her honestly. "I don't deserve anything from you."

"Fletcher, am I allowed to testify?"

I glance over my shoulder at the attorney. "Yeah, Jamie, you can unless Mr. Ballard's attorney has any objections."

"None from us," Saul says.

"Thank you," I say to her.

She stands and I follow, still loving that I'm a head and shoulder taller than her. "Aren't you worried about me lying on the stand?" She smirks as she steps past me.

I inwardly groan. I wasn't, but I am now.

## 12

## JAMIE

The look of pure shock — or maybe it's realization — on Ajay's face is priceless, yet I feel like a complete shit for saying what I did. He has every right to tell the truth about what happened that night. I never asked him to lie for me or withhold information. When I committed the act, I knew he'd take the fall... that was the kind of guy he was. But he's changed since then; he has a career and even though this is petty, not only the charges brought against him but the act itself, it could probably tarnish his image.

Fletcher takes me by the elbow and leads me out of the courtroom and down the hall to a small conference room. He shuts the door once we're inside and sighs. "What the hell is going on? Why are you even here?"

"I had some business to take care of this morning," I tell him. "It's not like I planned this. I don't even know what possessed me to go into the courtroom."

"Curiosity?"

"Of what? Seeing my ex?" Fletcher shrugs. "Yeah, I had enough of that the other day when he and his perfect girlfriend came into Bailey's." I start pacing back and forth in what little space is available. I should've never walked into the courtroom, but something told me I needed to be in there. I shouldn't care what happens to Ajay because as far as I'm concerned this is payback for ditching out on me. Maybe there's some deep-seated jealousy on my part. He's living the life, the one I thought we'd live together, while I'm still in Bailey working in a bar. That must be it. I'm angry at him for leaving me behind.

"So now what?" I ask Fletcher. "Do you put me on the stand?"

He nods as he thumbs through some papers. "If I don't, Ajay's lawyer does. You can either testify for the State or for him."

"If I testify for you, I lie up there."

Fletcher looks at me, his face pensive and almost sad. His dirty blond hair is kept short and styled neatly. "Or you tell Harvey you forgot."

"Isn't that the same as lying?"

He shrugs. "It was a long time ago, memories are hazy. You don't remember whose idea it was or when it happened."

I nod and continue to walk back and forth. I've definitely gotten myself into a jam before but nothing like this.

"What I don't get is why your name isn't mentioned anywhere in the police report."

"You and I both know that the police report was recently filed, likely when my father and Harvey sat around the poker table, smoking cigars, and plotting the demise of Ajay as soon as they heard he would be passing through town, all for something he did years ago. What I don't understand is why? Why would they even care at this point? It's not like Harvey's house sustained any damage."

"It's because of you, that's why. Your dad must somehow think that this is payback for what Ajay did to you. Fletcher tosses the folder down onto the table. "This case is nothing but a waste of my time. I shouldn't even be in court right now."

"Harvey clearly has a vendetta, which I don't get."

"I'm going to ask you why you targeted him. Is that something you can answer?"

I nod, even though I don't want to tell the story of how Harvey tried to coerce my mother into sleeping with him. After I decorated his house with two-ply and the dozen eggs that had been in my truck for a week, she got a raise and he left her alone. I hadn't expected that outcome but whatever. Message sent and received as far as I was concerned.

"What else will you ask me?"

"Some basic questions, name, age, those types of things."

"Nothing about Evelyn, okay?"

He looks at me like I just pulled his puppy dog's tail. "Why would I do that?"

"I don't know but Ajay doesn't know about her and I'd like to keep it that way."

"Think he'll be upset?"

"I'm not sure," I say, shrugging. I stop and stand at the end of the table. "When I lost..." I pause and take a deep breath. "I just don't know how he'll react, and I don't think he should find out in court."

Fletcher nods and goes over the night in question. I tell him everything, how it was my idea, how Ajay begged me to leave but I refused, and how the only thing he's guilty of is driving the truck away from the scene. What I leave out is what we did afterward even though I can still clearly remember us together that night. The relationship Ajay and

I had was explosive, some even called it toxic because I was a rebellious teen. Many blamed him for my bad attitude. When we were in the room together, the sexual tension radiated off us. All we had to do was look at each other, and people would tell us to get a room. A room we rarely had, and I often wondered how we never got caught having sex in public. If anything, we should be on trial for indecent exposure or public fornication, not teepeeing someone's house.

"We need to go back in. I think under the circumstances; you should be prepared for Ajay's lawyer to come down on you hard. I'm sure they're eager to get the heck out of town and back on tour."

"Then the feeling's mutual because I'm just as I'm eager for him to get out of town."

Fletcher opens the door and I follow him out. Ajay is standing in the hall with his girlfriend by his side, and two people who I know aren't his parents. I try to smile but all he gets from me is a grimace.

Once in the courtroom, I sit directly behind Fletcher. He tells me that as soon as Harvey brings court into session, he'll call me to the stand. I feel Ajay walk beside me and do everything I can to keep my gaze on Harvey's black chair even though Ajay's cologne is overpowering my senses and making me tingle. My body is a traitor, yearning for his touch, when all I want it to do is be repulsed by him.

"He has somebody," I whisper, hoping my senses can understand that he's off limits. Not that I would even go there to begin with. My life doesn't need the complications that one roll in the hay with him would bring.

The bailiff tells us to stand and gives his spiel about Harvey being honored and all that. I roll my eyes and Fletcher glares at me from over his shoulder. I shrug, letting him know that I can't help it. Harvey is the least honorable judge in our county and needs to retire, but he won't because he likes the power he has over us "common people".

"Mr. Oakes, please call your first witness," Harvey says as he settles into his chair.

Fletcher stands and clears his throat. "The State would like to call Jameson Foster to the stand."

Being the dramatic one that I am, I stand, straighten my shirt and saunter to the seat. Once I'm in it, I avoid looking at Ajay.

"Raise your right hand and repeat after me," the bailiff says. I do and that's when it hits me that if I lie up here, I could end up with a fine or worse... *jail time*. Right now, I want to take back everything I said to Fletcher; I don't want to testify. My palms start to sweat as Fletcher comes closer.

"Please state your name for the record."

"Jameson Foster," I say into the microphone.

"May I call you Jamie?"

"You may."

"Jamie, do you know why you're here?"

"I do."

"And you can say confidently that you're familiar with the case?"

"I can."

Fletcher returns to his table and picks up a piece of paper. "Jamie, on the night in question, can you tell us who was responsible for the vandalism?"

Something compels me to look at Ajay, and I wish I hadn't. He looks sad, defeated, like the world is against him and the last time I saw him like this was when his grandma died, leaving him with no one. I remember when he cried on my shoulder and I begged my father not to call child services because they would take him away from me. I was the only family he had, and I had to protect him. However, telling the truth now will put me in the same situation he's in.

"Ms. Foster?" Fletcher calls my name to get my attention. I smile softly at my friend.

"Spouses can't testify against each other, right?"

Fletcher looks at the sheet of paper again. "At the time of the incident, you were not married to Mr. Ballard," he points out.

I glance at Ajay, who is focused intently on me. "This is true, but we did marry."

"And subsequently divorced, therefore your testimony is admissible."

I drop my head and look at my hands. The dollar store ring Ajay had bought me is resting somewhere at the bottom of some river I drove past on my way home from Nashville. The green iron stain that it left behind on my finger disappeared slowly, day after day, until one day I noticed it was gone. That was the day when everything became a reality for me. The love of my life was no more. The cheap ring that signified our life was gone and I had nothing to hold onto.

Looking back at Fletcher, I try to grin, but my cheeks barely move. "Ms. Foster?"

"I invoke my spousal privilege or whatever it's called."

Fletcher steps toward me just as Ajay leans forward. "There isn't anything to invoke," Fletcher says. "You and Mr. Ballard have been divorced for seven years."

I sit up straighter in my chair and close my eyes. I have no choice but to come clean. Even if I were to file the papers today or tomorrow, he'd get a copy and know that I never followed through with the divorce in the first place. I chance a look at his girlfriend who is watching me intently, probably wondering what the hell's going on. I spotted her ring earlier and could feel a small bit of jealousy course through me. The rock could cut a piece of glass and it could've been mine. I stop myself from thinking what should've been because who knows if Ajay and I would've made it? I used to dream that we would have.

"Your Honor, if you would please instruct the witness to answer the State's question," Ajay's lawyer stands and says.

"Ms. Foster, please answer the question."

I mentally flip Harvey off.

"Like I said, I invoke spousal privilege because Ajay Ballard and I are still married."

The small group in the courtroom erupts. Immediately, my eyes are back on Ajay. He stares at me, stunned. The lady he came with has her hand over her mouth as she looks on. The man is saying something to the lawyer, and Ajay's girlfriend looks pissed. I have no doubt that once we leave here, she's going to demand the papers be filed so they can get on with their lives.

Harvey, on the other hand is having a field day with his gavel. He keeps slamming it down and yelling "order" even though it's fairly quiet in the courtroom. I'm not sure what the big deal is, other than the obvious, but it's not like I confessed to murder or something equally egregious. Ajay and I are still married when we thought we were divorced. Seems like a simple fix.

"Your Honor, in light of the newly revealed information, I move for an immediate dismissal against my client."

"Not so fast, city boy," Harvey says. He turns and points his gavel at me. "Listen young lady, I will not tolerate these lies from you."

"As if I care."

His lips go into a fine line and I can see that he's grinding his teeth. "Very well, then. Jameson Foster and Ajay Ballard are hereby remanded to the Prineville County jail until the facts of the matter can be verified by the county clerk."

My mouth drops open and before I can say anything, he slams down his gavel and walks off toward his chambers.

"What just happened, Fletcher?" I ask, standing up.

"He just put you in jail for mouthing off to him."

The bailiff walks behind me and pulls my arms together. "Can he do that?" I screech as the cuffs go around my wrists.

"He just did."

Fletcher turns his back on me as the bailiff pulls me toward him. Ajay and I make eye contact and I try to convey some remorse, but he turns toward his girlfriend just as I'm pushed through the wooden door.

## AJAY

*T*he words *"Ajay and I are still married"* keep replaying over in my head as I'm driven back to jail. Leave it to Whiskey to smart off to the judge and leave it to Harvey to be a major piece of shit by having me locked up again. As soon as the cell door slams shut, I can hear Pate laughing. I'd really like to take one of my drumsticks and put it where... no, my drumsticks are too good for the likes of him.

The cell door opens, and Whiskey is pushed inside. I'm stunned by her presence. The bailiff looks at the both of us and says, "Harvey thinks you two need to spend some time together and get your story straight." He shuts the door, leaving us in the cell together.

I don't ask if she's okay or what the hell she's doing, lying on the stand like that. I do feel like confronting her, telling her that she needs to tell the damn truth so I can get back to my job. But I don't. Instead, I sit down on the edge of the cot and rest my elbows on my knees. I've worked so hard to keep a clean image, this is surely going to get my ass booted from the band. And once that happens, I'll have nothing.

Whiskey sits across from me and cries softly. It's a ploy. I know her. She's not crying because she's hurt, it's because someone with authority has pissed her off and she didn't see it coming. My girl was — and still is by the looks of it — a con artist. I'm not falling for it though.

Whiskey stands and goes to the bars. Of all the times we broke the law, I never imagined us locked up together. Yet, here we are, and for what? Harvey has such a bone to pick with me, her, and apparently *us,* that he has no qualms about putting us in here when the information he needs is probably right in front of his face.

"Pate," Whiskey yells, "turn your damn television down, I can't think!"

"Shut up, Jamie. You ain't the boss of me."

"Asshole," she mutters as she sits across from me again. "You're quiet."

I shake my head slightly. "Not much to say."

"You don't have *anything* to say to me? No questions? Nothing?"

"No, I do, but I'm not sure I can find the words until my temper cools down."

"Fair enough," she says.

"Actually, I do have something to say." When I look at her, I want to tell her that I love her, that I always have and have wished for years that things hadn't ended between us, but they did, and at the time I thought it was for the best. I remember the nights when we were apart and I needed her, when all I wanted was to wrap my arms around her because feeling her pressed against my body made the world seem fair. And then I remember the night she showed up in Nashville and how I was hurting her and remind myself I made the right decision, even if it's something I've regretted every day since.

"Go ahead then."

I sit up straight, pressing my back to the wall. "Why can't you just tell the truth, Whiskey? Why did you have to lie about us being married?"

"Who says I'm lying?"

Why does she want to play these stupid games? "Whiskey, you're messing with our lives here. I could be on my way to wherever the hell I'm supposed to be by now if you would just tell Harvey that it was you who vandalized his house. And, while you're at it, tell him that maybe he shouldn't be such a dick to the next group of kids that do the same thing."

"Is that what you want? To get out of here so you can carry on with your life?"

"I have obligations."

"Right, most of us do. It's called being an adult."

My eyes cut to hers. "And you're acting like a child, Whiskey. Harvey is going to figure out you're lying, he's going to think I put you up to it, and we're both going to become Bubba's bitch in jail."

She laughs, but there's nothing funny about the situation. I stand and go over to the wall. There's a small window at the top and I can just about see a glimpse of the sky. It's bright blue with no clouds. A perfect day in my opinion.

"What if I told you we're still married?"

I sigh. "I signed the papers, just like you asked. You were there; you watched me do it."

She stands again and moves to the opposite end of the cell. The space between us is small, but it feels like miles apart. Only God knows how much I want to pull her into my arms and kiss her senseless. The slap in the face that would follow would be worth it just to feel her lips pressed against mine one last time.

"I never signed the papers and I didn't file them."

Her voice is small, nothing like the strong, confident woman I know.

"What?" I ask. Her back is facing me and I'm waiting for her to turn around. "Whiskey, what did you say?" She turns slowly and looks at me. I've seen this before. It's the face she makes before she breaks down and cries. "Jamie?"

She smiles sadly. "The other night after I saw you, I pulled out a box of our stuff. I found your diploma, by the way, and if I had my purse, I'd give it to you. I thought that maybe you'd want that."

"Thanks."

She nods. "Anyway, there they were, at the bottom of my memories, folded up nice and neat. The only thing was, they were the originals, not the stamped copy you get back from the clerk after you file them... and lo and behold my signature was missing from them."

"Is that what you were doing earlier when I saw you?"

"Yeah."

"But you were crying. Why?"

"Because I'm stupid. Because life sucks sometimes. Because my dad can be a total jerk and as much as I hate you, you don't deserve this."

Hearing her say she hates me makes my knees wobble. I grab hold of the metal bed railing and ease myself onto the bed. Deep down I knew she did but hearing her say as much is like a punch in my gut.

"You *should* hate me, Whiskey. What I did to you, to us... I have never forgiven myself."

Whiskey sits down across from me and relaxes against the wall. "We were young, stupid—"

"And in love," I finish her sentence for her.

"I was going to say naïve, but I suppose 'in love' works as well."

"I was naïve about life, still am sometimes, but I know without a doubt I was in love with you."

She repeats the word "was" quietly to herself. What she doesn't know is that I'd profess my love to her without any hesitation if I thought it would mean anything to her. But I know it wouldn't be fair to her, she has a life and I don't plan to interrupt that for her.

"So," she says, rubbing her hands down the front of her legs. "Speaking of life, how goes it?"

Nice change of subject, I'll give her that and appease her request. "Life's good."

"Yeah, big time drummer in a fancy band."

I smirk. "Band is anything but fancy and I'm just the drummer."

"Not according to Dhara. She says you're on tour with the man of her dreams, 4 something. I honestly don't pay attention when she starts talking about music."

"4225 West is who we're on tour with. Their drummer is one of our lead singer's dads." She looks at me oddly and I shrug. "Made better sense in my head." I look away, unable to keep my eyes on her out of fear that I'll end up sitting next to her, begging her to give me another chance.

"I'm sorry, Ajay."

"For what?"

"For messing up your life like this. Your girlfriend, who, by the way, is hot... and I'm *totally* jealous of her tits... looked pretty pissed off when I blurted out that we're still married. I suppose I'm screwing something up there as well. I'm going to tell Harvey that we need the decree signed off on right away so you can get on with your life. I'm sure the date is coming up soon."

"What are you talking about?" I ask her once she's done rambling.

"Your wedding."

"What wedding? Who told you I was getting married?" I know exactly what she's doing, and I have no intentions of stopping her. I like when she's like this, flustered and digging for information without being bold enough to ask me outright.

"I saw her ring. It's gorgeous."

I look at her hand and see nothing, not even a tan line. I shouldn't care, but I do. She's right about Elle's ring though. It's big and flashy, and it makes me wonder if Whiskey thinks that could've been hers if we had stayed together. Thing is though, right now I can't even afford that. With Sinful Distraction just starting, funds are still mediocre, but Elle promises us that things will get better. Our sales are increasing every day and royalties are starting to come in. I'm hoping that I can move out of Quinn's house soon and into my own place. It's not that I mind sharing with him and Nola, it's that I want to finally have something that's mine. Something I've paid for myself, with my own money. I've never owned my own anything. Even the car I drive is leased.

"She comes from money," I say with a shrug, letting her believe whatever her mind spins up. "Tell me about you. What have you been up to since I walked out on you?"

Her eyes jump to mine but quickly turn away. I own what I did. I had no right leaving her like that, not after everything she had done for me. I think in my head, I planned to go back, but after seeing the ugly side of the industry, I knew I didn't want her to experience what I was experiencing.

"I work a lot."

"Boyfriend?" As much as I don't want to know, I have to ask.

"Yes, sort of."

"Is it one of those 'we're in a relationship' type of things where you both pretend you don't know what you want?"

"When did you become an expert on relationships?"

I shrug. "Since I joined the band and have to listen to mushy love songs. Answer the question, Whiskey."

"No," she says, rolling her eyes. "He's a Marine and is busy. It's not serious in the sense that we're moving in with each other or planning a life. We have fun. We see each other on the weekends if he's free."

"Whiskey girl, are you afraid of commitment?"

She mocks me. "Clearly after the number you did on me."

"Touché."

"Way to dodge my question about the wedding."

I shrug. "Talking about you is more fun. I missed this," I point back and forth between us. "We always had good banter but amazing—"

"Don't you dare say it, Ajay." She gives me a stern look. She's right. Some things should stay in the past and this is the last place where I should recount our many sexual encounters and experiences, although going through them with her would be a nice trip down memory lane.

"So, when's the wedding?"

"Don't know."

Whiskey throws her hands up in the air. "You're a lot of things, Ajay, but I never took you for the guy who leaves all the planning up to someone else."

I love this game of back and forth we're playing and so I decide to up the stakes. I stand and go over to the cot she's sitting on and take the spot next to her. Our arms and thighs are touching, and it feels like I'm being electrocuted from the energy moving between us. Fuck, how I missed how she used to make me feel so alive. She's my muse and there will never be anyone else like her.

"I don't know because we're not getting married. The woman who you are jealous of," I purposely leave out the part about Elle's boobs because one, she's my boss, and two, I much prefer Whiskey's over anyone else's, "is the manager of my band, Sinful Distraction. The couple you saw with her are her parents. Her father is my mentor and drummer of the band Dhara likes. Her mother," I pause again to gain some composure. "She's been like a mom to me this past year."

"She has?" Whiskey's voice breaks.

"For the first time ever, I had a Christmas with a stocking and presents under the tree."

"And that brunette is your boss?"

I nod. "Your dad thought the same thing and I didn't correct him because it was better that you thought I had moved on. The notion backfired, however, when you dropped the bomb that we're still married."

*Because I'm not sure I'm willing to give that up.*

14

JAMIE

*W*hy do I feel so much relief from what he's telling me? He had his first real Christmas, something I was never able to give to him and part of me wants to be petty and jealous. I want to tell him that if he had stuck around, he would've had many first holidays with me because I was his wife and we were a family. Yet, I'm so incredibly happy that he found someone to love him like a son because that's all he's ever wanted in life, to be loved. My mom tried, but he never felt at home with her. And as much as I don't want to admit it, to hear he's not getting married, that the beautiful woman is nothing more than his boss, relieves me. I'm happy and I shouldn't be because what he does or who he's with is none of my business. It stopped being my business when I asked him for a divorce even though it seems I wanted to keep his life tied to mine because I never signed or filed the damn papers.

Before I know it, his thumb is rubbing along my cheek bone and my head is leaning against his hand. "Don't cry, Whiskey," his voice is husky and makes me long to get lost in the sound of it, to hear him call out my name and tell me that he loves me... that he needs me and that I'll always be his one and only. But I can't. That ship, the one that rocked us back and forth until it capsized, has sailed and is not one that either of us should be wanting to board right now. I stand and move away from him, wiping angrily at my tears.

"Pate," I yell to avoid the ever growing elephant in our cell. "Turn down your damn soap opera!" From behind me, Ajay chuckles.

"Shut up, woman!"

"He's an ass," Ajay says. He kept the TV volume so loud the night I was here I couldn't sleep. Not that I really wanted to, though, because each time I closed my eyes I saw my life imploding."

Leaning against the bars, I reach behind me and grip them tightly. My hands need something to do because they're itching to touch the man who is only a foot or so away from me.

"Tell me about California."

Ajay sighs and leans forward to rest his elbows on his knees. He's dressed in a suit and looks dashingly handsome. The only time I ever saw him dressed up was for our prom and even then, he wore a suit from my dad's closet. For our wedding, he wore jeans. I wore shorts. I should've known it wouldn't last.

"I don't know, it's a lot like North Carolina in a way. It's hot but not overly humid. Too many people though. Beaches are crowded. Lots of surfers. And it's pretty expensive."

"And the band? Is it everything you dreamed of?"

He shrugs. "It's tiring, rewarding, stressful and exactly where I want to be. Playing the drums is therapeutic for me. Knowing that someone is counting on me to do my part helps me get up in the morning. It gives me something to look forward to."

"You make it sound like Nashville saved you."

He hangs his head and is quiet for a moment. He takes a shuddering breath and looks forward. "After you lost the baby... something broke inside of me. I thought that I somehow failed you because I couldn't take the pain that you were feeling away. I was suffering in silence, trying to bury my feelings. I know the experience is different for mothers because they carry the baby, but I wanted our child so badly because it would've been the best parts of you and to have another you in the world would've only made my life better.

"Going to Nashville was a way to hide the pain, to take my anger out on a kit instead of yelling at you... to get drunk and forget about everything."

"Did it work?"

"Not at first. I knew going there was a long shot, but I had to do something because the alternative was to quit us."

"Which you did anyway."

He nods. "Once I got there, I had every intention to come back to Bailey, pack up what little shit we had and hit the road. I had aspirations, and those only increased after I talked to other musicians. They told me stories about how they were making money, getting gigs right and left, how they travel with well-known solo acts. I was determined to land a gig until every place I stopped at slammed their doors in my face. I had nothing to offer these people except for an ability to play the drums, and we both know I was mediocre at best.

"I had almost given up but the thought of coming back to Bailey to face your dad with no money in my pocket was making me sick. I couldn't provide for you, no one was hiring here, and other than being able to bang on a drum, I had no skills.

"I stopped at a bar that was just off music row and met a manager. He told me he'd give me a chance. That night you saw me, I was a week into a contract with him, and I signed it without reading it because I was so damn excited that I was finally earning some money to be able to provide for you. The fine print was clear, the band received half the gig money, divided equally. I was making a hundred or less a night, depending on who I was playing with while that bastard was taking the rest."

"I never cared about the money, Ajay."

He looks at me, his eyes are bloodshot, and his cheeks are wet. I do everything I can to remain where I am.

"It wasn't all about money, Whiskey. It was about eating, sleeping. While people in the bands had homes, I slept in alleyways. I ate one meal a day just so I had enough to buy new sticks because after a week they were so beat to shit, I needed new ones. Never mind the fact that groupies would try and steal them if I took my eyes off them for a second. I couldn't provide for myself, let alone you. That night you came to Nashville, I wanted to run home with you, but I was stuck. I owed this man three years and there wasn't any way he was letting me out of my contract, so I did what I thought was right and told you to go back home. I didn't expect you to hand me divorce papers."

"You signed them without a moment's hesitation." His eyes meet mine and I see sadness, loss, and heartbreak. I'm not the only one who suffered even though I've felt that way. "Why didn't you come back after your contract was up?"

"I hooked up with a band and started making decent money. Still wasn't a lot because we had to pay for our shitty van and gas as we traveled from gig to gig. I did that for a couple of years until I saw a flyer for a drum contest that was happening in Malibu. It was some charity event and by then I was pretty good with the drums so when our tour ended, I hopped on the Greyhound and went out to California. That's when I met Harrison."

"Who's that again?"

Ajay smiles. "He's the drummer for 4225 West and my mentor. It was his contest that I entered, a drum battle in the blazing sun. At night, I'd bathe in the ocean and sleep under the dock. Then get up and play the drums."

"Did you win?"

This time he looks at me and smiles widely. "Yeah, I did. Winning that competition was a life changing thing for me. It's how I met Elle and she put me in her band. And yet somehow now I'm back here and in jail with my Whiskey girl." He winks and my insides turn to mush.

"I'm really sorry for what my dad has done to you, Ajay. You don't deserve it."

"But I do. I skirted my responsibilities to you. The only excuse I have is that I was young and so in love with you that I thought you were better off without me. I lived like a vagrant for a long time and that was no life for you."

"I could've worked, kept food on the table."

"At the time I had too much pride to allow or even ask you to do that. And your father..." he pauses and gathers himself. "After we eloped, he told me I better take care of you, that you were his princess and deserved to be treated as such. He said you had dreams and that I was to make sure they came true."

My mouth drops open as I listen to Ajay, realizing my father is likely the catalyst for him leaving me.

"And then after you lost the baby, he all but blamed me and my 'stupid music career' for causing you stress."

I choke back a sob. "Your career wasn't stupid and it's *not* the reason I lost the baby, I just—"

Ajay stands and walks to my side, pulling me into his arms. My head rests perfectly against his chest while his hand cups my head. I can feel his lips press into my hair as he tries to soothe me.

"I'm so sorry for everything, Jamie. I really, truly am. You'll always be the last person I ever want to hurt, and you'll always be the one woman I'll ever love."

I step away from him and brush the tears away. "I'm sure you've loved others."

Ajay leans against the bars, his lips purse as he shakes his head. "Never."

"You don't have a girlfriend?"

"Not since you. I've gone on a few dates recently, but that's all they are, dates."

I don't know if I want to believe him or not, but the old me says Ajay would never lie to me. The new me, though, is about to say something sarcastic but when I open my mouth to do so, the bailiff walks in.

"Judge Harvey is ready to make his ruling."

"On what?" I ask as he unlocks the cell door.

"How would I know, I'm only told what to say and do around here. Now, do I need to cuff you both or will you walk to the courtroom without incident?"

I look back at Ajay and wink. "I don't know, Ballard, what do you think?"

He laughs. "I have a tour bus waiting, it probably won't get us far but it's worth the try."

"Very funny you two." The bailiff motions for us to walk in front of him. When I feel Ajay's hand on the lower part of my back, I automatically lean into him and even though I want to put as much distance between us as possible, I can't.

In the courtroom, Fletcher is sitting at his table and Ajay's lawyer is at his. I really don't know where I'm supposed to go so I go back to sitting behind Fletcher.

When Harvey comes in, he tells us to stay seated before calling Ajay and I up to stand in front of him.

"After due diligence by our esteemed clerk, it has been determined that Ajay Ballard and Jameson Foster are indeed still married."

"Great, I'd like to file the petition to have our divorce finalized," I say to Harvey.

He huffs and continues speaking, "After a meeting with a lawyer in our family division, it's also been determined that due to the circumstances surrounding your current situation, Ms. Foster, in conjunction with Mr. Ballard's financial status, the law precludes me from granting a divorce without filing new paperwork."

"What situation are you in?" Ajay whispers to me. I shake my head, hoping he understands that I'll tell him later, even though I won't.

"Your Honor, my client is prepared to file the necessary paperwork today for dissolution of marriage, however it should be noted that he will not agree to pay alimony nor spousal support due to the length that they were separated before his career started, as well as the fact that they are only currently still married due to the negligence of Ms. Foster," Ajay's lawyer blurts out. Ajay turns and mumbles something under his breath.

"Shark, huh?"

"He's paid a lot to protect us."

Harvey clears his throat and clasps his hands together.

"As much as I'd love to see the both of you pay for your crimes behind bars, I feel this is going to be punishment enough: For the next ninety-days you will stay married and spend at least three days together each week. Mr. Ballard, you're allowed to travel with your group, however, I suggest you make your schedule amenable to this sentencing. Ms. Foster, you will accept the terms of Mr. Ballard's schedule, provided it falls in line with my sentencing, and see to it that yours does as well. You will both appear before me at the end of your sentence and at your request I will sign off on your divorce. Until then, you're a married couple and your lawyers can figure out the rest."

"Your Honor, you can't demand that they spend time together," Fletcher says.

"But I just did. It's either this or I sentence them both for vandalism."

"This will be fine, your Honor," Ajay says, much to my dismay. Before I can object, Harvey adjourns court and slams his gavel down.

"What just happened?" I ask anyone who can hear me.

"Looks like you're still my wife."

"The fuck I am," I say, storming out of the courtroom.

## 15

# AJAY

The way Whiskey storms out of the courtroom sends a very strong message. It's abundantly clear that she doesn't want to be married to me. It's fine, I get it. She has a boyfriend and wants to move on with her life. I can't really blame her, but is it really *that* bad to have to spend a few days a week with me for ninety days?

Katelyn is by my side, hugging me tightly as I watch Whiskey's retreating backside disappear through the door. Elle's in front of me as well and Harrison is talking to Saul.

"What a mess," Elle says.

"Let's go to lunch and talk about things," Katelyn says, motioning for all of us to get moving. Once we get outside, I look everywhere possible for any sign of Whiskey, but the foot traffic here is light and she's nowhere to be found. It pains me to think that she went running to her boyfriend, but honestly, she probably did. I'm simply the pain in her ass that won't go away.

The drive over to Bailey's is short but it feels like an hour. I'm watching the passersby, trying to spot Whiskey. I want to talk to her before I have to leave. I need to tell her that I will do whatever she wants during the time we have to spend together. If that means I'm sitting in Bailey's while she works, so be it. It's not what I want, but I lost the opportunity to have a say years ago.

As soon as we step into the restaurant, people gasp. Beside me, Elle mutters, "Great, lunch will be lovely with people asking for my dad's autograph every five minutes."

"I am so glad it's not me," I lean down and tell her.

She smirks. "It will be soon enough. Enjoy the quiet while you can."

This is one of the reasons why Elle is such an amazing manager, she has faith in us. Not only as a group but also with our individual crafts.

The hostess takes us to our table and tells us that our waitress will be by to get our drink orders.

"Excuse me," I say, grabbing her attention. "Is Jamie working today?"

"She is, but she's not here yet. Do you want me to let you know when she gets here?"

"Yes, please."

"This isn't a PR nightmare, right?" Elle asks. I don't know who she's talking to, so I keep my mouth shut. "What am I supposed to do with this?"

"Nothing," Harrison says. "So, Ajay's married, it's not like it's the end of the world."

"But married and seeking a divorce?" Elle sighs. "The rag mags are going to be all over this. I swear that judge has the biggest bone to pick with you," she says, looking at me.

"I have a meeting with him in about an hour," Saul adds. "I'm going to see if we can get the divorce pushed through. It's not going to do either of them any good to prolong this for three months."

"We could offer him money," Katelyn says, much to

Harrison and Saul's disagreement. I like her, she's feisty, and the fact that she wants to pay off a judge so I can get a divorce is comical.

I sit there while they decide my fate, halfheartedly listening while watching for any sign of Whiskey. It's not going to matter what I say, they're going to make the decisions for me because when it comes down to it, Elle owns my ass.

"Until we get this resolved, we need to figure out Ajay's travel schedule. I have to submit it to the courts," Saul adds.

"What about the wife's schedule? Surely, it shouldn't be Ajay's responsibility to always be here?" Elle asks.

"I think because of financial situations, Ajay needs to take the brunt of the travel," Saul tells her.

"That's bullshit."

"Don't cuss at the table, Elle," Katelyn admonishes her daughter causing us all to laugh.

The same waitress I had the other day sidles up to our table and takes our drink order. After we've gone around the table, she puts her pad away and looks at Harrison. "Are you Harrison James?"

"I am," he says.

"Wow, just *wow*. Like, *oh, my God*, you're in Bailey's and I'm your waitress. Like, wow!"

"Don't you know any other adjectives?" Elle asks.

"Elle James, what has gotten into you?" Katelyn wants to know.

Elle shrugs and picks up her phone.

"Um, do you think we could take a selfie?" the waitress asks Harrison.

"Maybe after lunch?" he suggests politely, but by the look on her face, you'd think he just killed her pet rabbit or something and not put her off for an hour.

As soon as she's gone, Saul starts to figure out a back-up plan on how to I get out of the sentencing.

"It's fine," I say. "It'll be a pain, but I can handle it."

"I'll talk to Liam and JD, see if we can make sure the jet is available or at least let you use it when we're not."

"Thanks," I reply. "I appreciate it."

"This is really going to hamper the tour, Ajay. We need to either find a way to get this decision appealed," Elle mumbles the last part as something catches her attention on her phone. "Well someone's already let the cat out of the bag that you're here trying to get a divorce. I bet she called the Enquirer."

"She wouldn't do that," I say in defense of Whiskey. "She couldn't care less about media attention."

Just then she walks in and rushes toward the back. "When do we leave?"

"After lunch," Harrison says. I nod, get up from the table and head toward the bar. When Whiskey doesn't come out, I go through the doors into the kitchen. "Where can I find Jamie?" I ask one of the cooks. He points with his spatula at the door that says "Manager" on it.

I knock twice and she tells me to come in. I do so, opening the door slowly. She's sitting at the desk, hiding behind a computer. Her eyes meet mine and even though I smile, she frowns.

"What are you doing here?"

I motion toward the dining area. "Lunch."

"No, back here. Why are you back here?"

"I wanted to talk to you. You ran out of the courtroom before we had a chance to discuss the schedule."

"What schedule?"

"Whiskey," I say her name, dragging it out.

"Look, Ajay. I don't give two shits about what Harvey

said, okay? You have your life, and I have mine. They're not going to magically mesh together and become some cohesive unit for a couple of months. His sentence is stupid, and I've told him as much. You can go back on tour and I'll do my thing here. I'll tell him you came back if that's what you want."

It's not what I want, at least it wasn't until now. Sitting in the cell with her made me realize how much I've missed her and want her in my life, and yet here she is, offering me an out. She's willing to lie for me, just so she doesn't have to see me again.

"I don't think it's going to work that way, Whiskey. My lawyer said something about checking in with the clerk every time I come to town." I shrug and hope she buys my lie.

She throws her pencil down and rests her head in her hands. "I hate Harvey. I swear to all things holy, I'm going to get him back for this."

Ouch, am I really that much of a bad guy that she doesn't want to spend a couple of days with me each week?

"What're you doing tonight because I think we should go over to his house and spray paint it."

My eyes widen, and I start shaking my head back and forth as my mouth opens to tell her no.

"I'm just kidding, Ajay. I wouldn't... well, yes I would... but I won't."

"That's good because I'm not sure I have enough bail money saved up if you were to get thrown back in jail."

"You'd bail me out?" she asks, lifting her head from her hands.

"In a heartbeat," I tell her.

Whiskey sighs. "Look, you don't have to be nice to me or hang out with me. Come to town, show your face

113

around here. I'll do my part so neither of us gets into trouble."

"I have to leave tonight, but I'll be back."

"Will you miss shows because of this?"

I nod. That's the unfortunate part, unless our schedule shows we're lucky enough to have three days off between shows. It's unlikely though. "Harrison will cover for me." Which also means I won't get paid. However, she doesn't need to know that. "I'm going to keep my room over at the Inn, and like I said, I'll be back in a few days and maybe we can talk?"

"About what, Ajay? I think we said all we needed to say earlier today."

I frown. She's right but I want more from her. I want to know about her life while I was gone, and she's kept that from me. Probably with good reason. I think of anything to say, anything that will give me an excuse to stay in her office with her for a bit longer.

"The door says 'Manager'. Is that you?"

She nods slowly. "Yeah. The owner lives in Florida so it's just me. I work most days but cover the nights on the weekends because the tips are better, and the bartender can't handle the rush we get."

I go over to her cork board and look at the flyer for their house band. A couple of the guys listed are people I used to play with. "Lee Johnson's still playing?"

She laughs. "The other day I ran into Jolene Johnson and she said you stopped by her house to talk to Lee, asked him to join your band."

"Why would I do that?" I ask her, completely confused.

"Dunno, but I knew she was full of it."

"Sinful Distraction has one of the best young guitarists in the industry right now. He's called Hendrix."

"Really?" she asks. "He's that good?"

"Yeah, and he knows it. Cocky little shit. Anyway, how would Jolene know?"

Whiskey laughs. "She's married to Lee. You should see her, she's a Parton wannabe with kazoos out to here." Whiskey holds her hands out from her breasts to mimic the size of Jolene's.

"Wait, Jolene Johnson married Lee Johnson?"

"Yep, and she hyphenates her name."

"Wow, that's some seriously small town shit."

"Yeah, it is, but hey, so is getting married at eighteen and getting knocked up..."

And just like that the mood in her office changes. Our mistakes are laid out on the table to remind me of what I've done, as if I could ever forget. I don't know if she did it on purpose or what, but her tactic was effective. I move toward the door and rest my hand on the knob. Without turning around to look at her I tell her, "I'll call ya, Whiskey, and let you know when I'll be back in town."

I leave, shutting her door behind me. In the dining room, my pseudo family is deep in conversation and I don't really want to talk to anyone right now so, I send Elle a text letting her know that I'm heading to the Inn to pack my bag and let Mrs. B know that I'll need to make a block booking on my room. As soon as I open the door, I'm greeted with her million-dollar smile.

"Is it true?"

"That I'm a famous musician and woman are madly in love with me?" I wink at her. She pats my arm and chuckles.

"Always were a charmer."

"Mrs. B I can't even charm a snake, let alone a beautiful woman."

Again, she pats my arm. "I heard you and Miss Jameson Foster are still married."

"Apparently," I say, correcting her. "Seems our divorce never went through. We just have to wait out a couple of months and then she'll be free of me."

"Oh, nonsense. That young woman is madly in love with you, just you wait and see." I would love to agree with her, but something tells me that Whiskey will keep me at arm's length for the entire ninety days.

"I need to leave town for a few days, but I want to know if I can rent my room until the divorce is final. Judge Harvey is forcing Jamie and I to spend time together."

"He always was a sneaky bastard," she says, causing me to laugh.

"I agree, Mrs. B."

"Your room will always be here, Ajay. Don't you worry. But I have a feeling you'll be moving in with Jameson and Evelyn before too long."

"Evelyn?" I ask as I try to run through the names of her family members and friends that I can remember.

Mrs. Buxley sets her hand on my forearm. "It's best she tells you about Evelyn." She walks off, leaving me confused. At this point Whiskey would rather eat rat poison than tell me anything.

## 16

# JAMIE

*A*s much as I don't want to admit it, I've missed Ajay. It had taken me years to forget him, although I never really forgot, I just pushed him aside as a part of my life that didn't work out. Once I had Evelyn, she became the only person who dominated my thoughts. And now, as I sit at my desk, watching Ajay through the security camera, I'm wishing he would turn around so I can see him one more time before leaves. He says he's coming back, but he said that before and it's taken him almost eight years to make good on his word... and he really only did so because my father arrested him.

As if he knows I'm thinking of him, his face lights up on my phone. I groan as the device vibrates, moving slowly across my desk as a result. I choose not to answer. I know he has Evelyn today but the conversation we need to have has to happen face-to-face. Even my father knows this.

I shut off my monitor, gather my things and head toward the kitchen to let the guys know I'll be back later. Being the manager has its perks. I can come and go as I please. The downside is that in a small town like Bailey, employees are limited so when someone calls in sick or needs a day off, I am usually the one to cover. For the most part, I don't care, but sometimes the hours can be a bit too much, especially for Evelyn.

The drive over to my parents is about fifteen minutes from the bar. They live close to the ocean on the outskirts of town, while Evelyn and I live in town near her school, the park and our small downtown. I enjoy being part of the community and want Evelyn to grow up surrounded by these people. My little spitfire of a daughter is loved by all around here.

"Mommy!" she screams as soon as I get out of my car. She runs toward me, launching herself into my arms. I hold her tight to my body. "I missed you," she tells me even though she's only been at school for half a day today.

"I miss you always. How was school?" I set her down but grab her hand as we walk toward the front door. My dad is standing there, leaning against the doorjamb. I can't look at him out of fear that I'll lash out in front of my daughter. She doesn't need to hear me say things to her grandfather, at least not the kind of words that I'm holding back.

"School was boring," Evelyn sighs heavily. "No recess and I had to do spelling."

"Do we have words to work on?"

She nods and skips over a hole that's likely a result of my parents' dog doing some digging. "Ten of them. But I already know them."

"Of course you do, because you're so smart."

We climb the steps leading to the wide wraparound porch. This was a must have for my mom who loves sitting out here to watch the sunrise and listen to the ocean as the waves lap against the shore.

Dad steps out onto the porch and picks Evelyn up. He

whispers something in her ear to make her giggle and when he sets her down, she's off and running. He must know that we need to talk and that it's going to get ugly. I decide to sit on the steps, as doing so gives me a clear shot at my car if I need to make a quick escape because right now, I feel like running. Running to find Ajay. Running away from life. Just running, never stopping, and never looking back.

He sits next me and lets out an audible sigh. "Jameson—"

"Unless the next thing out of your mouth is 'I'm sorry for putting my nose in your business', don't say anything."

He sighs again. "I *am* sorry. I just wanted to scare him. I had no idea Harvey would pull this shit."

"Really?" I ask, looking at my dad. "Did you really not know? Because I'm having a hard time believing that. At what point did you think arresting Ajay would be a good idea?"

He doesn't answer. He doesn't even look at me.

"You have no idea what you've done," I say to him. "Things are good here for Evelyn and me, and now... now I'm forced to spend time with Ajay all because you have a vendetta against him. I accepted that things between us were over a long time ago. I grew up. I became a mother. Ajay's doing his thing – and we shouldn't begrudge his happiness or success - yet, here you are interfering with his life. He made a choice, one that I found a way to make peace with, and you need to as well. You don't act like this with Evelyn's father and what he did was far worse."

"At least he pays child support."

I roll my eyes. "Is that what this is about, money? Does Ajay owe you some? Because if he does, I'll tell him to pay you and we can be done with this crap. Neither of us want to be married to each other, and yet something as simple as

Harvey signing the papers to end this farce of a marriage is too much to ask."

"I've already said I'm sorry."

"Yeah, well sometimes sorry isn't good enough, Dad." I glance at him, he's staring down at his hands. "Three days a week for three months, that's how long I have to spend with him. And he's determined to fulfill the sentencing. What am I going to do with Evelyn?"

"You know she can stay here."

"Not the point."

"So, introduce them."

I shake my head. "I don't want to see the hurt in his eyes, Dad. He wanted *our* baby, and he has no one, except for his band, while I have her."

I leave my dad on the steps and go inside to see what my mother is doing. I find her and Evelyn at the table, working on a craft project. I don't ask questions, I just sit down and immerse myself in glue, glitter, colored cotton balls and construction paper. At times, I have to excuse myself because my eyes start tearing up, and I can't stop them. I'm so angry with my father, and yet there's a small piece of me that is happy he did what he did because I saw Ajay. Seeing him, however, has opened old wounds, wounds that have never fully healed. I could use our time together to gain some closure, but knowing my heart, it's highly unlikely that will happen. It's always belonged to him and as much as I'd love to close the door, I'm not capable... it remains wide open for him to come in and destroy me.

Instead of returning to the craft table, I sneak out back and walk the steps my father built down to the beach. My mom has two chairs and a small table out here, but I choose to sit closer to the water.

The cold, wet sand feels good as I dig my toes into it.

The waves come close, but barely touch me except for the errant one that envelops me. I don't care that I'm wet and sandy, right now it's the only thing that can distract me from my aching heart.

"He meant well," my mom says as she sits down next to me. She hands me a bottle of beer with the top already twisted off.

"I have to drive home," I tell her.

"Not until after dinner and one beer won't hurt you."

Still, I hesitate before taking a drink. It's one of her fruity beers, something I don't particularly care for. Maybe that's why she gave it to me, knowing I'd nurse the bottle instead of finishing it.

"Did you know about this?"

"Not until this afternoon when Tina called. Why didn't you tell me he was back in town?"

"Because I thought he would be gone after today, that I wouldn't have to see him again."

"And what were you going to do with your divorce papers?"

I try to peel the label off the bottle even though I know it won't come off. Back in high school, Ajay and I used to do this. We'd save them, saying that when we had our own place, we'd make wallpaper out of all the labels. Good thing that idea lasted as long as our marriage... well the initial part of our marriage.

"I was going to sneak into the records and put them in there. Blame the clerk for not filing them correctly."

"So, Ajay comes back, and you revert back to your old ways?" she asks. I shrug. Sometimes being bad is fun. "I used to think he was a bad influence on you but maybe it was the other way around."

"He definitely encouraged me."

As my mom and I sit, she points out different birds that land near us and talks about how the tide is shifting. She tells me that the craft project that we were working on was for the senior center and that it was Evelyn's idea to make glitter cards. I remind her that last week Evelyn's class went on a field trip there and that's all Evelyn talked about for days.

"Why'd he do it, Mom?"

"Who, your dad or Ajay?"

I close my eyes briefly. "Both."

"Well, I can't speak for Ajay, but I imagine he just got lost and couldn't find his way back home. Your father... I don't know, Jamie. We watched you struggle for so long after Ajay left; I think that always played in the back of his mind. He's a father after all, and he's protective of his daughter."

"How did he know where to find him?"

"There was an ad in the paper for the concert. I threw it away but found it later on his dresser. He had circled Ajay's name. I tried to talk him out of whatever he was planning, but you know your father. Once he sets his mind to something there's no stopping him."

"I'm the one who teepeed Harvey's house. Ajay just drove my truck. I did it because I heard what you told Dad about Harvey hitting on you and I got pissed."

"You were such a delinquent back then, but I thank you for sticking up for me." She bumps her shoulder into mine. "What are you going to do if Evelyn takes after you?"

"Lock her up," I say with a shrug. "Tell her that whatever she's thinking of doing, I've already done it so she can't outsmart me."

"She's definitely smart."

"Like her father."

My mom looks at me. "She asks about him a lot."

I nod. "I know. I don't know what to tell her about him. She shouldn't have to know that he chose his family over her."

"All you can tell her is that you didn't know what he was really like."

I scoff. "No matter what I say to her, I look like the asshole who had an affair with a married man."

"Don't be so hard on yourself, Jameson. A one-night stand hardly constitutes an affair on your part... he on the other hand, needs his balls cut off."

"He was just another mistake I made."

"But the result was worth it in my opinion. Evelyn is the light of our lives, and you gave her to us. You brought that beautiful little girl into this world; her father be damned. She's ours and we get to keep her to ourselves."

Mom shrugs. "Maybe it's time to make up a fairytale about him. I'm sure between the two of us we can create a Prince Charming who lives with a wicked witch in a cold, dark dungeon and only a fire breathing dragon and unicorn can save him."

I look at my mom with bewilderment. "She's going to see right through your story."

Mom shrugs. "It's the beer talking," she says, taking another sip.

## 17

## AJAY

*W*hen I walk onto the stage, everyone stops tuning their instruments. Dana rushes over and hugs me, while Hendrix mumbles something about being the only man alive who's allowed to touch his woman, earning him a sly flip off from Dana. Quinn, Keane, and I shake hands, and when Hendrix finally gets over his little attitude, he comes over and gives me a half hug.

"What's the big house like? Did you shank anyone?"

I push Hendrix's shoulder and frown at him. "It was county lock-up, dude."

"So, no hard time?"

"No, man. Just a local judge being unreasonable, nothing the lawyers can't handle."

"Well, I, for one, am happy you're back," Quinn says. "Playing with my pops is fun and all until he starts critiquing."

"I heard that," Harrison yells from somewhere back-stage. I may have only been gone a week, but what a differ-ence it makes. Being surrounded by people that I love, who love me back, offers a whole different outlook on life.

"Sorry, man. I'll do my best to stay out of trouble."

"What'd you do anyway?" Keane asks.

"Stupid teenage stuff. It always comes back to bite you in the ass."

"Remind me to never go home then," Hendrix says.

"You're from Los Angeles, you moron," Dana yells out, causing us all to laugh. Hendrix is our jokester, the one who can and will turn any situation into a comedy routine. He's also the guy that will break your heart with his sob story about Dana and their failed relationship. His love for her, however, doesn't stop him from hooking up with women that he meets at 80's night karaoke. They all swoon when he sings the ballads.

I climb the ramp to my drum set and sit down on my stool. The caddy in front of me holds four pair of sticks. I pick them up and rub my fingers along the wood, thinking back to my conversation with Whiskey about how I couldn't afford to buy new sticks at one time and yet now, here they are, always waiting for me. Being with a band that's signed to a label is something I'll never take for granted.

While everyone finishes tuning, I make sure my kit is stationary, that every nut and bolt is tight, that the toms sound right, that my foot pedal has the right amount of tension, and that my bass drum sounds just the way I need it to.

Pulling a pair of sticks from the caddy, I go through a run, starting off slow until I build the tempo. I continue to play, pushing through the ache in my arms and wrists until our sound crew tells us they're ready for rehearsal.

As soon as Quinn strums his guitar, followed by Hendrix, and Dana sings the first line of our new hit, I'm lost in the beat. I play everything on auto pilot while I soak in her voice. I love this group, not because I'm in it but because of the songs Quinn and Dana sing. They mean something, not only to me, but to all of us, as well as the masses out there who are downloading our songs. I realize while I'm hitting my drumsticks against the toms that I want Whiskey to be here. I want her to see us play, to be a part of the experience. To do that, I'm going to have to play my cards right. I'm going to have to show her that despite everything, I want her to be a part of my life.

After rehearsal, we gather in the green room and chow down on the buffet provided by the catering company. It's always different from the previous location, which is a nice change.

When Betty Paige and Chandler, Keane's daughter, come into the room, I have to swallow a lump that forms in my throat. I could've been the guy who had a child on tour. He or she would be about seven or so, following me around, waiting back stage and living on the tour bus. Life for Whiskey and I could've been totally different than what we have going on now. I long to have the life with her that we were supposed to have.

After dinner, Keane and I stand backstage and listen to the local group opening the show. People are still finding their seats as they play. They try to entertain the crowd, but it's hard. The people aren't into it. They paid for the headline act, after all, not to see the openers.

"Tough crowd," Keane says.

"I was just thinking the same thing. I'm also thinking how lucky we are. Without Elle, Quinn and 4225 West, we're just like this opening act trying desperately to get some attention."

"Don't I know it. I've been the small fry before, as well as being part of the headline act. I'm perfectly happy where we are."

"How does Chandler like being on tour?"

"She loves it, although I probably would too if I got to fly everywhere. She gets along very well with Paige. She likes her tutor as well, which is good otherwise I wouldn't tour during the school year."

"It's almost summer vacation, right?"

He nods. "A few more weeks. I'm hoping to take her to Disneyworld when we circle back to Florida."

That's where I wanted to take Whiskey for our honeymoon. I told her it would happen, that I would save every cent I had to make her dream come true. I can do it now, but the meaning is lost. Maybe I'll make the offer anyway, to come as my friend when the time is right.

If the time is ever right.

As soon as the group on stage starts their last song, Keane and I head to our dressing room to get ready. Inside, Dana is pouring champagne for everyone.

Elle holds her glass up high. "I just heard that your new single will debut at number one on the charts this week. This," she pauses and looks at all of us, "is what we've worked for. The dedication each of you have put into this group, following my vision, and never giving up, has proven to be successful. I am honored to be your manager."

We clink glasses and praise each other. I set my flute down and go over to Elle, pulling her aside. "Can you get me Jamie's number?"

"Why?" she asks. I know she's meant to protect us from the people around us, even from ourselves, but surely she has to know that considering the situation I'm in with Whiskey, we need to communicate.

When I don't answer right away, she nods. "I have it. I'll text it to you, but please be careful, Ajay. Neither of you are in the same place you once were, and you don't need your emotions getting in the way of what you've got going on here."

"I know, Elle. My head's in the game. I promise."

She places her hand on my arm and gives it a squeeze. "It's not your head I'm worried about, it's your heart. I saw the way you looked at her... it's the same way I look at Ben. Just be careful."

"I will," I tell her although my voice lacks the conviction that I need to make myself believe it.

"Alright, unless you're in the band, please leave the room so they can get ready. We'll see everyone after the show." Elle shoos everyone out except for Liam, Harrison, and JD. We come together as a family, arms linked around one another, and pray silently until Liam breaks the silence.

"Another show, another victory. Make the night yours."

Seconds later, one of the staffers comes to our dressing room. She leads us to the stage, telling our sound and lighting people that we're on our way. As soon as the lights dim, the crowd starts to cheer.

"I love you guys," Dana says as she hugs us all while the rest of us high five. We walk out together, all except for Dana who comes on after the melody has started. As soon as I sit down at my kit, my phone vibrates. It's Elle, with Whiskey's number. I save it quickly under Whiskey Girl and send her a text: **I'd like to talk to you after my show tonight, around 8 or so. Will you be awake?**

I don't have time to wait for her response before I have to start playing. From the moment I slam my sticks down and the lights come on, I'm in my zone, and I'm fucking happy that in a few shorts days I'll see my girl, even if she doesn't want to see me.

Throughout our show I do nothing but think about Whiskey and how I miss her. I only spent one day around her and now I can't get her off my mind. Each song that we play reminds me of her, which is crazy because I haven't written a single one of them so there's no underlying influence. Maybe love is all the same and I've just been too deaf to really hear what Dana and Quinn have been singing about.

Once I've banged on the toms for the last time, I stand and walk to the front, tossing my sticks to some people in the crowd. As soon as I'm off stage, I pull out my phone and much to my surprise, Whiskey responded.

**Whiskey Girl: I'll be awake**

That's enough to make my heart pound with anticipation. I shower quickly in the dressing room and hightail my ass onto the bus. Elle is there, talking on the phone, the bus otherwise empty other than the driver. I have never been so eager to get on the road before, but this time I know it puts me one day closer to heading back to Bailey and my Whiskey.

Normally, I chill out in the front of the bus but tonight I head to my bunk. With my headphones on, I press Whiskey's name and wait for her to answer.

"Gone are the nights when you'd get done at one or two in the morning, huh?" is how she answers.

I can't help but laugh. "We aren't the headliners of this tour We play for about an hour and then we drive to our next stop."

"Where are you?"

"Ohio. We have a couple more shows and then I'll have a two-day break. That's when I'll come back."

"You seriously don't have to, Ajay. Harvey is stupid. I told my dad to fix what he did."

129

"I want to, Whiskey."

"Why bother?"

*Because I remembered how much I love you.* "Because I have a lot to make up for and even though we'll be divorced in three months, I'd like us to at least be friends," I say, knowing full well I'm lying to her. I have no intentions of being her friend. I want a second chance with her even though I don't deserve one.

"If I tell you we can be friends, will that change your mind?"

"Not in the slightest, Whiskey Girl."

She sighs and I laugh. "I promise to be that super annoying friend that only comes around when his schedule permits. Besides, if I ditch out, what kind of man does that make me?"

"So, this is a way to fix your image?"

"Only in your eyes. You're the only one that matters to me."

She goes quiet before saying, "I don't want you to get your hopes up, Ajay. You and I, we have vastly different lives and don't fit together like we once did."

All I have is hope. "No hope here, just doing my part to make sure Harvey signs off on our divorce. Three months, Whiskey, and then we'll be on opposite coasts, texting each other late at night when the mood strikes."

"I have to go, Ajay." She hangs up before I can tell her goodnight or that I'll call her again tomorrow and the next day and that I'll see her soon.

I'm still holding my phone when Keane walks in. "Am I interrupting?"

"Nah, man. Just listening to some music." He doesn't say anything as he crawls into his bed. I do turn some music on to drown out the noises from the bus, and against my better judgement, open Facebook, and search for Jamie's profile. Her name yields no results, so I look for Bailey's restaurant page and find a few pictures of her there. I type in Dhara's name and find a ton more photos, some of which are with a little girl who always seems to be holding Whiskey's hand or be in her arms. I stare at the angelic face, trying to figure out who she is and who she looks like. I see a lot of Whiskey in her, but surely, she'd tell me if she had a daughter. Studying the girl for a little longer, I find myself wondering what our child would look like. Would he or she be tall like me, have Whiskey's hair, my eyes... or look just like this little girl in the photo.

I end up saving a few of the pictures and setting one of Whiskey as my screensaver. Hers is the face that I want to stare at until I fall asleep.

## 18

## JAMIE

The early morning knock at my door sends my heart into a frenzy. I never asked Ajay how he got my number. I wanted to, but in the end, it seemed like a moot point. I'm required to spend time with him so it's conceivable that his lawyer gave him my number, which he likely got from Fletcher, which under different circumstances would call for me maiming my good friend. Lucky for him, since this whole thing was beyond his control, if it *was* Fletcher, I'll forgive him. However, if anyone told Ajay where I live, all bets are off. I hesitate before twisting the knob and opening the door slightly. I'm not ready to let Ajay into my life, that much I know. We can meet occasionally and have a cup of coffee together but hanging out at my house is out of the question. Mostly because this is my space and he's never been a part of it, but more importantly because of Evelyn. I'm concerned about his reaction in regard to my daughter when I know I shouldn't be.

Thankfully, when I peer through the tiny crack, it's Logan. He's holds up a white bag which can only mean fresh cinnamon rolls from the bakery he passes by on his way here.

"Do I get to come in?" he asks.

"I don't know. I suppose it depends on what's in the bag."

He laughs. "As if I'd come first thing in the morning without breakfast." He's right, he wouldn't. I swing the door open and step aside as he enters.

"Logan!" Evelyn screams his name as she comes running out of her room. He bends down to pick her up and sets her on his hip as he continues toward the kitchen. I follow, watching the two of them interact. He sits her on the counter and opens the cupboard to grab some plates.

"Did you shoot your gun this week?" she asks him. While Logan and I have been seeing each other, whenever he's with Evelyn, they talk about his job and her schooling as if what she did during the week was work too.

"I didn't."

"It's going to get rusty, ya know. My grandpa says you have to take care of your piece."

Logan chuckles. He helps her get down from the counter and takes all three plates into the dining room. "I'll make sure to shoot it when I get back to base. Tell me, how was work this week? Any new co-workers?"

Evelyn shakes her head. "Nope, but we had a substitute. What would they be called?"

Logan pretends to think for a moment. "Oh, I think we'd call them a 'temporary employee'."

"Yes, one of those. She wasn't very nice, which is probably why she doesn't get to work every day."

I snort and Logan chokes on his sip of coffee. "Could be," he says through gasps of air. "Or maybe she hasn't found the right job."

Evelyn shrugs and takes a bite of her roll. "My boss says we're getting a new co-worker next week."

"Who did they hire?" he asks her.

"Dunno. Probably another boy. You know boys have cooties, Logan, don't you?"

"Yes," he says, sighing. "I'm fully aware."

"Logan, did you know that I have a loose tooth?"

"I did not." He leans closer to her. "Let me see."

My daughter opens her mouth, which has left over cinnamon roll pieces in it, and puts her finger on her tooth. I look as well because this is news to me and sure enough, there's a little wiggle.

"You know what this means?"

"What?" Logan asks.

"That the tooth fairy is coming back!" She throws her hands up in the air.

Logan leans toward her again and in a quiet voice asks her, "Is your room clean?" I want to high-five Logan so much right now. He's been on the receiving end of many late-night calls with me frustrated over Evelyn's room. Every month I go in there and throw random toys out, pack old clothes and donate them, and still it's like her toys procreate when I'm at work. I don't get it.

She huffs and rolls her eyes. "No, but it will be when my tooth comes out. I'm broke." This time I'm the one choking on my coffee. She looks at me like I've insulted her or something. I stand, kiss her on her forehead and start clearing plates.

"Evelyn, do you want to go somewhere fun?" I hear Logan ask her.

"Dunno, Mommy has to work."

"Not until later tonight," he tells her. "Today, we are going to the fair!" I imagine that her eyes are wide, and her mouth has dropped open. Every time she sees the commercial, she asks if we can go.

"Will they have lions and tigers?"

"No, that's the zoo or the circus," I interject as I come around the corner.

"Oh," she says as her face falls.

"But there will be horses, cows, chickens and baby goats," Logan starts to tell her.

"Like the baby goats in the funny videos?"

He nods and smiles happily at her. "Why don't you go get ready?"

"What about rides?" she asks as she gets down from her chair. "Rides, right?"

"A bunch of them," I say. "Make sure you put on your walking shoes. We'll be doing lots of walking and Logan isn't carrying you."

"We'll see!" she yells as she runs off to her room.

"You're not carrying her." I turn to him, only to find him grinning from ear to ear.

"She's lighter than my Rucksack." He puts his hands up in the air. I know I've lost this battle before it's even begun.

As soon as Evelyn's ready to go, we pile into Logan's truck, which she declares is much cooler than mom's car. I think she likes it because he has to lift her up into it and she can see everything when she's up high. Not to mention he lets her play with the windows, which is something I won't let her do.

The drive to the fairground takes about forty-five minutes and during this time, Evelyn asks if we're there yet, approximately twenty-eight point five times. I grow tired of the question and cut her off half way through her last one, telling her Logan will turn around and go home if she asks again. Surprisingly, this works in my favor, although I expect her to call my bluff.

And of course, as soon as Logan parks and opens the door for Evelyn, he turns so she can hop on his back. I half expect my daughter to stick her tongue out at me for getting her way.

"This place is amazing," she says after we get our tickets. "There's so much to do."

"It's a complete sensory overload," I say quietly to Logan. He winks and hikes Evelyn up higher onto his back. "Why don't you walk for a bit? Logan will carry you when you're tired."

"Promise, Logan?"

"Have I ever broken a promise to you?"

She shakes her head, slides down his back and reaches for both our hands. We decide to start with the crafts, to see what everyone has brought to sell. We sample jams, mustards, and other homemade foods. Logan tries to convince me that I need the newest knife set that will cut through a tree, and Evelyn is convinced she needs every piece of jewelry she can touch.

It's when we get to the food trucks that I'm truly happy. Fried dough, deep fried Oreo's, corn dogs... there's a method to my madness, it's all stuff I won't eat at home, but at the fair it's fair game.

Speaking of games, each time we see one, Logan wants to play. The three-point shooting game is an epic fail, however, he wins the hammer one on his first try, earning a stuffed dog for Evelyn. I call veto when he tries to win a fish unless he plans to take it back to base. This starts a whole round of 'Can we get a dog?' questions from Evelyn. And when we come to the game where I can shoot the clown in the mouth, I happily slap money down.

Evelyn sits between Logan and me. The three of us are poised, our water guns are aimed, and we're ready to blow up the balloon. This game and darts are really the only ones I'm good at.

The buzzer sounds and I'm squeezing the trigger, wishing that the water would come out faster. When the alarm sounds, I look up to see if my light is spinning. It is!

"Woohoo!" I stand and start jumping up and down, much to Evelyn's dismay. I don't let it deter me and continue to dance as if I've the lottery.

"Mommy, you have to pick your prize." I tell the young guy working that I'll take the elephant.

As we leave the game, Evelyn takes my hand. She rubs her face against my arm and looks at up. "Mommy?" she asks sweetly.

I crouch down so we're eye level. I'm a master at her game and pretend to have concern for her right now. "What's wrong, sweetie? Do you have an upset tummy? Are you tired?"

"No," she says, falling into me. "Do you love me?"

Logan laughs loud enough for us to hear him. "You know I do."

She falls more into my arms. "Can I have your elephant?" she whispers into my ear.

I stand, forcing her upright. I have every intention of giving her the stuffed animal but now that she's trying to guilt me into it, I'm going to torture her a little first.

"I won this. He's mine."

She drops her head, but not before I see her lower lip jut out. "Okay, I'll be happy with the doggie that Logan won for me, but maybe your elephant and my doggie can be friends?"

"I think my elephant would like that."

Her sour mood lasts a whole five seconds when we enter the ride area. Logan buys a book of tickets that costs more than a week of groceries. We wait in line with Evelyn so she can ride the motorcycles. Once it's her turn, Logan secures her on the seat and comes out to stand next to me.

"What's wrong?" he asks.

I look at him funny and shake my head.

"I know you better than you know yourself, something's on your mind."

"I wouldn't even know where to start." I wrap my arms around the elephant and hug it with all that I have. "Life has thrown me a bit of a curveball."

"Can I help?"

"I don't think so," I sigh. "Do you remember when we first met, and I told you that it wasn't Evelyn's father who hurt me but someone I never wanted to talk about that did?"

I look at Logan. He nods so I continue. "That guy is back, no thanks to my dad and a grudge he's held onto for years. Old memories have resurfaced and the other night I went through a box of stuff that I had kept and turns out that—"

"Mommy, Logan, look at me!" Evelyn goes by and we wave at her.

"Turns out what?"

"That I'm married," I say, holding eye contact with him.

His eyebrows shoot up, his lips purse and he grabs ahold of the fence that we're leaning against.

"We got married when I turned eighteen. It didn't last long. I made him sign divorce papers and then it seems that I never filed them. I tried to the other day, but small-town politics are getting in the way." I continue to tell Logan the sordid details. Everything from my dad arresting my ex, to throwing him in jail, to Harvey being utterly ridiculous with this sentencing.

Logan doesn't say much except that he's sorry and will do anything he can to play mediator between Ajay and me, if that's what I want. That's not exactly the reaction I'm looking for. I fully expect him to fight for me, to tell me to ignore Harvey's sentence because I'm supposed to be Logan's girlfriend, but it's like he's giving up without even trying. Either I've been way off base about our relationship or it's clear we've run our course and it's best that we remain friends. I don't know what to think right now but am very thankful that I have Logan to lean on.

Every ride, he waits in line with Evelyn and makes sure she's secure before the ride starts. He tells me he doesn't trust the ride operator to do their job and I don't either which is why I'll never get on a ride at the fair that spins or goes upside down. I don't feel safe if I can't climb out just in case anything happens.

When Evelyn's exhausted all her tickets, Logan picks her up and ushers us to the exit. She's tired, my mood is shot to hell, and I know his is as well.

We're almost to the exit when my blood turns cold. Coming toward me, with his wife and children, is Evelyn's father. Logan's by my side, whispering in my ear to keep walking, to just ignore what I see, but I can't. My daughter deserves to know her father and her siblings. It's not her fault that her father is a liar and a cheat.

We make eye contact. He looks from me to Logan, and then to the back of his sleeping daughter's head. But he doesn't stop. He never stops. And even as I watch him walk by, he turns and gives us one more look before he returns his focus to his family... the only family that matters to him.

## 19

## AJAY

*H*arrison and Liam are by my side as we wait in the private lobby for their jet to be ready. The three of us are standing at the large window with our sunglasses on, almost as if we were spies. What a fun job that would be, traveling around and doing covert missions. Maybe in another life because the one I'm currently living is booked solid between gigs and spending time in Bailey.

"If you need anything, call me," Harrison says.

"Or me," Liam adds. "I'll be less fatherly, but you can still call if you need someone to talk to. I know a thing or two about being young, in love, and fighting for the woman you want to be with."

"So do I." Harrison leans forward and looks at Liam but unfortunately, I can't see his eyes.

Liam scoffs. "What do you know? You met Katelyn, wooed her, she got upset for a whole two minutes and forgave you. What Ajay's going through — I've been there, man — not you!"

Harrison waves Liam off. "You think you know everything."

"More than you," he mumbles. I try not to laugh but the two of them are pretty funny together. Add JD to the mix and it's a downright party with side aching laughter.

"All I'm saying is that I loved, lost, loved again and wifed Josie up as fast as I could because I wasn't letting her go."

"Wifed her up?" Harrison looks confused. "I think you've been hanging around the kids to much. Wifed her up," he mutters, shaking his head.

"When did you and Katelyn get married?" I ask him.

"Ha! They're not."

"We are... by law."

This time it's Liam waving Harrison off. "Common law, whatever."

"Wait, you're not married? But Elle has your last name."

"Katelyn and I decided a long time ago that neither of us wanted to get married. I think it makes us both work harder at our relationship to be honest. I adopted the twins when they were little, about six years old and she adopted Quinn."

"You can do that?" I ask. "Just adopt other people's kids?"

Harrison takes his sunglasses off and turns so he's facing me. "Peyton and Elle's dad—"

"My childhood best friend to be exact," Liam adds.

"His name was Mason. He died in a car accident when the girls were five. Liam had come back to his hometown for the funeral and decided to stay. Quinn and I came to see him for Christmas that year... and well, the rest is history. And Quinn's mom gave up her rights to him, paving the way for Katelyn to adopt him."

I nod slowly. "I think it all makes sense, at least a little bit. Peyton, what does she do? Elle and Quinn talk about her every now and again."

Liam chuckles. "Peyton is married to my son, Noah. You'll meet him at a stop soon."

"Oh wow, is that weird?" I ask them.

Both say no.

"So, you guys are best friends, bandmates and now fathers-in-law to each other's children?"

"Yeah, pretty much," Liam says. "When I first moved to Los Angeles, I was paired with Harrison for the group. We just clicked. We're family, right along with JD. He's married to my wife's other best friend, Jenna, who you haven't met yet. They have a daughter, Eden, who competes in surfing competitions, so she travels with her a lot."

"Wow, this is band thing is a crazy dynamic. I remember Elle talking about the band becoming your family when we first started out."

"It's important because you spend so much time with each other that when there are wives or husbands, as well as children, it's invaluable to keep everyone included in everything, to make sure everyone feels involved in the decisions the band makes," Harrison tells me.

"What do you mean?" I ask him.

But it's Liam who answers. "If Harrison needs time off to tend to something, the band takes the time off. We put rehearsing on hold when Peyton and Noah got married, and when football season starts, we all go to my son's games as a family. We put real life in front of fantasy. I didn't always and almost lost the love of my life as a result."

I listen to everything that they're telling me and begin to wonder if I'll have an opportunity like this or if Whiskey's going to be adamant about following through with the divorce. If she is, I'll give her whatever she asks for because that's the least I can do, even though she got us into this mess.

The plane moves slowly down the tarmac and comes to a stop. The aviation clerk tells us we can go outside now, and just as we open the door, Quinn comes barreling toward us.

"Oh good, you haven't left."

"Everything all right?" Harrison asks him.

"Yeah, just gonna hitch a ride south. I thought Ajay could use some support and Nola's at her parents so she's going to drive up and meet us there."

I pat him on the back. "Thanks, man." I don't even know if I need help but the fact that he's here means the world to me. Quinn and I make our way out to the plane and board, leaving the guys behind.

"How is 4225 West getting to the next stop?"

Quinn laughs. "This isn't their plane. My dad rented this for you so you can spend time with your girl."

"Are you serious?"

Quinn buckles himself into the seat. I choose to sit across the aisle and opposite him so we can continue to talk.

"If my dad hadn't, Liam would've. He's a sucker for a good love story."

I look out the tiny window to see if they're still in the lobby but can't really see anything but blobs. Leaning back, I close my eyes and think of Whiskey, and how hard I'm going to have to work when I get back to Bailey.

At some point, I fall asleep and jostle awake when the plane lands. I look out the window to try and figure out where we are to no avail.

"We're in Wilmington," Quinn tells me. "Nola is meeting us here with a car rental."

"Oh cool, I appreciate the ride to Bailey."

He laughs and pulls his bag from the overhead compartment. "I sort of told Nola what's going on, and she's determined to be a matchmaker or something."

"What do you mean?" I follow Quinn off the plane and down the stairs. We follow another aviation clerk into their lobby, where Nola's waiting for us. Well, technically, she's waiting for Quinn. I'm just the third wheel.

"Hey, Nola," I wave at her once Quinn's done hogging her attention.

She dangles a set of keys in front of me. "Your rental."

"Um, thanks."

"You can thank me after you see what I picked out." She takes me by the arm and leads us outside and right to a brand new matte black Wrangler that only has a bikini top.

"Whoa."

"Right?" she says, "I hope she likes going topless."

Quinn and I pause and look at each other, waiting for Nola to realize what she just said. She's opening the back door when she looks at us and asks what we're doing.

"Babe, do you know what you just said?"

She smiles. "I do, now let's go!"

WHEN THE SUN rises the next morning, I'm already up, showered and dressed. I've had a nasty tasting cup of coffee that I brewed myself, and paced the floor of my room with my phone in my hand, waiting for an appropriate time to call Whiskey. I had planned to do it last night when we got into town, but after stopping for dinner, visiting multiple antique stores, and driving along the coast, we didn't pull into Bailey until after sundown. I thought about calling Whiskey then, but figured she was at work. The thought of going over and seeing her played heavily on my mind as well, but I don't want to get in her way. I know I have my work cut out for me today, trying to convince her to take a day off from work. I don't know her financial situation and realize it might not be so easy for her to be carefree with me but I'm determined to try. Plus, being the manager at Bailey's Bar and Grill May make it difficult for her to take any time off.

As soon as the clock turns to eight, I press her name on my phone. I know it's still early, but I'm eager to hear her voice and desperate to see her.

"Ajay," she croaks into the receiver and instantly the image of her in bed, wearing nothing but my t-shirt, comes to mind. I close my eyes and wish not only that I was there, but that I could think of anything else because those thoughts will only get me into trouble.

"I'm sorry that I woke you."

"No you're not," she says. I chuckle because she's right.

"I wanted to let you know that I'm in town."

"I know."

"You do?" I open the door and stand on the balcony, wondering if she lives nearby and saw me.

"Mhm... Dhara. She's a huge fan and she saw one of your band members. I assumed he was with you."

"Ah, yes. That would be Quinn, which brings me to the reason why I'm calling. His girlfriend is with him and I'm wondering if you'd like to go to the beach with us today. I realize you probably have to work—"

"I'll go," she says interrupting me. "Can I meet you at Bailey's in an hour?"

"I can pick you up."

"No, I have to stop there for a few minutes so it's just easier if I meet you there."

"Okay, I'll see you in an hour."

145

"Okay," she says, hanging up. I don't want to question why it was so easy to get her to agree, but there's a lingering thought in the back of my mind that this conversation will probably be the only part of my day that will actually be easy. Of course, I want to believe she wants to spend time with me, but this is likely the last thing she wants to do. The rational part of me realizes she's only spending time with me because she has to.

I send a text to Quinn, telling him that Whiskey said 'yes'. He responds, saying that Nola has already gone to the store, the cooler is packed, and that they're ready to leave whenever I am.

I think I love Quinn's girlfriend. At first, when he told me he had let her know what was going on, I was a little upset. But she's his person, and she's trying to help me get my person so who am I to complain? If I'm successful, I'm going to have to do something special for Nola.

The hour goes by painfully slowly. I convince Quinn and Nola that we have to leave fifteen minutes early to drive across the street. I'm pretty sure they're humoring me when they both just smile and plays along with my insanity. While we wait for Whiskey, Nola plays with the radio, telling me that she's going to control the music from the backseat. Honestly, I don't mind because it's one less thing I have to worry about while driving.

I'm standing next to the Wrangler when Whiskey comes into the parking lot, she stops and starts for a moment before approaching.

"Is this yours?"

"It's a rental," I tell her. "But I might have to buy one because it's fun as hell."

She looks at Quinn and Nola, who waves. "Let me introduce you. Quinn James and Nola Boone, meet Jamie."

They shake hands. "It's nice to meet you," Nola says. "I'm excited you could come. Spending the day with these guys by myself isn't always fun, if you know what I mean."

"Yeah I imagine it's all shop talk or moody brooding."

Quinn and I both hang our heads. "Things could be worse, we could talk about video games all day," I tell the girls.

"In which case I would take your credit card and go shopping," Whiskey fires back. I know she's joking but I like that idea a lot.

Even though the doors are off, I walk Whiskey to the passenger side of the Wrangler and wait until she's situated before going back to the driver's side. I'm completely mesmerized by the way she swiftly puts her hair up and checks herself in the mirror.

"What time do you have to be back?"

"I don't," she says. "We should go before all the good spots are taken."

I do as she suggests. As I drive through town, Nola and Whiskey chat. It's easy when there's minimal wind and I like that I can hear them. I decide to take the back roads to the coast because it makes the drive slightly longer but more amenable to having a conversation. Once we're out of town, Nola turns on the music. Through the rear-view mirror, I see Quinn scoff at what's playing on the radio. I want to turn it off or tell her to play something different until I check out Whiskey, she's singing right along to Dana's voice.

"You know this song?" I ask her as we come to an intersection. Thankfully, we're the only car there at the moment so I use this opportunity to talk to her.

She nods. "Yeah, it's on the radio a lot. Let me guess, you know the singer?"

"This is my band," I say with a chuckle. I watch as her

face morphs into something that I can only describe as embarrassment. I lean toward her, my lips close to her ear. "Don't hide from me, Whiskey."

"I'm not," she says quietly.

She turns and looks at me. She's so close that I could kiss her. I want to kiss her, but I pull away. "I love that you know our songs. It means a lot to me." I reach for her hand, intending to give it a quick squeeze, but she holds onto it for some reason and there's no way I'm letting go.

## 20

## JAMIE

*W*hat the fuck am I doing? Why can't I ever say "no" to this guy? Why is it that when he touches me, my whole body ignites in flames? My skin aches for his touch even though the burns he left behind years ago haven't healed. How stupid can I be? How much more of this traitorous behavior will I be able to withstand before I finally force myself to stay away from him.

The problem is, I don't have an answer. He called this morning and I couldn't get out of the house fast enough to go see him. The rational side of me knows I shouldn't feel this way. I should want to see Logan. I should've called him and asked him to come back down after he had to make an emergency trip back to base last night. *He* should be my priority, but even he knows our relationship isn't going anywhere, and I hate that. I hate that both of us became so comfortable that we stopped trying somewhere along the way and instead developed an amazing friendship with partial benefits. Yesterday, when he left, we didn't reach for each other, we didn't declare our love for one another. We said "goodbye" at the door and I immediately went to check my phone to see if the guy next to me had called or texted. He hadn't. But I wanted him to. I wanted to tell him about running into Evelyn's father and how much I hate him. How everything that he did to me was nothing compared to what her father did. How the man who gave me my daughter is the worst kind of man to walk the earth.

I should've said all of this to Logan, but I didn't. Instead, I want to tell Ajay. But then again, I don't. I want to keep him shut out of my life. I want him to leave, to never come back. And yet I want him to love me like he used to and fall in love with Evelyn, too. I want him to choose love, a life with me and my daughter, and at the same time I want him to disappear from my life all together.

I have so many fucked up thoughts that while I'm looking at him, as we're stopped at this four-way intersection with his friends in the backseat, all I want to do is climb over the console and feel him deep inside of me. I want to feel the same way I used to when he'd make love to me, to know what it's like again to be so consumed with love that merely being near him isn't enough. Because I need more... I *yearn* for more. He wouldn't say "no". He might tell me to wait until we get to the beach though, and I would. I'd wait because loving him was the best part of my life until he left, and I don't know if I'll ever forgive him for that.

A car honks but I'm too busy looking at Ajay to know which direction it's coming from, and I don't care to find out because the only thing that matters right now is watching him. He tears his eyes away and pulls forward. The moment is gone but not likely forgotten, at least not by me.

I shouldn't be here. I should've never answered the phone this morning, and when I dropped Evelyn off at my parents, I should've heeded my father's words over my mother's. They're like night and day when it comes to Ajay.

My dad is adamant that I stay as far away as possible while my mother is pushing me toward him. She believes in the notion that everyone has one true love and knows that Ajay is mine. There was a time in my life when I believed the same. Last week, I would've said he wasn't. This week, I'm not so sure.

Ajay pulls into the first open parking spot that we come to. The four of us slide out of the Wrangler and walk to the back. The guys try to carry everything, but Nola and I take the bags, blankets, and the umbrellas from them. Ajay leads the way. He loves this beach, always has. This was our go to spot when we were growing up. We had many picnics, dates, make out sessions and even sex here. I want to be mad that he brought his friends here, a place that was special to us, but I'm not because some of our best moments were spent here and that makes me smile. Ajay is trying to make me happy.

While Quinn sets up the umbrellas, Nola and I lay out the blankets and Ajay digs in the sand.

"What are you doing?" I ask him.

"Fire pit," he says without looking up. I stand there watching him for a moment until he glances up. "Are you working tonight?"

"I don't know," I say, stupidly.

Ajay motions for me to come to him and I do. *Damn traitorous body of mine.* Once I'm close, his palm is instantly touching my bare hip and once again, I find myself on fire and ready to rip my clothes off for him.

"Let's just see how things go today, okay?" he asks, his voice incredibly sweet and caring. This is the only Ajay that I know. The one that told me a divorce would be best was not the man I fell in love with.

"I mean, I do have to work but..." I stumble over my

words, hating myself. I want to be strong, to show him that he has no effect on me, to show him that I'm immune to his charms, but I'm failing miserably. God, how do I love him and hate him at the same time?

Ajay drops the shovel and places his other hand on my hip, pulling me closer, turning me slightly so that his back is facing his friends. "If you're uncomfortable, don't make excuses, just tell me and I'll take you back. Don't worry about Quinn and Nola, they're just along for the ride. And don't worry about me, Whiskey. My motives are clear... I want to spend time with you, but I know we're not on the same page and I'm okay with that. I just need you to be honest with me and tell me when you've had enough of me, okay?"

*There will never be a time when I've had enough.* I smile and nod, knowing I should step away, but I can't muster the strength to do so. "Thanks, Ajay. I appreciate it."

He's the one to step back first. Feeling awkward just standing there, I go back to help Nola, who's setting up a foldable table, chairs, and a radio.

"Do you do this a lot?" I ask her.

She stops and looks around, a big smile on her face. "No, but I'm used to having a house on the beach, so everything is always readily available."

I swallow hard at what she just said. "You live on the beach?"

Her eyes go wide. "Oh gosh, no! Quinn's parents live on the beach and when he's not on tour or in the recording studio, we spend a lot of time there. He's been teaching me how to surf. We do have a condo that overlooks the beach ourselves," she says shyly.

"It's fine," I tell her. "I'm sure he's worked hard for it."

Nola grabs my hand and drags me back to the parking

lot. Trudging through hot sand isn't my favorite thing to do but I follow her anyway.

"You're sort of forceful," I say to her as we reach the Wrangler.

"It comes with the territory. I had to learn to stick up for myself, especially where Quinn's sisters are concerned, not to mention the fans."

"My best friend is a fan, so I get it."

"Anyway, I wanted to tell you that Ajay works hard, too. The band is making waves and their popularity is growing."

"I know."

"Ajay lives with us," she says. "You're more than welcome to come visit anytime. Malibu is breathtaking."

"I've never left this area, other than a trip to Nashville and that didn't turn out so well."

"I was the same way until I went to college in Idaho. After I graduated, I took a road trip to Cali, met Quinn, lost Quinn because I was stupid, and then came home with a broken heart."

"It doesn't look broken now."

She looks out to where the guys are. I follow suit and see that they're standing together, shirtless. Both are tan and perfectly fit with toned muscles and those mouthwatering hip lines that I know for a fact Ajay didn't have when we were growing up. Granted, he was eighteen the last time I saw him and still a boy. Now he's a man, a smoking hot, gorgeous man who's making my mouth water. I don't know if it's the fact that I'm still in love with him or all of the tattoos, but I sure can picture myself memorizing each and every one of them.

"I stare at Quinn like you do at Ajay," Nola says, breaking my concentration.

"I was looking at the ocean."

"Yeah, okay," she says, calling my bluff. "I get it, believe me. Try being around Quinn's dad, Liam, JD, Ben, and Noah. There isn't a lack of eye candy in that group, that's for sure. And don't get me started on the wives and Quinn's sisters. Everyone in their circle is gorgeous and perfect."

*Lovely.*

"Who's Ben?" I ask, changing the subject.

"Elle's fiancé. He does all the band's promo and advertising."

For some reason it's a huge relief to know Elle has someone. "I thought she was Ajay's girlfriend."

Nola shuts the back of the Wrangler and adjusts the bag in her hand. "They're like siblings. Quinn's parents have sort of adopted Ajay."

I remember him telling me about his first real Christmas with them and while I was happy he had that, knowing it had never happened before broke my heart. Thinking about his parents infuriates me.

"You'll probably be overwhelmed when you meet everyone, but it's one huge family."

"Who says I'm meeting everyone?"

Nola chuckles. "I said the same thing when I started dating Quinn." We walk a little way until she stops. "Why does Ajay call you Whiskey?"

"My name is actually Jameson. Everyone but Ajay calls me Jamie."

"It's a cool nickname."

"It's not a nickname though. It's just his name for me and I'd probably punch anyone else if they ever tried to use it. It's only his."

"That's really sweet. I'm really Eleanora, but when I moved to Los Angeles, I called myself Nola. It stuck, unless you're with my parents and then everything is prim and proper," she rambles on until we get back to the guys. Ajay meets us half way and takes the bag from my hands. I wish I could say the band changed him for the worse, but ever since I've known him, he's never let me carry anything if his hands were empty.

Our little space on the beach turns out to be pretty cool. We have enough shade to keep us from burning, a cooler stocked with water, soda, and beer. There's music playing and when a Sinful Distraction song comes on, I find myself singing right along with Nola.

"Whiskey, you surprise me," Ajay says from behind me. As if on cue, my body betrays me and all I want is for him to touch me even though I know it's wrong.

"Why's that?" I ask through the lump in my throat.

"Because from the way you acted last week, I would've thought you never heard of my band or didn't know it was my group."

I adjust slightly so I can look at him. He's so fucking hot with his tanned skin and small pebbles of sweat on his chest. "I blame Dhara, she tells me everything. At first, I resisted..."

"And now, Whiskey? Are you going to resist?"

*For the love of all things holy, please tell me he's talking about music.*

"Ballard, I rented us some surf boards, let's go." Our moment is interrupted by Quinn. I want to scream at him for his imperfect timing and thank him all the same because I need a drink... preferably something cold. Of course, watching him walk away with a board under his arm isn't exactly helping my situation.

## 21

# AJAY

*I* should be pissed that Quinn took me away from Whiskey, however I'm thankful for the reprieve. As much as I hate to admit it, I need a break from her because I'm the guy that wants to forget the last seven years and pretend like I never left. I want to show Whiskey the man I've become instead of having her remember the boy I was.

Quinn and I paddle out and wait... and wait... for the waves to grow, but they never seem to take shape or start to swell. The water isn't choppy and doesn't seem ideal for surfing.

"I think we're wasting our time," I tell him, looking around for the other guys I saw earlier. Most are doing exactly the same thing as Quinn and I, just sitting on our boards.

"It's like the ocean is speaking to us," he says.

I scoff and look over at him. "Are you spouting some weird hippy shit?"

He laughs. "No, honestly that just slipped out. This shit's an omen, man. I'm going back in." Quinn lays forward on his board and maneuvers until he's facing the beach. I follow and start paddling, only looking back a few times to see if the waves have changed. Quinn's right, it's an omen. Of what, I'm not so sure. Maybe this is the calm before the storm, and I make a mental note to check my phone to see if a hurricane is brewing out near Bermuda or something.

Back on shore, we walk around blankets and other set-ups with our heads down, anything we can do to keep from being recognized. Honestly, I'm surprised we don't have permanent spine and muscle damage from keeping our heads down all the time. There are times when I don't care if someone doesn't notice me, and there are times when I want them to and they don't. That's a real shot to my ego, but in the end, it always seems to work out for the best. Go out with Harrison, Liam or JD, on the other hand, and we're sure to have fans coming up to us. JD, specifically, loves the attention and will tweet his location to people and act surprised when they show up. On days like today, I don't want to be recognized and even if I am, I'd like to be left alone.

Whiskey and Nola are lounging in the sun when we reach them. I'm jealous that Quinn can lean down and kiss his girl when all I can do is smile at mine. Believe me, I'm grateful that she's here, but damn it if I don't want more. I know how lucky I am right now and shouldn't look a gift horse in the mouth, but I can't help it. The way Whiskey is sitting there, staring at me, has my hormones working in overdrive and I have a feeling that she knows it.

"Hey," I say to her as I set my board in the sand.

"I have to say, Ballard, I'm a little upset that I didn't get to see you surf."

"Excuse me?" I'm slightly caught off guard by her tone together with the fact that Nola is snickering.

"Yeah, I mean after the way Nola described Quinn while he's in the water, I could only picture you being the same and was excited to see it."

"How exactly did Eleanora describe me?" Quinn asks. The only time he uses her real name is when he's being serious.

"Oh, you know," Nola says with a coy shrug.

"No, actually I don't," he says to her.

"I'd like to know as well," I say. "Maybe it's something I can do that might win me some brownie points with my girl."

Nola and Whiskey start laughing. Both of them double over in laughter while Quinn and I stand there, watching them act like silly fools.

"I guess we're missing the joke," I tell him.

He nods. "I guess. I'm thinking you and I should head south and leave these two here."

"We could. We have the Wrangler. That would save us some time," I add.

Nola stops laughing and looks dead straight at Quinn. She slowly stands and puts her hands on her hips. "You wouldn't leave me."

He shrugs.

"Ajay would leave me," Whiskey says. Her words hurt my feelings even though they're true because that's the guy she remembers. I was young and stupid.

I choose not to play her game or continue the banter that's going on around us. I walk past her and over to the cooler where I pull out a bottle of water and the necessary stuff to make a sandwich. I figure if my mouth is full, I can't say anything stupid. I feel her beside me before she even says a word, and when she touches my arm, I do everything I can to not pull away from her.

"I'm sorry," she says. "That was really insensitive."

"But true," I remind her. "What you said was true. I left you, but I'm back now, Whiskey."

She sighs and tries to smile, but her lips barely move. "I don't know if you being back is a good or bad thing."

"I suppose for you, it's a bad thing. I'm interrupting your life. If I had my way, we would forget the missing years and start over. I know it's not that easy though. Even though Harvey has essentially given us a second chance at making things right, you have a boyfriend which is sort of a roadblock."

"Logan... our relationship is different. We're a weekend thing, maybe a couple times a month, and we mostly just hang out. Yesterday, he came down and took me to the fair."

"Does he know about me?"

"He does now. I hadn't told him before because I never thought I could bring myself to talk about the hurt I went through. He knew someone had hurt me but not the story behind it."

"I will never stop telling you how sorry I am for what I did, Whiskey. I do hope that someday you understand why though."

She looks away and I go through the motions of making myself something to eat even though I'm not hungry and my appetite is gone. I hate knowing she has a boyfriend — or a "friend" — and I have to keep reminding myself that I shouldn't care even though I really do.

"Do you think we could go for a walk?" she asks. "There's something I want to show you."

"Yes," I blurt out, probably too eagerly. I scramble to put everything away and offer her a bottle of water, which she declines. I guzzle mine and put the empty bottle in the box that Nola designated for recycling.

"We're going for a walk," I say to Quinn and Nola, who are looking at a magazine together.

"Don't get sand in your... ouch," Quinn mutters. "Geez, Nola."

"You're not Liam or JD, don't be crass."

I chuckle and fall in step next to Whiskey. We walk for a bit and let the waves hit our bare feet. Neither of us are talking and while normally the silence would be deafening, it's nice to just be in her presence and surrounded by not only her beauty, but the scenery as well.

We come to a bend and have to climb over a few rocks. Doing this barefoot is not ideal, but she seems to have it mastered so I say nothing about turning back or finding a different route.

When we get over the formation there's a small cove waiting for us. We have to wade through knee deep water, but it's worth it.

"Wow!" I follow Whiskey to the small beach and sit down next to her.

"We can only be here as long as it's low tide."

"How have I never been here before?"

"A couple of years ago we had a massive hurricane. A lot of people lost their homes, even in Bailey. Somehow from all of that, this happened. Mother Nature created it."

I figure I can sit here and talk about the cove and how serene it is, or I can ask about her, and since she's always been my favorite subject the choice is easy. "Tell me about your life, Whiskey. I've filled you in on everything about mine."

She pulls her legs closer to her chest and wraps her arms around her knees. "After you left, things were hard for me. Even though I was only eighteen, I had lost everything. *You* were my everything. For as long as I could remember, you and I were always together, and then we weren't. It took a lot of drinking and a few drug induced nights to get you out of my mind."

My heart twists painfully when she says drugs. I can't imagine her doing something to harm herself.

"I went to therapy for a while. The whole, 'it's not me, it's you' thing worked until..." she trails off and seems to get lost in her own thoughts.

"I had to get a job and Bailey's was hiring. I took every shift I could, doubling up most days for about seven months, and then the owner asked me to bartend. He said I was good at keeping peace among the regulars. For a while the tips were really good but then the storm hit. After the hurricane, they wanted to sell and asked me to buy it but I couldn't with my credit... and it wasn't like I had the money to put down on it. I begged them not to sell but they wanted to move to Florida. As a last ditch effort, I suggested they make me manager. I'd run Bailey's in exchange for them paying the rent. It's been a few years now."

"Where do you live?" I ask her.

"I have a house not far from work. It's a rental, but it's mine. Own my car though."

"That's a step above me. I lease a car and rent a room from Quinn and Nola."

"On the beach, I heard."

"Do you want to come to California?" I ask, looking over at her. "I'd really like to show you the area."

She glances at me briefly and then turns away. "I don't know if that's such a good idea."

I adjust the way I'm sitting by pulling her legs over mine, leaving her no choice but to look at me. I trail my fingers over her cheek. "I know Harvey says I'm the one who has to come here because of your job. It makes sense, but I'd really like for you to see my life, to see how you could fit into it."

"Why?"

I swallow the lump resting in my throat. All my cards are about to be laid out.

"Because I don't want a divorce, at least I'm not pushing for one. You're the love of my life, Whiskey, and I think we have an opportunity to start over."

"We were young and stupid."

"And now we're older and probably not a whole hell of a lot smarter." We both laugh. I reach for her hand and weave our fingers together. "Life would be different with me, I know that. I live in California and while I could commute, I'd want you there with me. It's where the studio is, where I rehearse with the band. I know it's a lot to ask, for you to give up your life, but I promise that if you do, you won't be sorry."

"Ajay, what makes you think I still want to be married to you?"

"Because you're here. If you didn't want to spend time with me, you would've told me to come to Bailey's while you're working or told me to ignore what Harvey says, but you didn't. You didn't even hesitate." I let my words sink in and wait for her to tell me I'm wrong. She opens her mouth a few times, but words never seem to come out.

"I love you, Whiskey. I always have."

"I know and I think I love you too, but life is complicated."

"So uncomplicate it."

"It's not that easy, Ajay."

"Logan, right?"

I expect her to agree, but she shakes her head. "Yes-terday when I told him about you, he offered to play mediator." Whiskey shrugs. "He wasn't mad that I'm married, didn't ask me not to see you, nothing. I think this is the out we've both been looking for but didn't realize it until now."

I don't care what sign he was waiting for but I certainly know one when I see it. My hands cup her face and pull her toward me until our lips come together. Her mouth parts and her tongue seeks mine. From the moment we touch, I'm consumed with nothing but desire and yearning, the need to show her how I've changed and what life can be like together. We fall back into the sand, my arm cradling her head. Her body presses to mine as her hands roam over my torso. I find myself needing to be with her, to mark her, claim her as mine and only mine, but not here. Not now.

As if she's reading my mind, she pulls away and sits up, panting for air. "That shouldn't have happened."

"I disagree."

"Logan... he's still my boyfriend."

With my hand around the back of her neck, I guide her to meet my gaze. "Break up with him and let me be your husband, Whiskey."

## 22

# JAMIE

*I*'ve always been the girl who falls in love first, asks questions last, never thinks about the consequences and ends up ass over tea kettle because I'm not cautious. As much as I want to roll around in the sand with Ajay, to add sex in the sandy cove to the list of "Stupid Shit Jamie Does", I can't. I'd love to be foolish right now, to blame my emotions on making rash decisions but I owe it to myself, to Logan, and to Evelyn to proceed with caution and to not be *that girl*. But being that girl, the one who doesn't care, can be nice. I hate being a responsible adult right now, and I blame Ajay. It's his fault. He brings this reckless behavior out in me. If it weren't for him, I'd be sitting behind my desk, processing inventory, or standing behind the bar, pouring drinks, and listening to people's problems.

Except, I'm here with my legs between Ajay's, my fingers digging into a muscle on his back and looking into his eyes. He asked me to give him a chance at being my husband. Do I owe him that? I'm not sure that I do. Do I want to be married to him? Again, I don't know, but I'm not positive giving up on a chance to be with him again is something I want either. Life with and without him is complicated. He's never been far from my mind especially with his band doing so well — plus Dhara, despite being my best friend, made sure I knew everything even though I had no desire to know.

"Whiskey?" he says my name and it echoes all around. "Whiskey, look at me."

My eyes shoot up to his and I'm lost in the deep sea of blue. I'm waiting for him to say something profound, like to tell me he loves me again or wants to make love to me... maybe tell me that if he's not buried inside me immediately, he's going to die or something like I've read before in a book or two, but he doesn't say anything. He leans forward and kisses me softly. After years apart I've never forgotten the way his soft lips feel against mine. That must mean something right?

"I think we should get back," I tell him before any of my fantasies start to come true and I'm left with no option except to tell him no. I don't want to have sex with him on the beach... the Wrangler, maybe... but not here. Not now. Not tomorrow either. I have to get my life in order. But I can't lie and say I don't want to have sex with him, and yet I know I shouldn't.

On the way back to our spot on the beach, he holds my hand and our arms sway as if this is the most common thing between us, as if we've been doing this for years not minutes.

Ajay stops down by the water, away from his friends. We're ankle deep in the water when he turns to face me, blocking me from seeing the people behind us. "I'm freaking out a little. It's starting to feel like the cove wasn't reality and as we walk closer to our friends, we're also going back to our real lives."

"That doesn't make any sense, Ajay."

He sort of rolls his eyes. It's not because I'm being a smart ass, but because he's showing me his frustration. He's never been particularly good about expressing himself.

"I don't know what I'm trying to say, Whiskey. I just want you to know... look, I kissed you, told you that I love you. Those things still exist for me when my friends are around."

"Okay?"

His eyes roll again, and I place my hand on his cheek. "Are you trying to say—"

"What I'm trying to say is that the person I was in private is the same person I am in public. I won't hide my feelings for you, not from anyone."

His words bring a smile to my face. I like that he's open and honest about things and that if we were to stay together, everyone would know it. Our relationship wouldn't be a secret hidden behind a closed door.

All of this is great, but I still haven't told him about Evelyn. I don't know why I can't bring myself to do it. Mostly due to fear of what he might say, do or what questions he might ask. I don't want to see the hurt on his face when he finds out I have a daughter, not because I moved on but because she's not his. He used to tell me he only wanted children with me, and while I don't know if that still holds true to this day, I used to say the same thing to him.

Ajay squeezes my hand and directs us back to our spot. Nola's making lunch and offers us some as well.

"Actually, I need to go make a phone call," I say, without looking at Ajay for his reaction. I rifle through my bag and pull out my cell phone, thankful that no one has been trying to reach me.

I walk toward the parking lot and cross it to where

there's a shelter with picnic tables. Sitting down, I press the button and wait.

"Hey," Logan says. "What's up?"

"I kissed Ajay," I blurt out.

"Oh," he says. That small word lingers on the line between us.

"I'm sorry. It was stupid. I just got caught up in the moment."

"You had a moment?"

"Nostalgia."

"Tricky little thing nostalgia is, isn't?"

"Yeah," I sigh. "Especially when you don't have closure."

"And yet, another tricky word."

"Logan, I'm sorry."

"Don't be, Jamie. I'm not mad. I get it. But listen, I'll be down in the morning, okay?"

"Okay."

"Jamie?"

"Yeah, Logan?"

"I don't want you worrying your pretty little head about what happened, okay? After everything you've gone through the last couple of days, I know your emotions are running high."

"You're too good to me."

He laughs, which means he's probably agreeing with me. "You should tell him about Evelyn."

I shake my head even though I know he can't see me. "He'll bail by the time our ninety days are up. I'm just going to wait him out." Despite Ajay telling me he's in this for the long haul, I'm not sure I trust him.

"I gotta run, Jamie. Are you working tonight?"

"Technically, no. I took the night off, but Ajay doesn't

know that. He brought me out to the beach with his friends. I figured I should make an effort if he is."

He laughs. "Be nice, tiger. I'll see you tomorrow." Logan hangs up, leaving me very confused. He's not mad about the kiss, tells me I need to be nice to Ajay, and thinks I need to tell him about my daughter. It seems like Logan is pushing me toward Ajay when he should be standing between us.

I continue to sit under the shelter, needing a few minutes to get my thoughts in order. A limo pulls into the parking lot and stops. The doors open and a wedding party gets out, followed by the groom and his bride. Her dress is mermaid style and I find myself laughing as she tries to keep up with her group. It's when her husband scoops her up into his arms that my heart skips a beat.

*"Are you sure you want to do this, Whiskey? You don't even have a dress."*

*"I'm tired of my daddy treating you like crap," I tell Ajay as he drives us to the courthouse. "Besides, it's my birthday and I can't think of a better birthday present."*

*"Your daddy's going to kill me," he mutters.*

*I wave him off. "Eh, after today he won't be able to chase your naked ass down the road with a shotgun anymore."*

*"Don't remind me. But he* can *tell me I can't live with you."*

*"Then we'll move to my grandpa's. He's got that trailer on his property, we could live in that. Hell, we could pull it with the truck and move someplace else."*

*"I don't want you living in a camper, Whiskey. Not with the baby coming."*

*I look down at my stomach. There's a tiny bulge there, but only Ajay and I notice it. After we're married, I'll tell my parents. I know they'll be pissed but there isn't anything they* can do about it. I'll be Mrs. Ajay Ballard and they'll just have to accept my choices.

Ajay reaches across and places his hand under my shirt, his palm on my stomach. Every night since I failed the most important test of my life, he's laid in bed and spoken to our baby. He even bought me a book on what to expect and we've read it together.

I am so in love with the man next to me. I can't wait to be his wife and the mother of his child.

"We'll be fine, Ajay. My daddy will come around. Once I tell my mom she's going to be a grandma, she'll force Daddy into submission. You know deep down he's just a big ole softie, like a bear."

"Like a grizzly, while they're cute and fluffy, one swipe with a paw and I'm out cold." Ajay pulls up along the curb and shuts my truck off. "Are you sure about this, Whiskey?" He asks me again, "Marriage... it's forever."

"Stop fighting me on this, will ya?"

Ajay looks out the window and finally back at me. "I have nothing to offer you, Whiskey Girl. I'm barely passing school and my job stocking shelves at the mini mart doesn't pay shit."

"It pays enough to feed me and our baby. I'll worry about putting a roof over our heads." I take his hand in mine. I expect him to get out and drag my ass up the stairs of the courthouse, but he lets go of my hand and turns the truck back on instead.

"Where are we going?"

"Look, I can't afford much, but I do have a couple hundred saved up."

"For what?"

He looks at me and smiles. "For a ring."

"I don't need one, Ajay. Besides, I have a math test in fifth period that I have to be back for."

He doesn't listen and continues to drive us to the superstore. We walk hand in hand to the jewelry counter, all the while I'm looking over my shoulder for a sighting of either of my parents. They're going to be pissed I ditched out on school today, but not as angry as they will be when I tell them why.

The clerk comes over to help and Ajay asks to see the rings in his price range. I can tell he's a bit embarrassed but I'm not. I'm in love with him and want to be his wife.

"Which one do you like?"

I point to one of the three he's showing me. It's small, simple, and beautiful. He pays for the ring and a band to go along with it.

"What about for you?" I ask.

"Maybe next month, I don't have enough to buy all three."

"I should buy yours."

"Nah, I'll get it. Besides, after today, my money is yours."

"And mine is yours," I say, giving him a kiss in the parking lot. Standing at the truck, his hand rests on the handle. "Everything okay?"

He nods and drops down to his knee. "Whiskey Girl, will you marry me?"

I throw my arms around him and we almost fall to the ground. We're laughing as he slips the ring onto my finger.

"Come on, we gotta hurry." He helps me into the truck and makes his way back to the courthouse. Inside, we have to show our driver's licenses to prove we are of age.

"Does your daddy know what you're doing, Jamie?" the desk clerk asks.

"Sure does. Told this boy to start acting like a man. What a better way to be a man, right?"

She cocks her head to the side and gives us an 'uh huh' as she continues to process our paperwork. We sign our names and she tells us that Judge Harvey can see us in ten minutes. Frankly, that's too long but I can be patient.

As we wait, Ajay's leg bounces up and down. "Cold feet?"

"Nah, just scared she called your daddy and he's about to burst through that door with his shotgun loaded and aimed at my head."

"Well at least you're dressed this time."

"Funny," he says, but he's not laughing.

"I'm an adult and this is what I want."

"Most eighteen-year-old's ask for a car."

"Got that already."

"Jameson Foster and Ajay Ballard, you're next."

I stand up and drag Ajay behind me. Judge Harvey doesn't look too pleased to see us standing in front of him and I suppose it's because he knows I'm the one that teepeed his house not too long ago. I have no doubt that it was a bitch to clean up because his stupid sprinklers came on, soaking that tissue right where I left it. Plus, it rained for the next few days which meant he couldn't really clean it all up.

"I don't even want to pretend I know what's going here."

"Works for us," I tell him.

"Do you, Jameson Foster, take Ajay Ballard to be your lawfully wedded husband?"

"I do."

"Ajay Ballard, do you take Jameson Foster to be your lawfully wedded wife?"

"I do," he says proudly.

Judge Harvey sighs, scribbles his name on our marriage license and looks at the both of us. "I hope to hell you both realize what you've just done," he pauses to shake his head. "I now pronounce you husband and wife."

He doesn't tell Ajay he can kiss the bride, but Ajay does anyway. "Mrs. Ballard," he whispers against my lips.

"Best. Birthday. Ever."

## 23

## AJAY

*T*he day at the beach hadn't really gone like I had planned. After Whiskey walked off to make her phone call or do whatever she had to on her phone, she was different when she returned. Her normal jubilant, smart ass banter disappeared, and she acted reserved and somewhat standoffish, shooting off one-word answers instead of engaging in conversation. Still, I did what I could to make the rest of the day and evening enjoyable for all of us.

Today, though, it's a different story. My calls to her have gone unanswered and my texts unreturned. I suspect it has to do with the fact that I kissed her, knowing she belongs to someone else. I don't even know the guy, but I know they're not in love with each other. If they were, she wouldn't have come out to the beach with me for the day or would have invited him to come as well. I know her better than she knows herself. She's loyal, maybe to a fault. That's something I've always admired about her. What I find odd is that she owes me nothing and earlier in the week didn't give a shit about following the sentence from Harvey. In fact, she told me she was willing to lie. I, however, am not. I want this marriage and find it comical that we're "forced" to spend time together, mostly because Harvey knows he has no basis to order us to do so. Saul called me the day after I left Bailey and told me he was filing an appeal and that he was confident the divorce settlement would be imminent. I told him not to bother, that I wanted the three months to try and win her back and if she thought she had to see me, she wouldn't be able to tell me no.

It's an underhanded plan, but I'm desperate. I'm in love with this woman and I need all the help I can get. I was stupid to ever let her go, but the thought of living on the street with her, or in a sleaze bag motel, disgusted me. It's not what I wanted for us and by the time I could actually provide something decent, I had been gone far too long. Proving that I've changed and that I never wanted to leave her in the first place is going to be an uphill battle...one she's currently fighting with me.

I step into Bailey's hoping to see her. Unfortunately, there's a man behind the bar, wiping the top down.

"What can I get you?" he asks as I pick a stool. There are very few people in here and I assume that's because it's a Sunday. Everyone is probably still at church or at home cooking family dinners.

"Coke?"

He nods. I look around and find a few girls staring so I pull my cap down and keep my attention on the bar. The barkeep places my drink in front of me and sets a menu down, telling me to let him know when I'm ready to order.

"Is Jamie working?"

"Not today, she took the day off."

"Gotcha." I'm not going to let it bother me that she's been off all day and couldn't return my calls. I need to remind myself that what she does is none of my business, regardless of how much I want it to be. What I could've done though, was head off with Quinn and Nola. They're driving to her parents for the day and invited me, but I didn't want to miss an opportunity to see Whiskey. Now I feel like a fool. I should've taken the hint she was silently sending me.

After I finish my drink, I ask for a beer. I need something stronger, and I need food if I'm going to drink. My other option is to eat my lunch and head back to my room to enjoy my pity party for one.

I'm three drinks in when someone taps me on my shoulder. I'm half tempted not to acknowledge the person next to me, until they sit down next to me.

"Ajay Ballard, is that you?"

I lift my hat a little and apprise the guy next to me. "Lee Johnson, how the hell have you been?" I ask him. He looks like an older version of the guy I left behind. Lee was the guy who everyone thought would make it big. He made such a big deal about playing in the garage band, almost as if it were beneath him. If I remember what Whiskey said correctly, he married Jolene Johnson.

"Heard you were back in town."

"Yep," I say, finishing off my bottle. I show it to the bartender who nods in my direction. "Just passing through mostly."

"Really? Jolene said she ran into Jamie at the park. She said Jamie told her you're back for good and looking for a gig."

If I had beer in my mouth, I would've choked. I shake my head slowly. "Funny story, Lee. I heard Jolene told Jamie that I came by asking if you wanted to join Sinful Distraction."

His eyes go wide. "Oh wow, I mean I'm flattered but—"

I hold my hand up, interrupting him. "Lee, no offense but we're not looking to add to the group, and I think we both know I'm not in town to ask if you want to play in my band."

The poor dude hangs his head, and now I feel bad. Back in the day, Lee and I weren't exactly close. We both had an affinity for music and wanted to make a career out of it. Lee had won a few talent shows and everyone thought he was destined for stardom. I, on the other hand, was the kid who was going nowhere, who didn't have a home, and could barely afford to feed myself. Guess life has a funny way of working out in the end.

"So, you married Jolene, huh?"

He nods. "Yeah, we have a little boy. Being a parent is pretty awesome, man," he says, patting my shoulder.

"I heard." The youngest kid I know is Chandler, Keane's daughter. She's pretty awesome, but mostly keeps to herself.

"How are things? Married? Kids? The band is successful. Jolene's a big fan."

The bartender sets a fresh bottle of beer down in front of me and Lee orders water, saying something about performing later. I think I'm in the clear and can avoid answering Lee's questions, but unfortunately he's looking at me, waiting for me to unload about my life.

I sigh, take a drink, and give him the dirt. "Band is great. We are on tour right now, but I'm trying to spend my off days in Bailey. No kids. One wife."

"Congratulations, man. Who is she?"

This time I laugh. "Her name is Jameson." I let her name hang in the air, along with a cheesy grin. Lee studies me; I suppose he's waiting for me to crack up with laughter, but I don't.

"You're joking, right? Didn't you guys get divorced years ago?"

Slowly, I shake my head while bringing the bottle of beer to my lips. "Doesn't seem that way. Jamie forgot to file the paperwork to end our marriage."

"Well ain't that some shit. So now what are you going to do?"

"I don't know," I say, shrugging. "Judge Harvey has a stick up his ass and isn't granting us a divorce."

"Man, that guy."

On the inside I'm laughing, but to anyone watching me, I look like one pissed off dude who's forced to hang out in his former hometown. I'm going to play it off as long as possible, at least until I can convince Whiskey that being married to me is worth it.

"Does that mean she gets half your money?"

Lee's question gives me pause. I hadn't really thought about any financial implications but imagine that she wouldn't be entitled to anything. I signed the papers, proving that I wanted the divorce. Only now, since I've been back and have seen her, have my feelings changed.

"No, I don't think so." Even though I'd give her what-ever she asked for. "What's new with you? How's the band?"

Lee turns and nods toward the stage. "I'm part of the house band here. We're down a singer and a drummer tonight though. The flu has been going around."

"That's hard man." A few months ago, Dana came down with a cold and happily shared it with all of us.

"Hey, do you have plans tonight? We could really use you on the drums. Our acoustic performances aren't really that great, if you know what I mean."

I glance at the stage and find myself nodding. "Why the hell not? I don't have anything better to do tonight."

Lee claps his hands together and smiles like he's just won the lottery. When he motions toward the door, I crane my neck to see who he's eyeing.

"Speak of the devil," he says as I stare at Whiskey, the guy standing next to her and... the little girl holding her hand. It's the same girl in the pictures I saved from Dhara's profile.

Every hope I had about staying with my girl dissipates rather quickly. I know deep in my heart that the reason she's avoiding me is because she's in a committed relationship, despite what she told me, and was only with me yesterday to appease me. A reconciliation of our marriage is unlikely.

Turning away from the door and the look she's giving me, I chug my beer and ask the bartender for another one.

"Hey man, don't get drunk. I really do need you to play."

"I'll be good," I tell him. "Do you have any sticks for me?" I have some in my bag back in my hotel room but I'm afraid that if I leave the bar, I'm not coming back.

"Yeah, I'll make sure they're with the kit when you get up there. See you in about thirty?"

"One last question, what are we playing?" Lee digs into his pocket and hands me the set list. I look it over, confident that I know all the songs. "I'll meet you up there."

Lee leaves me at the bar and I immediately wish I had followed him because Whiskey's near me and being close to her is the last place I want to be right now.

And because I've had a little bit too much to drink, I can't keep my mouth closed. "Well, look what the cat dragged in," I say, taking a long pull off my bottle. I tip the bottle toward her boyfriend and smile.

"You're drunk, Ajay," she mutters through gritted teeth.

"Not yet but I'm thinking about heading in that direction really soon. Hey man, I'm Ajay, Whiskey's *friend*." I purposely leave out that I'm her husband because for all I know, she's lying to him about me and as much as I'd love to air our dirty laundry, I'm not about to hurt her. Right now, I'm not sure I believe her about much of anything. Yesterday, she made it seem like they weren't that serious but the little girl between them tells a different story.

This little girl... she's fucking adorable and looks just like her mom with blonde pigtails and hazel eyes. She's the same one from the photos I found on Facebook and subsequently saved on my phone. I didn't want to believe Whiskey had a child because I knew that once I did my heart would seize, and sure enough the stabbing pain I feel is my heartbreaking. She smiles and shows me that she's missing a tooth, but then turns shyly into her mom's side. I get it, stranger danger. I'm all about it. Whiskey's hand comes protectively around the girl's shoulder, pulling her closer to her.

"She yours?" I look at Whiskey and ask one of the hardest questions I've ever had to ask her.

Whiskey's eyes divert to her feet. I'm trying to hold it in, but my heart is fucking broken. Our child didn't thrive when Whiskey was pregnant, but hers with another man did. I never thought I'd care as much as I do, but this is painful. I wipe away at the tears forming in my eyes and stand.

"Where are you going?" she asks, finally breaking the silence.

I point to the stage and clear my throat. "Lee asked me to play with the house band."

"Oh great," the guy with her says, "Jamie tells me you're really good on the drums."

Swallowing hard to get rid of all the emotions threatening to take over, I nod at the guy who has won the heart of the girl I'm in love with. "I'm sorry, I didn't catch your name."

He offers me his hand to shake and as much as I don't want to, I'm going to be a bigger man and suck up my pride. "I'm Logan."

"Logan, right. Well I hope you enjoy the show."

"I'm Evelyn," the little girls voice rings out. "And today I get to come here because it's kids' day."

I crouch down and gaze into the eyes of Whiskey's daughter. "Well Evelyn, it's really nice to meet you. I'm Ajay." I shake her tiny hand and walk away as soon as possible knowing full well that if I say anything else, Whiskey will know she's gotten the best of me.

## 24

## JAMIE

*A*fter Ajay left for Nashville, I didn't mope. I didn't sit around waiting for him to come back. I didn't jump every time I heard a door slam or the phone ring. I went to work, earned money so I could help move us out of my parents' house. I fought with my dad, who took every chance he could to tell me how I made the biggest mistake of my life when I married Ajay, and I sat with my mother, night after night, watching evening game shows and laughing at corny sitcom television shows. All the while, I was wondering what my husband was up to because the phone wasn't ringing, he hadn't checked in and the calling card he took with him hadn't been used.

And then, finally, the phone rang. Only it wasn't Ajay but a guy looking for him, and I asked him when he last saw Ajay. He told me where he was performing. My husband had gotten a gig and hadn't called to tell me, hadn't thought to share the news with me. To say I was hurt was the understatement of our short marriage.

I told my parents I was going to Nashville. I needed to be with my husband. My father had another idea, and presented me with divorce papers, saying it would be for the best. Maybe part of me felt the same way because I took them with me, but I was determined to support Ajay, to stand by his side while he traversed the music industry. This was his dream and I was going to help him succeed. Only that wasn't what he wanted... and neither was I.

Walking into Bailey's tonight, Ajay is the last person I expect to see. I looked all over the area for the Wrangler he drove yesterday and when I didn't see it, I figured he had left, especially after I didn't answer any of his calls or texts. I don't know if I want him to leave or not, but I think it'll be easier for me. My heart is torn and my resolve is breaking. Ajay's getting the best of me and there isn't anything I can do to stop it. After one week, I'm ready to jump all in with him and not look back, except I know I can't make rash decisions... not when I have Evelyn to think about. She's my one and only priority. And I've been hiding her from Ajay. Not because I'm ashamed, because I knew how he would react to seeing her.

As soon as the three of us stepped into Bailey's and I saw Lee talking to someone whose back was to the door, my heart dropped. I knew instantly that it was Ajay. We should've turned around and left. I should've told Logan that I didn't feel well, anything to get the hell out of there, but Ajay had spotted us and had seen Evelyn. There was nowhere to hide.

I fully expected Ajay to be a real asshole, but he wasn't. He introduced himself as my friend, and when he spoke to Evelyn, I could hear the agony in his voice. He tried to hide his face from me, but I saw his tears. I wanted to hold him, and tell him all about Evelyn, but I couldn't bring myself to say anything. For a moment, I was back in my bedroom, curled in fetal position with him holding me tightly, his tears mixing with mine as we cried over the baby we lost. I was one week shy of my second trimester and hadn't felt very well. Dhara's mother is a nurse so I went and saw her. When she couldn't find the baby's heartbeat, she sent us to the hospital. The whole way there, Ajay told me that everything would be fine. That day, he never let go of my hand.

Fingers snap in front of my face and I come back to reality. "You still with me, Jamie?"

"Yeah, sorry, just really lost in thought."

"Logan said he's going to dance with me later," Evelyn says from beside me.

"Is that so?"

She nods happily. "I'm the best dancer."

"There's no doubt about that," I say to her, but my eyes are trained on the stage. I can't recall the last time I saw Ajay playing the drums. I think it was a garage band or might have been someone's summer party, but it was shortly after I lost the baby. We were so in love, but our hearts were broken. We wanted to use our loss as a fresh start, which is why he said he wanted to go to Nashville to land a good paying gig, to get us out of Bailey. I believed him.

Evelyn crawls over my lap and meets Logan at the end of the table. He takes her out on the floor and swings her around.

From where our table is, I have the perfect view of Ajay. His hat is on backward and the flannel shirt he had on earlier is either on the floor or wrapped around his waist. I'm hoping for the latter. That was always my favorite look on him for some reason. Maybe because it made him look rugged. Ajay's watching Evelyn and Logan on the dance floor. Every so often he looks in my direction, we make eye contact and he immediately looks away. We have to talk before he leaves because I want to explain - I want him to know that if he wants me, he has to love her, too.

"Phew, I'm tired." Evelyn wipes her forehead with the back of her hand and starts to climb over my lap.

"Would you like me to move so you can get to your seat?"

"No thanks, I can do it." And she does, but not before giving me a Charley horse.

"Do you want to dance?" Logan asks just as the lead singer tells us he's going to slow things down a bit. Logan holds out his hand and I take it, appreciating the help in getting up since my thigh is killing me.

"Grandma and Grandpa are on their way. Don't leave the booth, okay?"

"Okay, Mommy."

With my hand in his, I follow Logan onto the dance floor. I don't look at Ajay, I can't. I've seen enough hurt in his eyes tonight to last me a lifetime.

"We need to talk, Logan." He nods as we continue to sway to the music.

"I'm going to make this easy, Jamie. I'm deploying next week. The orders are really unexpected, but I'm needed overseas. I found out the other day, which is why I've been down here as much as possible. I wanted to show you and Evelyn a nice time before I went away."

"Logan—"

"Jamie, I don't want you to wait for me. I would never ask you to. I know your life is with someone else and I'm okay with that. I just want us to stay friends. I need someone to be the person I call when shit is bad."

I nod and fight back the tears. "I'll always be that person, Logan. Always." He pulls me close and I nestle into the crook of his neck.

"I don't want you to think I'm hurt because you're in love with your ex. I get it."

"I'm so sorry."

"I'm not," he says. "Knowing you and Evelyn has been the highlight of my life so far. Even if I wasn't deploying, I'd step aside."

Looking at him, he has me wondering why he would do that. "Why? What makes you think you can't compete?"

He smiles. "When he was just a ghost, it was easy. I knew you had been through something earth shattering but I was willing to put your fragile pieces back together. For a couple of years, we've been at this relationship, neither of us willing to make a big move. It's like you've always been present but never really here, until this week. I think on some level you always knew he'd come back."

My feet stop moving even though Logan is trying to keep us dancing. His words replay over in my head and I find myself questioning them.

"You okay?"

"Yeah, it's just that what you said there gave me pause."

"He's your soul mate, Jamie. I can see the connection between you. No one can compete with that."

"Oh," I reply as I start moving from side to side again. Once the song stops, Logan and I walk back to our table where my parents are now sitting. My dad's sitting in my seat, forcing me to sit across from him where I can't watch Ajay play.

"I thought he left town." Dad motions toward the stage and even though I know better, I look over my shoulder at Ajay.

"Some of the guys are sick, so Lee asked Ajay to play."

"I suppose he has to stick around for as long as possible, huh?"

"He wouldn't, if you'd tell Harvey to knock his shit off," I say.

"Don't curse in front of Evelyn, Jameson," Mom scolds.

"Yeah, Mommy. You're not allowed to say bad words." Great, everyone is ganging up on me. Logan decides now is the time to tell my parents that he's leaving. My mom cries and tells him she'll send him boxes all the time so all he has to do is tell her what he needs. My dad mumbles something about war and how it's gone on far too long and needs to end. You won't hear me complaining there. But it's Evelyn who has all the questions. She doesn't understand why he has to leave, why he can't come see her for a long time, and why he has to go so far away that they can't talk on the phone. Most importantly, she wants to know if he's bringing her a present back and if he is, she asks if it will be a puppy or a kitty.

When Dhara and Fletcher show up, my parents decide it's time to go and take Evelyn with them. The goodbye between Logan and Evelyn is sad and he asks her to send him lots of pictures so he can decorate his wall with her drawings. Fletcher is pissed that his friend is leaving and Dhara promises to take him to a concert when he comes back.

When last call is announced, the four of us get up and make our way outside where Dhara, Fletcher and Logan share a tearful goodbye.

"You ready?" he asks, motioning toward his car.

"I think I'm going to stay." I look back at the door. Logan pulls me into his arms and kisses the top of my head.

"He's one lucky guy. Do me a favor?"

"What's that?"

"Keep me updated. If he doesn't get his shit together, I'll come back and beat his ass."

I laugh into his chest. I have no doubt Logan will do exactly as he says.

"I'm going to miss you."

He hugs me tighter. "I'll email and text when I can."

One more kiss and he leaves me standing in the parking lot. I wait for him to drive away before I contemplate going back into the bar. The guys from the band are starting to file out so I stand near the door, waiting for Ajay.

He's the last one to come out and stops in his tracks when he sees me leaning up against the light pole. "You shouldn't be out here alone."

"I'm not alone if you're out here with me."

Ajay smiles and drops his head. When he stands up tall, the grin is gone. "It's late. I have a plane to catch tomorrow so I'm going to go."

I walk toward him, determined to keep him out here as long as possible. "I thought we could talk."

"I don't have a whole lot to say right now, Whiskey. I mean..." he pauses and breaks eye contact. When he hides his face, I know he's fighting back his emotions.

I go to him and wrap my hand around his wrist, pulling his hand away from his face. There are tears in his eyes, tears that I know he's shedding over our lost child.

"She's five and the love of my life," I start off with. "I had a one-night stand with a guy I met at a management conference. My boss took me, thought it would be a good idea to show me the ropes. This guy was in the bar. He bought me a few drinks... I was still broken from our relationship and it felt really good to feel something again. Her father, he knows about her and pays child support, but he's married, has a family, and doesn't want his wife to know. Evelyn asks about him all the time and I say nice things because I don't know what else to say but when she asks what he looks like, I describe you."

"Your boyfriend isn't her father?"

"No, he's not, and as of tonight, he's not my boyfriend either."

Ajay chokes back a sob. "You have a daughter, Whiskey. One who looks just like you and I sat there wondering—"

"What our baby would've looked like?"

He shuffles his feet instead of answering me, which is fine. I already know that's what he was thinking because I've often thought the same myself.

"I'd like for you to spend some time with her... if you want."

I expect him to jump at the opportunity but instead he steps away from me. "I don't think that's a good idea, Whiskey."

"Why not?" I step closer.

"Because I don't want to get attached."

## 25

AJAY

*M*y fingers are digging into my thighs, surely poking holes in my pockets from the ache I feel on my legs. There's so much rage building inside of me, mostly aimed at her daughter's father. I know what it's like to not have a father, to know the man who conceived you wants nothing to do with you, and I can't fathom ever being that way with my own child. I don't even know her daughter but I want her to be mine, to give her a set of parents that care, that love her. I know I'll love her because she's Whiskey's, but the thought of loving her from afar isn't the life I desire.

Right now, all I want to do is pull Whiskey into my arms and tell her that everything will be okay. In a few short months, I'll be gone and she can go back to her life. At this point, it makes sense for Saul to file the appeal so we can just be done and both of us can move on. The fact that I'm standing here, thinking about being a father to a little girl that I just met is ridiculous. Whiskey wants to go through with the divorce. We want separate things from life. Hell, we live vastly different lifestyles. And the fact remains that I want her as my wife, but she wants me as an ex.

"What's so wrong with getting attached, Ajay? I happen to think my kid is awesome."

"I don't doubt that she is, but you don't want her close to someone like me, Whiskey. Once we're divorced, I won't come around again. I can see how me being here has messed up your life enough already."

"What if I want you around?"

"Woman, you're toying with my emotions here and it's late, I'm tired and..." Behind me the door to Bailey's opens and shuts, causing me to turn around. The guys coming out ask Whiskey if she's okay or if she needs help. One guy sizes me up and the dude is big. There's no doubt in my mind that he'd beat my ass, so I tell Whiskey I'll call her later and head across the street to my hotel. It pains me to walk away from her, to leave her in the parking lot, but I'm confident her employees will protect her. When I get to the porch, I turn around and stare at the well-lit parking lot. She's not there and I can only hope she in her car and on her way home or safe back inside Bailey's with the doors locked behind her.

Thankfully, the nighttime desk clerk of the Inn isn't anywhere to be seen when I walk in. I climb the stairs two at a time and fish the key out of my back pocket. I had to move it there in order to play tonight. Nothing like having a rigid piece of metal jabbing you in the leg each time you push down on the foot pedal.

After unlocking the door, I step in and let it close on its own. I left the sliding glass door open earlier and decide to go out onto the balcony to take one last look at my little hometown. Once I leave tomorrow, I'm not coming back. I'm going to ask Saul to file the appeal and have the divorce processed immediately. It's what Whiskey has wanted from the beginning and it's the least I can do for her.

Back inside, I start to pack because sleeping right now is out of the question. Whiskey's single and I'm leaving. It doesn't seem to make much sense in my mind, but in my heart it does. She needs time to figure things out and I'm only in the way, pulling on her heart strings when I beg for time with her.

"You know you should really make sure the door closes when you walk into your hotel room."

I jump and place my hand over my heart. My breathing is sporadic and coming in short bursts. "What the fuck, woman?" I manage to say. "You just about gave me a heart attack."

Whiskey walks further into my room and takes a seat on my bed. "You're the one who didn't shut your door."

"What did you do, follow me?"

She nods and a sly smile plays on her lips. "I couldn't let you leave, not like that."

I sigh and sit down next to her. "I have to go, Whiskey. We have a tour stop tomorrow and I need to be there."

"When will you be back?"

The carpet of my hotel room is green with black, white, and red specks mixed throughout. I hadn't noticed them until now, but I'd rather study them and look for a pattern than to see the disappointment in Whiskey's eyes.

"Like I said, I'm not coming back."

"Why not?"

"Whiskey..."

She moves from sitting by my side to sitting on the floor where I have no choice but to look at her. The last thing I want to do is hurt her, to make her suffer through anymore

191

bullshit, and forcing her to spend time with me is just increasing the animosity she feels for me.

"Did you hear what I said back there? When we were in the parking lot?"

I shake my head slowly, telling her the truth. "All night I've been hung up on the fact that you have a daughter. I guess I sort of knew but wasn't sure."

"How did you know?"

Pulling my phone out, I open the photos app and show her the pictures I found. "Dhara has them on her profile. The little girl, she looks a lot like you, so I assumed, but you hadn't said anything, and I was too afraid to ask you."

"Her name is Evelyn."

"I know, I just have a hard time saying it because part of me doesn't want her to be real. She's named after your grandma?"

Whiskey nods. "Grandma passed away when I was about seven months pregnant. At the time, I really hadn't thought of a name or decided on whether I was going to keep her. I was really messed up back then."

"That's my fault."

Whiskey reaches for my hand and presses it against her cheek. "You may have triggered things, but you weren't the only issue. Imagine my surprise when I finally tracked down my baby daddy and he tells me under no certain circumstances will he be part of our lives. I spent the last few months of my pregnancy going back and forth with him. He finally agreed to pay child support if I kept my mouth shut."

"What a fucking douche."

She nods. "Yep, a rich, stupid douche bag, living the high life in his fancy house with his fancy wife and his private school educated kids. But I won in the end."

"Because you have Evelyn?"

Whiskey smiles when I say her name. "She's the best, Ajay. She's smart, funny, and can turn a shitty day into something salvageable."

I tug on Whiskey's hand and nod toward the spot beside me. She sits down and rests her head on my shoulder. "I don't have much experience with kids," I tell her. "Chandler's seven and hangs around the studio some, and then there's Betty Paige who I see back stage. That's about it."

"Who's Chandler and Betty Paige?"

"Chandler is Keane's daughter. Betty Paige is Liam's teenage hellion determined to put her father in an early grave... his words, not mine."

"Chandler is a girl?"

I nod. "Her mom was a *Friends* fan, according to Keane. She's wicked cool though. Loves to read and draw and hates the spotlight."

"I have a feeling Evelyn's going to love the spotlight."

Hearing her say that makes my heart twist. "Whiskey, I don't think it's such a good idea to mix her in my world. People pry, they spread rumors, they take photos of you while you're eating. They'll follow you around and shove their cameras into your faces, post shit about you on social media. Is that what you want?"

Whiskey stands and goes over to the slider door. She leans against it, staring out into the night. Bailey is quiet now, everyone's gone home to get ready for their week to start. Bright and early, Nola and Quinn will pull up in front of the Inn and we'll drive to the airfield where Quinn and I will fly back to the tour bus, and Nola will go home to Malibu.

"I've been through a rollercoaster of emotions with you in my life, Ajay. Literally every single one you can think of and probably some that don't even have names. When your group first played on the radio, I loved the song and then I found out who was in the group and hated every bit of it. Dhara was relentless, though, and would play your music even though I hated it. But when she wasn't around, I'd listen to it willingly. And then I'd start to wonder what life would've been like for us, for Evelyn, because despite her being another man's child now, she would've been ours had we stayed together."

My girl turns and faces me. "There used to be this show on about a female movie star or musician — I don't really remember which because it didn't last long — but I pictured myself as her, walking down some random street with people following her. She acted like she didn't care, and I thought I could've done that. But then I would read articles about celebrities having issues and I started thinking life is too crazy when you're famous."

"It's the only part that I hate. Thankfully though, I'm still a nobody and people don't bother with me as much as they do with Dana and Quinn. Quinn grew up in the spotlight, he's used to it. Dana craves it. Me, I just want to play the drums."

"And Evelyn and I want to be with you." She walks toward me until she's standing between my legs. Her arms are resting on my shoulders and her fingers are playing with the back of my neck. I don't know where to put my hands. Do I leave them on the bed? Put them on the back of her thighs? That's where I really want to put them, and it seems that my hands know better than I do now. The feel of her legs pressing into my palms is enough to make me forget everything that's hanging in the balance.

"Evelyn doesn't know me, Whiskey. She may hate me because I'm not Logan. They looked like they're pretty close earlier. There's no denying that they have a connection. She may resent me for taking time away from her when it comes to you. She may hate me because I'm not here. I live in California and there's no changing that. Have you thought about that? That being with me means you give up your life in Bailey and relocate? Or do you want me to travel back and forth? While that may sound ideal, it doesn't work, not all the time. The studio we record in is in Los Angeles. I have to be there."

"You're the one who said you wanted to be my husband." She throws my words right back at me.

"You're right, I did. I was letting my heart get ahead of the bigger picture. I wish I could say that you having a daughter doesn't change things, but it does. I'm not going to ask you to uproot your life... *her* life... to accommodate mine. We aren't kids anymore. We have responsibilities. You have a little human that depends on you, and I'm not going to get in the way of that. I love you, Whiskey. I always have and I always will, but my life is there. Yours is here. I'm not going to ask you to give it up for me. I did that once and look at how things turned out for us."

"We were young," she says. "I could've fought harder."

I nod in agreement. "And I could've as well, but neither of us did. What does that tell you?"

She slides off my lap and stands in front of me. We're silent for a long time before she speaks. "What time is your flight?"

"Quinn will be here in a couple of hours. I think it leaves at five."

"I should probably let you get some sleep."

I stand and pull her into my arms. "I love you, Whiskey Girl."

"Then stay," she whispers into my ear.

"I can't."

## 26

# JAMIE

*I*t's been a month since Ajay left. I thought he was bullshitting me when he said he wasn't coming back, but he wasn't. My father says I got played. I don't believe that. I know Ajay's busy and this is part of his life, one that I have to accept if I'm going to be in it. And in it is exactly what I want to be. But that means seeing him, and he refuses to commit to a date. Maybe this week or next, maybe on such and such date, he's not sure. He has to ask Elle. Elle this. Elle that. I'm starting to think that Elle tells him when he's allowed to take a piss. I know that's not the case but that's how things feel right now.

We are under the sixty-day mark for the finalization of our divorce. Sadly, my father has a countdown on his phone, and he reminds me of it daily. He means well, I know he does, but he has to stop. Even my mother says so. I want to try and work things out with Ajay and would much prefer it while he's legally bound to me. I know how he thinks, and right now he considers us married. I can guarantee he's not looking at another woman, speaking to another female or even giving entertaining the idea of being with someone else. I'd say that's not how he was raised, but in a sense it was. He grew up knowing what a shit bag his father was and always vowed to be different.

Evelyn comes into my room and sighs dramatically. Call me evil, but over the last few weeks I've played Sinful Distraction's album continuously. She knows the words to most of the songs and I plan to have her sing to Ajay... if he ever comes back.

"What's wrong with you?" I ask her as she lays across my bed with another sigh.

"Today is the last day of school."

"You should be happy. It's summer vacation. We're going to do lots of fun things."

"Like what?"

"Go to the beach. Read books. Practice math. Hang out at the park. Spend time with Dhara and Fletcher."

Evelyn picks her head up, turns to look at me and flops it back down dramatically. "I like all those things except the reading and math part."

"Oh? Okay." I pretend that my feelings are hurt.

"Ugh, fine. I can read a book, but no math."

I jut my lower lip out and make a whimpering sound.

"You are a hard bargain."

"You drive a hard bargain," I correct her. There are times when I wish I could go back to when she was learning to speak and do the baby talk thing with her. I was so hell bent on her being a smarter person than I am that I didn't encourage it. I'd correct her and we'd work on saying words correctly. Hindsight is a bitch.

"Are you going to finish getting ready for school?"

She comes over to me, dragging her feet behind her. "I'm sad."

"Why?" I bring her to my lap, and she rests her head on my shoulder.

"Because I won't see my friends during summer."

"Of course you will, silly girl. Most of your friends will be around here, you'll see them all the time."

Evelyn picks up her head and looks at me. With her hand in the air, her face deadpans. "Not with all the math I have to do."

"Oh geez, Evelyn. Now you're just being silly. Go finish getting ready. Mommy has to meet Auntie Dhara for breakfast." I set her down on the ground.

"Can I go?"

"School, Evelyn Jameson Foster. You have school."

She crosses her arms and huffs. "I'm telling Grandma you three named me. She's going to be so mad at you."

As soon as she's out of ear shot, I let out a laugh. Tattling on me to my parents has become her favorite thing to do. "Mommy didn't give me bacon, didn't buy the right toothpaste, gave me a turkey sandwich when I asked for ham"... the list goes on and on, and each day my mother asks why I'm making my daughter's life so hard. Of course, Mom knows her little princess is just being a dramatic almost six-year-old.

After I drop Evelyn off at school, which consisted of me walking her in and helping her hang her backpack, I'm finally pulling into a small diner outside of Prineville. It's an old soda fountain with a white and black checkered floor and red vinyl seats. Dhara waves to me from the booth she's secured for us.

"Sorry, I'm late. Evelyn didn't want to go to school."

"Can you blame her? The last day of school is the worst. You know it's over once the bell rings, but the bell takes forever to get to that point. Then you say goodbye to your friends, and there's always one that doesn't come back because they move. School is torture," she says. She eyes me over the top of her mug as I give her my best "what the hell are you talking about" look.

"Did you have a conversation with her this morning or something? It's like the two of you are in cahoots to give me a headache."

"Nah, I would never." Except she would and often has. Still I love her like family. We spend the next few minutes looking over the menu and place our order when the waitress stops by to check on us.

"So, how is he?"

"Logan? He's okay. He can't tell me where he is, but he says he's safe."

Dhara leans toward me. "You know damn well I'm not talking about Logan, Jamie. How is *he*?"

I sigh but before I can say anything the waitress is back with a cup of coffee for me. I wrap my hands around the base even though I'm not cold, the hot ceramic gives my mind something else to think about other than Ajay.

"What's going on?"

"Don't know. His texts are vague when he responds. Calls are cut short because he always seems to call right before he's going on stage, going to bed or about to eat."

"And you're letting him get away with this?"

I glance at her to see her smirking. "As if I control him."

"You do, you just have to assert yourself, Jamie."

"I'm trying, Dhara. It's hard. Like he said, he has this whole other life, and that life is crazy busy. He lives on a tour bus, at least for another few weeks, and he's pretty much controlled by his manager. When we do talk, things seem good between us. He doesn't really ask about Evelyn and if he hears her calling for me, he suddenly has to go."

"Do you think he doesn't want kids?"

I shake my head. "No, I think he's afraid that he's taking time away from her. He never had parents that gave a shit and I think this is his way of showing that he does. I don't know. It's frustrating. He's frustrating," I sigh heavily. "I do know one thing."

"What's that?"

"I'm falling hard for him."

"Well you were already there. You just buried your feelings."

The waitress comes back with our breakfast: An omelet for Dhara and pancakes with fruit topping for me.

"The other day, I caught myself when I was filling out a form for work. I checked married instead of single and it felt good to do that."

"You know," she says in between bites, "I wonder what kind of tax implications there are. You've both been filing as single."

"I hope for my sake, none. Although I should probably ask Fletcher about it, see if he can refer me to someone he trusts. There's no way I can pay back the earned income credits I've received since Evelyn was born. Honestly, I hope no one figures it out."

"That would be best," she says in agreement. "So, back to Ajay. What do you want from him?"

I finish taking a bite and washing it down with my coffee. "I want a chance. I want a chance to see if we can function as husband and wife."

"You just want to get laid," she blurts out loud enough for others to hear.

I do everything I can to fight back my smile, but to no avail. "Believe me the thought has crossed my mind many times. He's just so..."

"Yummy? Hot? Delicious? Tantalizing? Sexy AF."

"Okay, first, it sounds like you want to eat Ajay, and second, yes to all those and so many more. His tattoos alone, I want to spend time getting to know each one. He does a good job hiding them from me."

"Fletch thinks one of them is your name."

"Doubt it." Although, how sexy would that be? "I'm sure he has done everything he can to forget about me over the years."

"Text him and ask," Dhara dares me. To prove that she's wrong, I do it.

**Do you have my name tattooed on your body**?

He responds before I can even put my phone down.

**Well good morning to you too ;)**

"He ignored my question." I show Dhara my phone but the expression on her face speaks volumes.

"You may want to look at the photo he sent."

Pulling my phone back, I double click the smaller image to make it bigger. Sure enough, "Whiskey" is inked into his arm. Also visible in the picture is the date I miscarried our angel.

"Jamie, what the hell are you doing here?"

"Um... eating breakfast?" I slip my phone into my pocket, unsure of how to respond to him.

"Girl, you're so damn lucky. I wish I had a man who tattooed my name on his body."

I scoff at her. "You have Fletcher, and while he may not be the type to get a tattoo, he's madly in love with you. You're just too blind to see it."

Dhara shakes her head. "I'm not blind, Jamie. I see him. I see every part of him but am afraid of ruining our friendship. He's been my friend for so long... what if we try and fail? I lose my best friend, and nothing is worth that."

"Not even a chance at love?" I ask her. "I could give up on Ajay, knowing full well that he's my soul mate, out of fear that we won't work because we've been apart for too long or because of his job, but then where does that leave me? It leaves me searching for a love that may or may not come. Ajay and I can be together and the ticket is Evelyn."

"What?" she asks. "You going to use your daughter to trap him?"

I laugh. It sort of feels that way, but no. "Absolutely not. Right now, he's worried about her getting attached if we don't make it. I'm not. I think once Ajay is part of our lives, those lingering feelings will disappear. He doesn't want Evelyn hurt in any of this. He still remembers his mom choosing a man over him — the wound is fresh, and it's not what he wants for Evelyn. He wants her to choose him."

"So, what's your plan?"

"That's just it, Dhara. I don't have one. I know Ajay is getting a few days off coming up, but he says he'll be in Los Angeles doing some press tour things so coming here isn't possible and there's no way I can go out there."

"Why not?"

"Money. I looked up flights and I can't swing two tickets. I thought about asking my parents, but my father isn't keen on me taking Evelyn to see Ajay, so I'll have to wait for him to come here."

"Have you withdrawn your petition for the divorce yet?" she asks.

I shake my head. "No, I haven't."

## 27

## AJAY

*T*he tour bus travels down the freeway after our last show, heading toward home. It'll be nice to sleep in my bed for the first time in... I don't remember how long. But the idea of being home is very appealing. It's where I think best and right now there are a few decisions that need to be made about my life.

Since leaving Bailey, I haven't felt right. It's not that I'm sick, I'm pretty sure I'm heartbroken even though it's of my own doing. Ever since I told Whiskey I couldn't stay I've wanted to take the words back, but haven't found the words to do so. I really couldn't stay, but only because of my job, not because of her or her daughter. I want to be there — or I want them here — I'm just not sure Whiskey's willing to move to California.

I can't sleep. I stare out the window at the passing signs, each one getting us closer to the studio which is our central drop off location. Dana, Hendrix, and Keane will go their own way, while Quinn, Elle and I will ride together to Malibu. I'm hoping Ben will be there to drive us because we're due to arrive in the middle of the night.

Every so often my mind plays a trick on me and I think I see "Bailey ten miles" or "Prineville Next Exit" only to realize they're actually signs for upcoming streets. That's how you know you're in the city besides an upswing in traffic: You're no longer looking for towns but the right street exit to get you closer to your destination.

The bus slows down as it moves through the city streets, careful not to hit any of the parked cars along the road. When we're about a block away, the interior lights come on, and Elle and Keane start to stir. I think I'm the only one fully awake right now, unable to sleep because my mind won't shut off. After our last show, I packed my bags and carried them to the front of the bus. Why? I have no idea. It's not like I can leave until Elle and Quinn are ready. Maybe it's because I'm eager to get off this bus and start figuring out my life.

We come to a stop in the middle of the road, due to cars parked along the curb in front of the studio. Even with the streetlights, the red flashers from the tour bus are bright and somewhat mesmerizing. Our driver opens the door and I step off into the stifling night air that is Los Angeles.

The only people out right now are the transients and a few walking home from a late-night club or after party. Thankfully, no one seems to care that we're here, which is nice.

As a group, we work to unload our equipment and get it back into the studio. We were lucky enough and grateful that 4225 West lent us their sound and lighting equipment for the tour, otherwise we probably would've had to rent some which would've lowered our paychecks in the end.

Once everything is back in place, the sun is about to rise. The sky is pink and gray as the night sky starts to burn off. I'm tired and ready for bed. Today will be nothing more than a day to sleep, do laundry, watch television and lounge around in my boxers while I take pity on myself for being alone. I should've taken a flight back to Bailey to surprise Whiskey, but honestly, our relationship has felt a bit off since I left.

Oh, who am I fooling? What relationship? I all but shut her out when she was telling me that she wants to try. I know trying is the next realistic step, but I want it all. I want her here, living this life with me. She's the one who encouraged me to follow my passion, the one who believed in me as a person and yet she's the one who isn't here. I want her to be, but I can't ask her to uproot her life to appease mine.

I doze off briefly on the drive to Malibu, opening my eyes as the Pacific Ocean comes into view. It's fucking gorgeous and a sight that everyone needs to see once in their lifetime.

Nola greets us at the door and inside, the house smells like breakfast. As much as I want to go hide in my room, I sit at the table and eat with the two people gracious enough to let me live in their house. After I finish, I help clean up the kitchen and finally make it down to my room. I pull my curtains to the side, open the sliding glass door, and flop on my bed like a fish out of water.

Just as I'm about to fall asleep, my phone rings. I'm tempted to let it go to voicemail and shut the damn thing off when I look at the number. I don't recognize it, but I know it's a North Carolina area code. My first thought is that Whiskey's in trouble for doing something to Harvey's house again, but then I think she wouldn't do anything stupid like that because of her daughter. Still, I can't help but wonder.

"Hello?" My voice is groggy, a combination of sleep and exhaustion.

HEIDI MCLAUGHLIN

"Oh shit, did I wake you up? Fuck, sorry. I can call back."

"Um... no. I'm up. Who is this?"

"Huh? Oh, it's Dhara. Sorry, I figured you'd have my number." Why the hell would I have her number?

"Is Whiskey okay?"

"She's fine, why?"

"I don't know, you're calling me out of the blue and... well, we aren't exactly the best of friends."

Dhara sighs. "True, but I figured since you're nabbing pictures off my profile, we might as well have a little chat." I smile at what she says about the pictures. That means Whiskey told her and the fact that she's talking about me is a good thing.

"Anyway, I'm calling because you left our girl heartbroken."

That makes two of us.

"And I think that if you're in love with her, like I have a feeling you are, you need to do something to show her."

"And I'm guessing you're going to give me an idea of what that 'something' should be?"

"You're damn straight I am."

I get out of bed and go sit on my little patio. I can't see the ocean from here, but I can hear it. It's peaceful and the waves are much more active here than they were when Quinn and I tried to surf in North Carolina.

"Bottom line, she wants to come see you while you're on break, but she can't afford to fly her and Evelyn out, pay for a hotel and all that — and there's no way in hell she's going to ask you to pay for them, so you're going offer."

"I am?" Don't get me wrong, I'd do anything Whiskey asks me.

206

"You are," Dhara confirms. "She wants you to get to know Evelyn."

"Look, it's not that I don't want to know her daughter or spend time with her, I do. The problem is—"

"That your life is there and hers is in Bailey. And you're afraid Evelyn will get attached and you won't be able to make it work, am I right?"

"In a nutshell."

"Have you asked Jamie what she wants? I do believe she'll move to be with you, if you want her. There isn't anything holding her to Bailey."

"Her family, friends and her job are there."

Dhara scoffs. "But the man she loves is in California and I don't know about you, but I think love trumps all."

"I wish it were that easy."

"It is. Now, listen to my plan." Dhara starts in on her idea and while it seems farfetched, it could work. Of course, she's thrown herself and Fletcher into the mix and has asked for tickets to the 4225 West concert at the Hollywood Bowl next week. And because Dhara doesn't want Whiskey to know that I'm paying for everyone's flights, she's going to tell Whiskey that she won a contest. I, however, am supposed to play it off like I won't be in town.

"I hope you're right," I tell her. "I'm not sure Whiskey will fall for this."

"She will," Dhara says. "I am a die-hard fan and before you stormed into town, we had tickets to see you guys in concert."

"Wait, Whiskey was going to go to my concert?"

"What, no," she scoffs. "Logan, Fletcher and I were there, sort of. Jamie would've never agreed to go, but now that she wants to bang the drummer, she'd probably change her mind." Dhara giggles and I can't help but grin like a fucking fool.

"Are you in?" she asks. I tell her I am, and that I'll be in touch with travel arrangements for them. She squeals and tells me I'm the best. I have a feeling it has nothing to do with me and Whiskey, but rather Dhara's desire to meet Liam Page. As soon as we hang up, I send an email to Elle asking her if she can pull this together for me, and then send one to Harrison asking for the tickets. I haven't told anyone about Whiskey's daughter.

Back upstairs, Nola's out on the deck reading. "Hey," I say, interrupting her. "Can I talk to you for a second."

She closes her book and sets it down on the table in front of her. "What's up?"

"Is it okay if Jamie stays here for a few days?"

"Yeah, of course."

I nod and think about how to ask the next part of my question. I have no idea whether she and Quinn even like kids or if they want one running around the house.

"Thing is, Whiskey has a five-year-old daughter who will come with her. If you'd rather they stay in a hotel, I completely understand."

Nola's eyes go wide as she grins widely. "How come you didn't tell us she had a daughter? She could've come to the beach with us."

I run my hand over my hair and half smile. "I didn't know until my last night in Bailey. I sort of had an idea, but Whiskey was so evasive with her answers about her life that I didn't come out and ask her."

"Have you met her?"

"Briefly."

"Does this complicate things for you?"

I nod. "It's easy to ask Whiskey to move here, but to ask her to uproot her child, that's a whole other situation."

"Yeah, and I'm sure the girl's dad might have an issue it."

"The Dad isn't in the picture. Whiskey says he's married with a family and wants nothing to do with Evelyn."

"Evelyn? That's her name?"

I nod.

"Oh, it's so pretty. I can't wait to meet her."

Honestly, neither can I. At least a meeting that equates to more than just a quick handshake between us. Still, I fear that I will want more, and Whiskey can't give it to me. She wants me to stay in Bailey, and I can't.

"So, you're okay with her being here?"

"Absolutely. What are you going to do while she's here?"

"I don't know. Before I came out to ask you, I had just gotten off the phone with her best friend who told me in no uncertain terms to shit or get off the pot where Whiskey's concerned. Thing is I haven't asked Saul to file the appeal. I meant to, to give Whiskey her life back, but I like saying she's my wife and haven't been able to say that for a long time. When I had to chance to call her that, it was short-lived. Now things could be different, but I have her little girl to worry about as well."

"It's an instant family, lots of responsibilities. Are you up for it?"

"I think so, unless her kid hates me."

"Not possible," Nola says. "Look at Chandler, she seems to adore you. Maybe call Keane and see if y'all can hang out together. The girls are close in age."

"Yeah, that seems like a good idea."

"What is?" Quinn asks from behind. He steps out onto the deck and instantly goes to Nola to kiss her. They make me jealous. I want what they have and while I know it's within my grasp, I don't know how to pull the trigger.

"Ajay's wife has a daughter; they're going to come visit."

"She does?"

"Yeah, Evelyn, she's five," I tell him.

"Damn, married and a step father," he pauses and starts laughing. "You're the 'ninety-day stepdaddy'."

I glare at him while Nola's eyes go wide. "Oh, I think I have that book." She bolts from her chair and heads back into the house while Quinn and I stare at each other. He finally sits down and looks at me.

"What are you going to do?"

I tell him what I know about Evelyn and her father and how I'm concerned with all of the impending decisions I need to make. I want Whiskey as my wife but not at the expense of her daughter's happiness.

"Take it from me, if her father doesn't want her and you fall in love with this little girl, adopt her. My mom adopted me, and it was the best thing for my life."

I hadn't even thought about what Quinn is suggesting, but I like the idea. However, I'm not going to think too much into it until I can spend time with Evelyn and see how well we mesh. I won't put Whiskey in a bad spot where her daughter is concerned. I love her too much to hurt her that way.

# JAMIE

The idea of waking before the sun is up is not my idea of a good time, even worse is trying to rouse Evelyn out of bed. This child refuses to budge and keeps slapping my hand away when I try to tickle her. I should've told Dhara no, that I didn't want to go to her stupid concert with her, but Ajay convinced me to come even though I will only see him for a day. Technically not even a full twenty-four hours, but something more like five. Five hours together after not seeing him for six weeks feels like a lifetime apart when I don't take into account our earlier separation. But I'm trying to forget that period of my life and focus on the future, which is challenging considering Ajay's elusiveness. I have hope that once I'm out there, things will be different. I'm going to use my time wisely to show him that the three of us deserve a chance at happiness with each other.

"Evelyn, don't you want to go on the airplane?"

When Dhara told me about the contest she won, I called bullshit. It seemed obvious that she didn't actually win but rather found something to hold over Ajay's head to get tickets. That was until he told me Sinful Distraction wasn't even going to be in town, but that he'd find a way to come see me while I was in Los Angeles. I tried to tell Dhara that I wasn't going, that it was a waste of my time, but she cried and went on about how she already gave them our names and things were nontransferable. I finally relented but am still leery of the whole thing. It's just too convenient to be a coincidence.

"Mommy, I tired," she says, rubbing her eyes.

"I know, sweetie, but you'll be able to sleep on the plane, and I think it'll have a TV so you can watch some shows. You'll be able to color and read your book."

"But no math?"

"Nope, no math. Not on this trip."

Evelyn sits up but keeps her eyes closed. She lifts her arms so I can remove her pajamas and put her sundress on. "It's warm in California," I tell her. "But not humid like it is here."

"What else is there?"

"Well I don't know, but I imagine it's a lot like North Carolina with palm trees and the ocean."

"Sounds boring."

"I know, but Auntie Dhara asked us to go to a concert with her. It'll be fun."

While she's still in bed, I sit behind her and pull her hair up into a ponytail. Normally, I'd ask her what she wants but this is just easier for the trip. I'm afraid she's going to be miserable. Not only is this her first flight, but mine as well, and despite reading testimonials from people who have flown before, I'm not certain I'm ready for this.

The loud knock on my door has me scrambling through my darkened living room. Fletcher and Dhara are standing there under my porch light and the only one who looks even remotely happy is Dhara.

"I think I'm still asleep," Fletcher says as he enters my house.

"Me too. Evelyn's a zombie. I'm really afraid she's going to be unbearable."

"Y'all are worrying for nothing. We'll be fine. We can sleep on the plane and we have a really nice hotel where we can nap and have room service," Dhara says as if winning a big contest is an everyday thing for her. "Where are your bags? I'll put them in the car," Fletcher asks. I point to my room and he disappears down the hall.

"I'll go get Evelyn but be prepared, she's crabby."

"Eh," Dhara says as if a tired five-year-old means nothing. Instead of waking her up again, I scoop her into my arms. She's heavy but I only have to carry her to Fletcher's car. Dhara locks up after I step out onto the porch and when Fletcher sees me, he comes rushing over to take her.

The drive to the airport usually takes about an hour, but with no traffic Fletcher gets us there in forty-five minutes. He drops us off curbside and tells us to wait for him while he goes to park the car. I'm thankful he had the wherewithal to do this because Evelyn is still out cold.

"Shit, I forgot to put her shoes on," I say aloud as I start going through her bag. Luckily her flip flops are in there, but I decide to hold onto them until after she goes through security.

When Fletcher comes back, he reaches for Evelyn and picks her up. "You don't have to." I tell him, but he doesn't seem to mind.

"It'll be easier for me to carry her while we walk to security."

"Maybe you can try to wake her up before we get there. I don't think they'll let you carry her through the detectors."

Our airport is small and there aren't too many people

traveling this morning, so it doesn't take us long to get through the line and to the TSA agent who checks our identification and boarding passes. Somehow Fletcher manages to get Evelyn to wake up, although the scowl on her face looks like she's about to start the next world war.

By the time we're called to board, Evelyn's awake but moody. I'm silently kicking Dhara in the rear for suggesting an early morning flight. I get it, we want to get to the other coast as early as possible but I'm not sure this was such a good idea for Evelyn.

I get her situated in her seat with her pillow and blanket and tell her that once we're up in the air she can have some breakfast. Except she never makes it that far because she's out like a light before the plane takes off and so am I.

By the time the plane lands, I'm second-guessing the trip. It's nice to get away, but the only reason I would come out here is to see Ajay and knowing that our visit is only a few short hours makes this trip really not seems worth the hassle. Dhara should've asked her friends from work to go with her. I wouldn't have been upset at all.

There is, however, one shining light right now: Evelyn's awake and pulling her luggage behind her while she carries her stuffed elephant. I have to stop every few feet to remind her to keep walking because something catches her attention.

"There's a car waiting for us," Dhara says as we make our way toward the exit. When we step outside, I take in the many cars waiting for everyone. The traffic at the airport alone is insane.

I grab hold of Evelyn's hand and tell her not to let go as we follow Dhara through the mob of people. They bump into us without any regard for our well-being. I don't like it and I'm ready to turn around and go back home. But I know having those thoughts is not productive. If I want to be with Ajay, this is where I have to be, unless I want us to live apart. I don't. I want a chance at the fairytale I thought I was getting when I turned eighteen. Of course, in my mind that fairytale didn't include one of the busiest airports and the feeling of helplessness I have going on right now.

"Mommy, why does that man have our name on his paper?" Evelyn stops us in our tracks and points to a man holding a sign that says, "Foster."

"I'm sure he's waiting for someone else. We're going with Auntie Dhara," I say as I turn to follow her.

"Actually, you're not." That voice, the one I've known and have had memorized for most of my life, has me frozen in spot. I turn slowly to find Ajay standing there with a bouquet of roses and a stuffed Minnie Mouse toy in his hands.

"Ajay," I say softly. He steps forward, leans down, and places the roses strategically between us.

"Can I kiss you?" he asks quietly. I nod and tilt my head toward him, welcoming the soft sensation of his lips against mine. He pulls away far too soon.

"I thought I wasn't going to see you until tomorrow."

He smiles shyly and drops the roses from shielding me. I know he did it so Evelyn wouldn't see us kiss, and I love him a little bit more for that.

"That was a ruse," he says as my mouth drops open. "Dhara and I have been in cahoots to get you and Miss Evelyn out here."

"So, she's not going to the concert?"

"Oh no," his eyes go wide, "She is, but you're not unless you want to."

"I don't think I want to. And you're here the whole time we are?"

He nods, leans forward, and kisses me on my cheek before dropping down to his knees to face Evelyn. "Hi, do you remember me?"

Evelyn turns shyly into my leg. Ajay shows her the stuffed Minnie and she takes it slowly. "I'm Ajay, a friend of your mom's."

"I know," she says.

"And I was wondering if you'd like to go meet Mickey and Minnie Mouse tomorrow." My eyes go wide, but he's not even paying attention to me. "You see, they're friends of mine and have asked me to ask you if you'd like to come have breakfast with them tomorrow?"

Evelyn looks at with the widest eyes possible. "Mommy, can I?"

I nod and crouch down. "I think you have to tell Ajay that you want to go."

"I do, Ajay. I really, really do."

"Well okay, then. But first we have to go to my house. I have some friends who want to meet you. Do you mind if I carry your suitcase for you?"

"Nope," she says happily. Ajay points to the car we're going to ride in — it's a limo where the man standing by the car is sure enough holding a sign with our name on it. "See, Mommy," she says when she reaches the man. "It *is* for us!"

Ajay steps closer and hands me the roses. I lean in and smell their heavenly scent. "These are beautiful."

"Not nearly as beautiful as you."

"You're biased," I remind him.

He nods and reaches for my bag. "I'm happy you're here, Whiskey."

I turn in front of him and place my hand on his side, clutching at his t-shirt. "I almost didn't come but the thought of seeing you for five hours when I haven't seen you for six weeks was too good to pass up."

"I've had some things that I needed to take care of here first," he tells me. "But now I'm all yours until you decide to leave."

*Until I decide to leave.* Not when I leave or at the end of my trip, he's just left our relationship completely open ended with one comment.

Ajay and I get into the limo, only to find Evelyn sprawled out on one of the bench seats. I remind her that she still needs to put her seatbelt on, and she does, along with putting one on Minnie Mouse. I send a text to Dhara, thanking her and promising that we'll find a way to meet up later. She sends a picture back of her and Fletcher, drinking champagne in the back of a car and tells me to have fun and enjoy the drummer and his stick. She's utterly ridiculous.

But she's right, I do want to enjoy him. I put my phone away and rest my head against the back of the seat, angling myself so I can stare at him. It takes him a moment until he mimics my position. My hand reaches for his and he holds it without hesitation. It feels good to hold his hand, and while I know Evelyn's watching me and I need to explain to her that this man is the love of my life and part of our future, I don't want to stop looking at him.

With my free hand, I reach over and stroke his cheek. He leans into my touch and kisses my palm.

"We're almost at my place," he says.

"I thought you lived with your friends."

He shakes his head. "I rented a condo. It's not on the beach, but it has a pool and a playground. It's a gated community so people can't just come and go. There are sidewalks so Evelyn can ride her bike."

"Ajay, I didn't bring her bike. Just enough clothes for a few days."

He nods and smiles. "I bought her a bike with training wheels and a helmet. She has clothes hanging in her room. Miss Katelyn bought them for her, along with Elle and Peyton. They also bought you some clothes, with Dhara's input, in case you want to stay longer."

He's left me speechless and in complete awe. When I last saw him, he was unsure about how this would work between us, but it seems like he's pulling out all the stops to show us that we can live together as a family.

## 29

# AJAY

*T*elling Whiskey about the condo I'm renting and how the James's went shopping for the girls in my life is something for me to be proud of, but the real highlight comes when I watch Whiskey's face as we drive through the complex and pull into my driveway.

Of course, as soon as the limo parks, Chandler's outside and waiting in my yard for us to get out of the car.

"Who's that?" Evelyn asks as she gets out and stands next to me. I half expected her to leave her Minnie Mouse in the car, but she's holding on to her tightly. Better yet, she's talking to me and that makes me feel good. I want her to like me — no, I want her to love me — because I want to be in her life as her dad. I want her to grow up knowing she had a dad that wanted to be in her life.

"That's my friend, Chandler. Her dad and I work together."

"Oh," Evelyn says.

"Chandler this is Evelyn. Do you want to show her where she can put her stuff?"

Chandler nods and comes forward, reaching for Evelyn's hand. "Your room is pink, come on let me show you." Evelyn looks back at me, making me wonder if she's seeking my approval or wants me to follow. I choose to follow and pull Whiskey right along behind me.

"Is this Keane's daughter?" Whiskey asks me quietly.

"Yep, when the place next to him became available he told me about it and I put in an application." We follow the girls in, and as much as I want to show Whiskey around, I want to see how Evelyn likes her room. Chandler is talking to her the entire time they're climbing the stairs to the second floor, telling her about the playground and that there's a bunch of kids to play with. Chandler talks about the swimming pool and how she takes lessons there a couple days a week and asked Evelyn if she wants to go swimming with her.

Evelyn doesn't answer her and I think it's because she's stepped into her room. I wish I could take credit for the room, but I can't. It was all Miss Katelyn and Peyton, explaining little girls love pink, but it was Chandler who suggested the daisy comforter to go with the white bed because girls like flowers too.

"Ajay..." Whiskey gasps. Her hand is covering her mouth as she takes in the bedroom. "You did all of this for her?"

I nod and wrap my arm around her shoulders. "I want her to love it here."

"And what about me?" she asks.

I motion her to follow me down the hall. The room next to Evelyn's is mostly empty minus my new drum kit. I show her the bathroom, which has a stepstool in there for Evelyn so she can reach the sink, and finally the bedroom at the end of the hall.

"Wow," she says as she steps into the master bedroom. The king size four poster bed is in the center of the room with a white and navy color duvet. There are windows on each side of the room — one facing the front and the other facing the back of the condo. The walk-in closet is separated nicely with my clothes on one side, and her new things on the other. Her fingertips trail over the hangers of her new garments as she walks into the bathroom Where there's a stand-up shower built for two and a jacuzzi tub, along with a place for her to do her make-up.

"Ajay, this house is amazing."

"It's a good start," I tell her as I lean against the counter.

"A start? I'd say this is a home."

"You haven't seen the rest of it. Come on, I'll show you." I take her hand and we head back down the hall, stopping briefly to check in on the girls, who are on the floor playing with the dolls I ordered to make sure Evelyn had things to do while she's here. I know it's only for a few days, but I want her to be comfortable.

Downstairs I show Whiskey the living room with the sectional couch we always talked about owning because we said that we'd host parties once we had our own house and need the seating.

"Is there anything you haven't thought of or remembered?" she asks.

"No, I have a fairly good memory."

"Yeah, I remember."

Our next stop is the half bath, the laundry room, and I even show her the linen closet before taking her into the kitchen. She runs her fingers along the stainless appliances and stretches her arms over the granite countertop.

"I think I'm in love."

"Hopefully with me," I say as I pull her into my arms.

My hand cups her cheek and I guide her until our lips press together. I try to keep things PG, not wanting to heat up the kitchen, especially with the girls upstairs, but it's hard. I'm beyond happy that she's here, in my house which I want her to consider her own.

"Did you do all of this for me?"

"For us. For Evelyn. I know I said before I left that I won't ask you to uproot your life and interrupt hers, but I want you here. I know I'm not her dad, but I want to be, and I want us to be husband and wife... maybe even expand our family someday if that's something you would want."

The words I've said to her are heavy and full of life changes. I'm talking about us having a baby, living life here, and asking her to accept my crazy schedule.

"I want to tell Saul to withdraw the divorce petition — just say 'fuck it' and stay married. And I want to adopt Evelyn if she'll have me as her dad."

"Ajay," again she gasps my name, and I can't wait to hear it again later while we're in bed. "I really don't know what to say."

"Don't say anything. You have a few days here. You can observe how I am with Evelyn and the two of you can make a decision later. I'm not going anywhere."

"But you're moving to Bailey?"

As much as it pains me, I shake my head. "I can visit, but it would be for a month here and there and that's not the kind of life we want. When it comes to you, I know that much for sure."

"You're right, but I also have my parents to consider."

I push her hair behind her ear and gaze into her eyes. There have been times lately when I wished my life was different, and this moment is one of them. I'd love to pack up and move to Bailey to be with her but it's not possible. I'm living my dream butWhiskey's my dream too. Somehow the two need to mesh so we're all happy.

"Would you like to go for a walk?"

"Yeah, that would be nice," she says. I head upstairs and gather the girls, text Keane to let him know that Chandler is coming with us, and usher the girls outside.

Whiskey and I hold hands while the girls walk in front of us. Besides their height difference, you can't really tell there's two years between them. I like that Chandler is trying to make Evelyn feel welcomed. I want Evelyn to feel like she has friends here. She may only be five, but it's important to feel wanted at any age.

We walk along as a family, laughing and joking until we reach the pool. Evelyn wants to swim but Whiskey tells her that she can go later, maybe after dinner. I haven't told her yet that everyone plans to come over tonight. It wasn't my idea, but Miss Katelyn's. She said that it's important for Whiskey to know what she's getting into with this band stuff. The band is a family, who spends a lot of time together, and if Whiskey can't handle it, it might be better to know now as opposed to later. I don't agree or disagree, but just follow her advice because I trust her implicitly.

By the time we make it around the subdivision, Evelyn's tired. I offer to carry her, expecting her to tell me no, but she raises her arms so I can pick her up. I'm even further surprised as she rests her head on my shoulder and wraps her arms around me.

When we get back to the house, Chandler says she's going to go home. I walk past mine to make sure she gets in okay before turning back and meeting Whiskey at the now full driveway.

"Where did all these cars come from?" she asks.

"Well, that's the next surprise. I think everyone is here for an early dinner before they head over to the Hollywood Bowl for the concert."

"Liam Page is inside your house?"

I nod and wonder why she chose to mention him over the others.

"Oh man, Dhara's going to kill me if I meet him first." Whiskey takes off toward the door, laughing. I trail behind her and by the time I step in, Miss Katelyn is already hugging my girl. She takes over introducing Whiskey to everyone... and I do mean *everyone*. It seems everyone important to me is here to meet my girls, including Noah, who is in town visiting as well.

Up until this moment, I thought my condo was fairly large. I was wrong. With all my band family inside of it, the living room and kitchen feel incredibly small.

Evelyn picks up her head and looks around the room. I think I've figured her out; she's shy until she feels comfortable enough around new people.

"Do you want me to put you down?" I ask her but she shakes her head. "How about I take you around and introduce you to everyone? You can tell Miss Katelyn and Miss Peyton thank you for your pretty room."

"They did that?"

"They sure did. They picked out all the colors and I painted it for you. Do you like it?"

"I do."

I walk over to Katelyn and introduce her to Evelyn. "I have a wiggly tooth," she says, showing Katelyn which tooth is loose. "My mommy says I'll lose it any day now."

"Oh boy, we will have to call the tooth fairy and tell her where you are so she can come visit you when you do."

"Ajay, will the tooth fairy come here?"

"Of course," I say, trying to reassure her.

After we make our rounds and she meets everyone, she wiggles to get down. I watch as she goes from person to person, each one of them falling for her charm... the same charm her mother got me with so many years ago.

Josie and Katelyn recruit Whiskey to help them in the kitchen, while JD and Harrison man the grill. Whiskey fills Liam in on Dhara while he's in the kitchen with her and tells him how she's been a fan forever. Liam promises to give her the red-carpet treatment at the show tonight.

Outside, I hang with the guys. Harrison hands me a beer from the cooler, but I pass, opting for water. I don't know if Whiskey drinks in front of her daughter and I don't really want to put us in an awkward situation.

"She's a stunner," JD says.

"Thanks, man."

"Quinn really likes her," Harrison adds. "Nola was a bit sad that you moved out."

"Yeah, I know, but I needed to show Whiskey that I'm serious about her and Evelyn — and somehow, spending the night in one room of a place that isn't mine doesn't exactly scream responsibility."

"No, it really doesn't. What's the plan for tomorrow?" Harrison asks.

"Disney!" JD yells. "Eden is really excited. Jenna has the tickets."

"Speaking of, where *is* Jenna?" I ask.

"Eden, surfing, beach," JD says, shrugging. "She's always surfing but she's good and I love that kid more than life so whatever makes her happy."

I lean against the railing of my deck and look back into my house. Whiskey's laughing and she looks like she's in her element. In that moment, I realize how important her happiness really is to me... hers and Evelyn's.

I hear Evelyn yell for Chandler and a smile spreads across my face. Even if Whiskey decides this life isn't for her, Evelyn will have some great memories of her trip to California.

## 30

## JAMIE

*W*hen Ajay and I got married, he promised to take me to Disney World. It has always been my dream, so the fact that I'm walking into Disneyland with my daughter between me and my husband has my emotions soaring.

The clan is with us, including Dhara and Fletcher. It's the only way I can describe this enormous family properly. There are so many of them and the only time I can tell Peyton and Elle apart is when they're with their respective partners. Still, this is the family I've always wanted for Ajay and there is no way in hell I would ever take it away from him. I already know Evelyn's comfortable with him, and he with her.

This morning, I snuck downstairs and found them eating breakfast together; she was sitting on the counter and he was standing next to her. She was feeding him a banana while he read the paper. I watched them for a bit, just being together. She would ask him a question, he would answer and ask her one right back. I don't know how long they had been awake together getting to know each other this morning, but it warmed my heart to see and showed me that she and I can do this. My parents will miss us and that makes me sad, but it's my choice to make and this is where I want to be.

I stop at the entrance and take it all in, fighting back a wave of emotions. I have been dreaming of this my whole life and it's finally coming true. The people in our party are taking pictures, making the poor photographer work hard for his money. We each take turns posing and I already know my favorite is going to be the one of Ajay, Evelyn, and me. I don't care if my eyes are closed or if she's making a funny face... it's our first family photo.

I'm squeezing the life out of Ajay's hand as we walk out onto Main Street. My daughter is beside herself with excitement while I'm in awe.

"Have you been here before?"

"With Keane and Chandler. If I had known... I would've waited for you," he says.

"It's okay, we're here together now."

After two more rounds of photos, we finally make it to the castle where a cast member is holding a sign that reads "Ballard." Ajay goes up to her and they speak for a moment. When he comes back, he's grinning from ear-to-ear as he crouches down in front of Evelyn.

"Mickey and Minnie want to know if you're ready to have breakfast with them?"

Her eyes widen as her hand covers her mouth. "But I already ate."

"It's okay, they won't mind. Come on." He reaches for her hand and we follow the cast member through the park and into a restaurant not far from the castle.

"Mommy!" Evelyn screeches my name. "Mommy,

look!" She's pointing to the Disney Princesses who are lined up along with almost every single character possible.

Ajay glances around, looking slightly confused. He says something to the cast member and then turns toward Harrison. "You did this?"

"We did," Katelyn says. "We wanted her to have a special day."

The tears I had been fighting back earlier waste no time flowing from my eyes. I have never been so grateful for someone's generosity before in my life.

Chandler tells Evelyn to follow her, leading her over to the characters. Each one signs her autograph book and poses for a picture while I stand there, speechless.

"I really don't know what to say."

"Me neither," Ajay says. "I only arranged for Mickey and Minnie, but the James's..." He trails off as he looks over his shoulder at them. They're following the girls and making sure Evelyn is taking full advantage of this opportunity.

"They love you."

"They're amazing and they're one of the reasons why I can't leave, Whiskey. The love they show me, I've never had that before. I never knew what it was like to have someone care so much."

"I care that much, Ajay."

He looks at me, smiles and leans down to kiss me. "You should go be with Evelyn. Share this moment with her."

I do as he suggests and catch up with my daughter who is giddy beyond belief. She's telling each princess about her loose tooth and how Miss Katelyn has promised to tell the tooth fairy where she is in case she loses it while on vacation. Tomorrow, after the excitement has died down, I'm going to ask her what she thinks about living with Ajay. Honestly, it'll be a moot point because she's having such a good time, she'll want to stay. But I still want her to know her opinion matters to me and I want to make sure she understands that it means she won't see her grandparents every day. Broaching the subject with my parents will be difficult even though my mom is super supportive. It's really my dad that I have to worry about.

After this massive meet and greet is done, Liam suggests that if people want to split up, they should and that we can meet up for lunch. Keane says that he's going to hang with us because Chandler wants to stay with Evelyn, while everyone else seems to split off into groups.

"Daddy, can Evelyn and I go on the rides?" Chandler asks her dad.

"I think so," he looks at me for approval.

"She's only been on a few carnival rides. Can we start small?" I ask. Keane pulls out the map and shows us where we can find the smaller rides.

We go on everything from Alice in Wonderland to Autopia where Evelyn drives Ajay around the track. My favorite is the Buzz Lightyear Astro Blaster where Chandler and I successfully beat Ajay and Evelyn.

After lunch, Katelyn and Harrison ask if they can take Evelyn for a bit, giving Ajay and me a little privacy... well, as much as you can have while in one of the busiest parks in America.

Still we hold hands and walk slowly to rides, stopping along the way for more photos and ducking into gift shops to buy things for Evelyn.

"I still owe you a honeymoon," he says as he gives me a spoonful of his frozen lemonade.

"I think this about covers it."

"Not even close." He shakes his head. "I want to take

you on a real trip, just the two of us. Someplace romantic." Ajay moves his chair so he's closer to me. "I'm serious about us, Whiskey."

"Are you serious about Evelyn?"

"Without a doubt. I am falling hard for that little girl and want to be her dad, Whiskey. I can be there for her and give her a damn good life, one that includes a Mom *and* a Dad. Especially a Dad who isn't ashamed of her."

"Parenting is a big step, Ajay."

He smiles. "I was ready at eighteen. I know I'm ready now and can provide so much more than I could back then."

I lean forward and press my lips to his. "I love you, Ajay."

"I love you more, Whiskey. Stay here with me, let's be a family."

LATER THAT NIGHT, Ajay and I are listening to Evelyn recount her day at Disney while dressed in her new Disney pajamas that Ajay picked out for her. Honestly, I think he bought her an entire gift shop with the amount of bags that were delivered.

Her story includes hand gestures, crazy facial expressions, and the most animated voices I have ever heard come out of her mouth. When she finally sits down, she lets out a very dramatic sigh.

"Mommy and Ajay, this was the best day of my whole life."

"Wow, that's pretty huge," I say to her while trying to stifle my laughter.

"I'm tired. Can I go to bed?" she asks. Her question has Ajay and I moving rather quickly to appease her. It's a cold day in hell when your five-year-old asks to go to bed early.

Upstairs, Ajay stands in the doorway while I tuck her in. "I want Ajay to tuck me in too."

I look at him from over my shoulder and grin as he comes forward. He follows everything that I do and even leans down to give her a kiss.

"Mommy, is Ajay your boyfriend?"

I look at her for a long moment while I try to answer her question. Telling her that we are actually married will only confuse her.

"Hey, Evelyn, can I ask you a question?"

She shrugs. "Okay, Ajay."

He sits on the end of her bed, sliding all the way until his back touches the wall. "I've known your mommy a very long time and I really love her. So, I'm wondering what you think about me asking your mom to marry me?"

I'm not sure how I'm supposed to react, so I just stay still. It's a pretty silly question since we're already married.

"Do you love, Ajay, Mommy?"

"I do, angel. A whole lot."

"Do you love Logan?"

I stiffen at her question and am afraid to look at Ajay. But it's his voice that I hear answer her question.

"There are different types of love, Evelyn. We can love many people and have special places in our hearts for them. I love Miss Katelyn because she's like a Mom to me. I love Miss Elle because she's my boss. I love Miss Nola because she gave me a place to live when I needed it. Your mommy loves Logan because he was her friend for a really long time and now he's protecting all of us, which means I love him too."

"That's silly," she says, giggling.

"I know, but the love your mom and I feel for each other is different."

"We want to be a family," I tell her. "Ajay would like us to live here with him."

"Hmm," she shrugs. "I'll think about it after I wake-up. I'm really tired right now."

Shut down by the soon-to-be first grader, I give her another kiss and pull Ajay from her bed. He leaves the door slightly ajar and makes sure the hallway nightlight is on for her.

He follows me down the hall with his hands on my hips and his lips on my neck. I moan and he shushes me, telling me I have to be quiet until we get into the bedroom even though he's making it near impossible for me to function. He, somehow, manages to turn the knob of the door and ushers us inside.

His hands are everywhere, removing my clothes followed by his, and then finally picking me up and carrying me to bed.

"I love you, Mrs. Ballard," he tells me as his lips hover over mine. "Tell me you'll marry me again."

My hands cup his cheeks and I look deep into his eyes. "A thousand times over... I'll marry you every day for the rest of my life."

And I will, as long as Judge Harvey isn't the one doing the honors.

## AJAY

*A*sking Whiskey to marry me again was always part of the plan, but doing it today was not. However, I couldn't think of any other way to show or tell Evelyn that I'm madly in love with her mother. I have no doubt there's some confusion going on in her mind with the fact that Logan is suddenly not around while I am, and that's the last thing I want.

What I do want, though, is to be a family with these two beautiful girls and to do that I have to be a man, which means I need to talk to Whiskey's father — not an easy feat since we don't see eye to eye on a lot of things when it comes to his daughter. But he's important to Whiskey and Evelyn and without his support, Whiskey and I can't have a happy marriage. I know that's what she wants... what her parents have... and I want to give it her.

That's how I find myself back in Bailey. Not that I wouldn't come back just to see Whiskey and Evelyn, but while I'm here, I'm going to do what I should've done years ago.

My rental car idles in the driveway of the Foster's home

while I build up the courage I need to confront the Sheriff. I'm afraid that if I sit here to long, he'll come out with his shotgun and actually use it this time. He already tried to kill me once when he came home from work early and caught Whiskey and me in bed together. There was no way either of us could play it off as just talking, although she *was* saying my name. Her daddy, fully aware of what was going on, was beyond pissed and chased my bare ass down the road while trying to load his shotgun. I deserved it. I could stay in their home a few days a week if I kept my hands to myself, but there was no way I could do that. Not with the way Whiskey was turning into a woman. She had my hormones going crazy and all it took was one little shake of her ass, along with the come hither look she had developed, for me to drop my jeans and break every rule her parents set for us. Instead of apologizing for disrespecting them, I married their daughter, thinking I had beat her dad at the game. Boy was I wrong.

My legs shake as I climb the steps that lead to the wide covered porch. I can barely hear the ocean that Whiskey told me is behind the house, which they built a few years ago in preparation of Sheriff Foster retiring, over my rapidly beating heart. It's hard to imagine he would be the type to sit around day after day, but maybe after so many years at the same job, he's looking forward to it.

The front door is open; I can hear sound coming from the television and dishes clanking in the kitchen. No one knows I'm coming here, not even Whiskey. In fact, she doesn't even know I'm in town. She thinks I'm arriving tomorrow but I needed a day to make amends and put a plan in motion. I knock my knuckles against the wooden screen door and step back, waiting for someone to come to the door and silently praying for it to be Mrs. Foster.

The sound of footsteps has me looking through the mesh screen. Mrs. Foster is coming toward me, drying her hands with a towel. She pushes the door open slightly and smiles. "Well hello, Ajay. It's been a long time."

I tilt my head in shame and swallow the lump in my throat. "Yes, ma'am." My hands begin to fidget as I search for my words. I stuff them into my pockets to try and keep them still. "I'm wondering if I can have a few moments of Sheriff Foster's time and maybe some of yours as well?"

She smiles, nods, and pushes the door open so I can follow her in. "James, we have a guest."

I step in and let the screen door shut against my hand to keep it from slamming. The hall is filled with pictures of Whiskey and Evelyn — each one makes me stop and long for the life we could've had even though I know it would've been nothing like what I can give them now. Maybe if I had stayed, Evelyn would've been mine and not some piece of shit loser's who wants nothing to do with her.

"She's beautiful."

"They both are," I say in response. "I made a mistake the day I left her."

"She'll forgive you, Ajay," Mrs. Foster rests her hand on my arm. She motions toward the living room and gives me a wink. "His bark is worse than his bite, but be warned, he loves those girls more than his own life." She walks back toward the kitchen, leaving those words hanging in the air.

Stepping into the living room, I clear my throat. "Sheriff, may I speak with you?"

James Foster doesn't take his eyes off the television. He does, however, point the remote at it and change the channel to a hunting show. I continue to stand there, rocking back and forth on my heels. I clear my throat again, but he keeps his attention on his show.

"Sheriff Foster, I am hoping to speak to you about Whis... Jamie. I know I'm the last person you want to see standing here and I accept that, but I'm here to ask for your forgiveness. I was nothing more than a naïve boy who just wanted to be loved and Jamie gave me that. There's no excuse for what I've done... I disregarded your rules and hurt you and Mrs. Foster by whisking your only daughter off and marrying her without her family there. Then, after all of that, I left her. She was right to ask for a divorce, to move on with her life. I didn't deserve her."

"And you think you do now?" he pushes his recliner into a sitting position, turns off the television and stands. "Follow me," he says gruffly. I do as he says, nodding to Mrs. Foster as we walk through the kitchen. He walks to the edge of their property and stops. I do the same and look out over the small ledge. There's a staircase leading to the beach, with chairs set up around a small table. The view from here is breathtaking and retirement worthy.

"Evelyn loves the beach. She looks forward to building sand castles every spring. She can't swim yet though so if she goes in the water, someone must be with her always. Jamie," he pauses and continues to look out over the water, "she will sit down there for hours and read a book and when she's done, she'll walk the beach. Her mother tells me she's looking for love, for her fairytale. Personally, I don't believe in that crap. Do you want to know why?"

"Yes, sir."

He turns and looks at me. "Because she already found it. She found it at eight or ten, whenever it was that she met you. I always thought she would grow out of her infatuation with you, but she never did. You, on the other hand..."

"I needed to grow up. I needed to be able to provide for her."

"And you can do that now?"

"Yes, sir. I can."

"And Evelyn?"

"I love her. I want to be her dad, raise her as my own. I want to build sand castles with her, teach her how to swim, ride a bike, and walk her to school. I want to be there when she loses this next tooth and have her run up to me to tell me about her day."

"She's not yours, Ballard."

"Ever since I met her, I wish that she were. I regret ever leaving and want to make it up to Whiskey. I want to make things right."

He laughs. "I've never understood why you insist on calling her that, but I accidentally did it one night. I was comforting her and said it, boy did she let me have it."

"Sir, I would also like to ask for your permission to marry Jamie. I know I'm years late and we're already married, but your permission is important to me... and I know Whiskey would love your blessing."

Foster stands there, not saying anything. With my luck, he's probably going to tell me no. He's been waiting for the day when he could tell me off.

He inhales deeply and gathers himself. "You're taking my girls away from me."

I sigh in return. I tell him about my house and the neighborhood, and how Evelyn has a playmate in Chandler. "Whiskey doesn't have to work unless she wants to and when Evelyn isn't in school, they can come here whenever they want. Or you and Mrs. Foster could visit, maybe even retire out there."

He shakes his head. "I've never been out that way."

"It's much like here, just a bit cooler and not so humid."

"I have half the mind to tell you to pound sand and to

forget about Jamie and Evelyn, but I know that's not what my daughter wants. Tell me, does she know you're here?"

"No, sir. There are a few things I need to take care of before I see her and Evelyn, but I plan to tell her. I don't want to keep secrets from her. I love her too much."

The sound of a door opening and closing has us turning around. Mrs. Foster is walking toward us with her arms crossed over her chest. "Dinner is ready. Are you joining us, Ajay?"

I look from her to the Sheriff who nods slightly. "It'd be my pleasure."

She smiles and tells us not to be long. Once she's out of ear shot, Mr. Foster speaks, "if I were to tell you no, that I don't forgive you or that I don't want Jamie to take Evelyn away, I'd lose my daughter. She loves you and only she knows why. It pains me to know my girls are leaving, that they'll be three thousand miles away."

"It's more like two thousand six hundred but who's counting?" I shrug, realizing I should probably keep my comments to a minimum.

Foster smirks and shakes his head. "Some things never change."

"A couple of things have, sir. I'm more responsible, I'm better off financially, and I've grown up a lot. I'm also more in love with Whiskey than I ever have been. This ninety-day sentence was a blessing in disguise. If it weren't for Harvey being a tool, I wouldn't be standing here right now. I should thank him, but Whiskey would have my balls."

Her father laughs and places his hand on my shoulder. "All I ask is that you don't hurt either of them and when you and Jamie have your own child, you don't forget about Evelyn."

"Never... I plan to adopt her. She's going to know what

it's like to have a father and mother, something I've never known. And more importantly, when someone asks where her dad is, she can tell them instead of saying she doesn't know. Believe me, it's the worst feeling in the world when someone asks if my parents are proud of me or if they'll be at a show. I don't want Evelyn to ever experience that feeling again."

James Foster, the man who arrested me months ago, pulls me into his arms and squeezes me tightly. When he releases me, he steps away. "We best get inside, or the missus will have our heads for letting our food get cold."

"Does this mean you forgive me?" I hedge.

"Hell no, it just means I'm giving you a second chance. And you better not screw it up this time, son," he slaps the back of my shoulder and laughs as he walks toward the house.

It's a start. That's what I tell myself.

## 32

JAMIE

*E*velyn and I only spent a week in California, which was enough to realize that wherever Ajay is, is home, at least for me. Evelyn's still on the fence about it all, but she's giving up a lot leaving her grandparents behind. I wish I could tell her that moving is easy, but I've never had to pack up my stuff and move across country. I can't promise her that she'll make new friends, although I'm confident she will, or assure her that her teacher next year will be as nice as her kindergarten teacher. I can only hope and convey those feelings when we talk about our new adventure. She's scared, but so am I. I'm scared that I'm making the wrong decision about moving forward with Ajay even though it feels right. I wish I could go back to the beginning of our ninety-day sentence and start all over. I'd force myself to spend every waking minute with him, to tell him the truth about Evelyn from the onset, to make sure that he understood what staying together meant. I'd use those beginning days to get to know him, understand his life and immerse myself in it. Right now, I'm getting the crash course of what it's like to be with someone in a full-time band, and not a garage band that plays for a case of beer on a Saturday night. Those days of sitting on a milk crate and watching Ajay play were pretty amazing — I'm proud of what he's accomplished, though part of me would give anything to go back and beg him not to leave for Nashville. Our lives would be different, but I don't know if that's a good or bad thing.

The sound of someone clearing their voice brings me back to my reality. I'm about to leave a job that has kept me financially afloat and the thought of being dependent on someone else has my stomach in knots. I look up to find my boss in the doorway. He's come back from Florida to hire my replacement.

"You look deep in thought, any chance you're changing your mind?" he asks as he comes in and sits in the chair across from my desk, which is now technically his. He's tan, probably from his many hours out on the golf course, making me look like a ghost compared to him.

"I wish I could find a way to stay here and move."

"Me too, Jamie. I hate the idea of losing you."

I nod and choke back the lump in my throat. Everything about this job has been great and my boss has treated me fairly. He's taught me a lot about being an adult and was there when Evelyn was born. He felt responsible, in a small way, since it was a convention he had taken me to where I met her sperm donor.

"I have everything in order," I hand him a manila folder containing my day-to-day activities, schedules for the staff, time off requests, and delivery schedules. "I hope my notes are detailed enough but if not, you, or whoever you have coming in to replace me, can always call me."

"What are you going to do when he goes on tour and leaves you home for months on end?"

Worry my ass off for no reason because I know Ajay won't do anything stupid. He won't mess up what we're trying to build. "Explore California, lay in the sun, and help take care of Chandler."

"His son from another relationship?"

"No," I tell him while shaking my head. "Chandler is the daughter of one of Ajay's bandmates. They live next door and I told Keane that she can stay with Evelyn and me when they go on tour next or have a late night in the studio."

"And you're okay being a stay at home wife?"

"And mother," I point out. "I can work if I want to but I don't *have* to. Ajay said the decision is up to me. I think if I do, I'll find something part-time because I want to make sure that Evelyn is adapting well and our life there isn't about school and work. Besides, it'll be a bit before the band goes on tour. Keane doesn't want to tour during the school year because of Chandler and the band is going to start work on a new album soon."

My answers seem to appease him since he turns his attention to the folder. He opens it and thumbs through the pages, nodding and saying "uh huh" every so often. As I sit here, I feel like I'm facing a teacher with a final test, my fate in his hands. Do I pass or fail? Story of my life when I was in high school.

He sets the file on my desk and sighs. "You're going to be hard to replace."

"Thank you. That means a lot."

"I'm going to conduct some interviews today and would like for you to sit in on them, maybe tell the applicants about how you handle everything. Do you think of any of the current staff would make a good manager?"

I shake my head slowly. It's not that I don't love my staff, I do, but every single one of them has something going on and they're always missing work for some reason or the other. No one is committed beside the head chef and he only wants to cook.

"Yeah, I didn't think so when none of them applied for your job." We stand at the same time and he waits for me to walk out of the office. He follows behind until we enter the kitchen and he heads off in another direction. Out front, the crowd is light and even though I know Ajay won't be here until tomorrow, I can't help but scan the faces for his. Tomorrow we're going to withdraw the petition for our divorce. He offered to have his lawyer do it, but I thought it would mean more if we ripped the papers up together. It's unnecessary but ceremonial... a life changing event.

As soon as I see Fletcher walk in, I pull the tap for his beer. He sits down and sighs. We haven't spoken much about me moving, but I gather the news isn't sitting well with him. I set his pint down in front of him and rest my hands on the edge of the bar. "Where's Dhara?"

"Dunno, she had some meeting tonight."

"Is she meeting you later?"

"Didn't ask."

"Don't lie to me, Fletch. I know you, you asked."

He shrugs, picks up his glass and takes a drink. "She's out of sorts since you told us you've decided to move. I think she's been trying to process the fact that she's losing her best friend."

I lean forward and tilt my head slightly so he's looking into my eyes. "You can't give me a guilt trip here, Fletch. I'm doing exactly what you would do if Dhara decided to move. You'd follow her and you wouldn't think twice about it."

"She hasn't hurt me the way he hurt you."

"We grow from hurt. If I thought Ajay was going to do it again, I'd run the other way, but he won't."

"How can you be so sure?"

"Because, Fletcher... I've known him most of my life. I've seen him at his worst and now at his best, and he's seen me at mine. We're the not the same eighteen-year-old's that don't have a clue about being adults. We needed to grow up. It's easy for me to see that now and to admit that getting married so young was a mistake."

"Aren't you supposed to follow your heart and all that?"

"Oh, Fletch. Are you following your heart? Have you told Dhara how you feel? Asked her out? You had the perfect opportunity while in Los Angeles, but you didn't take it. Why not?"

He shakes his head and turns his attention to his beer. I feel like a shit for bringing up Dhara, but he's in the same boat as I used to be.

"She doesn't feel the same way." He sets his empty pint glass down and pushes it toward me. I leave him there, with those words lingering in the air, while I pour him another and help a couple that just sat down.

In the few minutes that I'm gone, I'm hoping life has smacked him in the head. "Have you asked her?"

"Nope," he says, drinking from his new glass.

"So how do you know she doesn't feel the same way?"

He shrugs. "Has she said anything to you?"

"We don't sit around like school girls, giggling about boys. Those days went out the window after I had Evelyn. But it's clear that she cares about you. She hasn't dated anyone in a long time. She spends most of her free time with you if she isn't with me. I would think that there's something there. Tell me, where did you sleep last night?"

"On her couch."

I shake my head and go check on my other patrons. They tie me up with a food order and a group of guys sit down at the bar, asking if I'll put the baseball game on for them.

When I finally get back to my friend, I ask him, "Do you want to order?"

"My usual." I put his order in and try to keep myself busy. Word is spreading that I'm leaving so people are asking questions and giving me words of encouragement. Of course, there are those few who are snubbing their noses up at me, but it doesn't matter. People like Jolene Johnson-Johnson will always find a way to be negative about a situation when it's a good thing for someone else. She was this way in high school and hasn't changed much during adulthood. I'm not going to let people get me down. My happiness — and Evelyn's — is far too important to me.

I continue to work the bar, checking in on everyone and giving Fletcher some time to think. I know our dynamic is changing but the only other option is for me to stay, and that's not possible. I want to be with Ajay. I want to grow our family and raise children together. Unfortunately, for that to happen, I need to move. Honestly, I'm looking forward to a fresh start with Ajay, in a place where people don't know us as a couple, and there isn't anyone around to give him the side eye for his previous actions.

When I head back to check on Fletcher, he's in the midst of taking a bite of his burger. I stand there and laugh at my impeccable timing. Contrary to popular belief, we are not trained to approach people while they're eating.

"Can I get you anything else?"

He nods and wipes his face with his napkin. "Can you ask Dhara how she feels about me?"

"You want me to do your dirty work?"

"I'm afraid of ruining my friendship with her so I'm

thinking if I have a little inside information before moving forward, I won't look like a fool."

"And what if she doesn't like you, Fletcher? Then what?"

He sets his napkin down and grips the handle of his beer before looking me dead in my eyes. "Then, I move. I've been offered a spot in the DA's office in Raleigh and I'm thinking about taking it."

My mouth drops open. "Fletch, that's amazing and heartbreaking."

He drinks from his glass, finishing off his beer. "I'd like to give them a valid reason why I should stay here or else tell them I'm coming. I want her to come with me, but what type of friend follows another for a job transfer?"

"None that I know of," I say sadly.

"So, if you wouldn't mind asking her or snooping around, I'd know how to proceed."

I rush around the bar until I'm standing next to my friend and pull him into my arms. "I feel like all these life changes should've happened years ago, but they're all happening now, and everything is moving so fast." Fletcher hugs me tightly before releasing his grip.

"Will you talk to her?"

"I will, Fletch. I believe you're supposed to be with each other so yeah, I'll find out what I can." I'll have to work fast, but one way or another, it'll happen.

## 33

## JAMIE

*I* jolt awake, open my eyes slowly, and reach for my phone to look at time. My heart is racing, and I believe it's from the loud bang that woke me. I turn my head slightly and look toward the window, not sure what I'm expecting to see, but anything would be better than thinking someone's breaking in or lurking around the outside of my house. It's just after seven and far too early for me to be awake, especially with Evelyn staying at my parents. I expected, or at least *hoped*, that Ajay would surprise me late last night but he didn't. He called though, to tell me that he was going to be later than planned due to some band thing. I did my best to keep my voice steady and to not let him know that I was upset. If I'm going to have a life with him, I can't let the little things bother me. He didn't cancel, he is just going to be late, and it's not like we had any major plans to do anything. He's only coming to help me pack and drive the rental truck across the country. Absolutely nothing life altering or major, at least that's what I keep telling myself.

The loud bang sounds again and again and my name is yelled. Now that I'm awake, I know it's coming from my door, and the only person who would do something like this is Dhara. "I'm going to kill her," I mutter as I get out of bed. As I make my way through my house, I think of all the ways I can maim her and how I know Fletcher will forgive me for hurting the love of his life once I explain to him why.

"What?" I screech as I open the door. My neighbor across the street is out. He's bent over, retrieving his paper when his head snaps up. I wave, hoping to convey a sincere apology for my outburst before glaring at Dhara. "What in the hell do you want?"

"We have appointments to get our hair done."

"Since when?" I ask as she side steps me to get into my house. "Come on in, I wasn't sleeping or anything."

"You can sleep later," she says as she makes her way to my bedroom. I follow her with the intent of going back to bed but find her rummaging through my closet.

"What are you doing?"

"Looking for a button up shirt."

"What for?"

"For you. Hair, remember?"

I roll my eyes and crawl back into bed. "You're not making any sense. Can you please leave or just come lay next to me? I didn't sleep well."

"Why not?" she asks loudly.

"Ajay, he called, and I thought he was going to tell me he was in town, but he was calling to say he wouldn't be here until later. My hopes were up and then down—"

"And then you laid in bed looking at your ceiling thinking about all the terrible things he might have been doing, to which you proceeded to second guess yourself

249

about all of your decisions?" She's standing at the foot of my bed with a flannel shirt in her hand; she tosses it to me. I bring it to my nose and inhale. Little does she know that it's Ajay's. I took it from him when I left his house. I needed something of his to hold me over until I saw him again.

Dhara sits down next to me. "Jamie, I love you. You're my best friend. But I want you to hear me and absorb what I'm telling you. Ajay Ballard is head over heels in love with you. I promise you that those stupid little thoughts you're having are very misplaced. That man will not do anything to intentionally hurt you ever again."

"I know," I say quietly, still cuddling his shirt. "I can't help it though. I read things."

"Stop reading the shit on the internet."

"You do," I point out.

"That's because I'm a fangirl. I read so I can pretend I'm there and part of the scandal."

"Dhara!"

She shrugs. "It's all a fantasy, J. I would never be the woman to break up a marriage. Ever. I'm not that person, I don't care how famous the person is. That's not how I roll, but I pretend. I picture myself married to guys like Liam Page because it's an escape from reality when the truth is that I met the guy and couldn't even form a sentence. Like, my rock God was standing in front of me, shaking my hand and smiling, and the only thing I could do was swallow. Fletcher saved me. He said everything to Liam and the other guys that I've wanted to say for years. It probably took me an hour, if not longer, to finally find the courage to move from the spot I was standing in and mingle. But by the end of the little party, I was comfortable."

"And more in love?"

"Yeah, with what he shares with his wife. She walked in and bam! The whole room shifted on its axis. I want a guy to look at me the way Liam looks at his wife." She nudges my hip with her elbow. "The way Ajay looks at you when you come into view. From the time we were kids, I've been jealous of you both. I knew early on what love at first sight was. It was Jameson and Ajay, two souls destined to be together, come hell or high water. You've already been through hell and he's going to be your ark to get you through the high water."

"When did you become so philosophical?"

Dhara smiles. "Let's go, seriously we have hair and nail appointments this morning."

"They're not even open yet."

"They will be by the time we get to Wilmington."

"But Ajay—"

Dhara tugs on my arm, pulling me upright. "We'll be back before he even gets to town. Come on, get dressed and wear that shirt. I want to beat traffic."

Until today, I have never been to a salon that has black drapes over their mirrors. The stylist says it's because there was a death in the family, and they were in mourning. Add this oddity to the fact that the salon sign says they're closed, cell phones aren't allowed, and no one asked me what I wanted my hair to look like. I'm fairly confident that when I leave here, I'm going to look like Frenchie from Grease and all Dhara can say is that I look beautiful.

She does, of course. Her hair is done in a French twist and her make-up looks flawless. From what I can tell, mine

251

is curled, braided, twisted, and pinned. After this, I'm not so sure she can be my best friend anymore. Who brings their bestie to a place like this knowing full well they're seeing the judge today? Mine, that's who.

"Close your eyes," the stylist says to me. I do, reluctantly.

"What's going on?" I ask anyone who is willing to give me a straight answer.

"We're being pampered," Dhara says. "Enjoy it."

"I feel like this is a set-up."

"It is," she laughs.

"What?" I turn my head quickly. "Shit, sorry," I tell the woman working on me. She doesn't say anything but mutters a few expletives that shouldn't be repeated in public. "Dhara, you need to start talking, immediately."

She sighs. "You're such a buzzkill. Ajay is taking you out to dinner tonight and he thought you'd like a day at the spa."

"This isn't a spa," I say through gritted teeth. "A spa means a massage, a mud bath, a mani and pedi. For all I know I look like Bozo the clown." I glance at the girl working on me and cringe. "Sorry."

"Well I needed my hair done, so this was an easy solution."

"Yeah, for you."

"Eh, whatever."

"What do you need your hair done for?" I ask her. "Are you finally going to tell Fletcher how you feel about him?"

Dhara doesn't have a witty comeback and when my make-up gal steps away, I turn and look at her. She's brooding and acting like she's engrossed in the magazine that she's flipping through... likely one she's already read.

"Fletcher loves you, Dhara. And I have a feeling you feel the same way. I think it's about time you both take a step forward before it's too late."

"Late for what?"

"He's leaving, D. He was offered a job in Raleigh and plans to take it. He wants you to go with him."

"And what? Be his roommate?"

I laugh. Leave it to her to play clueless. "To move *with* him. Don't play dumb with me right now, I'm sitting in this chair and don't have a single idea of what I look like."

"You're beautiful," she tells me.

"And you're biased and avoiding the elephant in the room. Fletcher loves you and you love him."

"As a friend."

I shake my head slightly. "I don't buy it one bit. He's your guy. He's your go to, the one you call for everything. He stays at your house almost every night, sleeping on the couch because he wants to be close to you when he has a perfectly great apartment of his own. You have dinner with him five out of seven nights. Meet for lunch, breakfast, and go shopping. You're in a relationship without being in a relationship."

"What we have is perfect."

"What you have is nice. It's far from perfect. It'll be perfect when you tell that boy how you feel, but first admit to yourself that you're in love with him."

"So, what if I am?" she asks defiantly. "If he's moving, what difference does it make?"

"It matters because he wants to build a life with you, and if he were to leave, you'd be devastated."

"How do you figure?"

"You're all done," my stylist says. I'm tempted to ask for

253

a mirror but am sure I'd be told no. I stand and go over to Dhara.

"I know because you haven't said anything about Evelyn and I moving. You haven't cried, complained, or told me to stay. You've helped me pack and each night gone back to Fletcher. If he leaves..."

I study her for a minute, looking for any sign in her eyes that my words are getting through. She closes the magazine and gives me a soft smile. "If I tell you that I love him will you drop this?"

Shaking my head. "Nope. I want you to tell him."

"And if I don't?"

"Then you'll finally understand the heartache that I went through when Ajay left, and believe me, Dhara, you don't want to experience that."

She doesn't say anything, except "thank you" to the staff. When we get outside, there's a limo parked in front of the salon with the driver standing by the door. "Let me guess."

Dhara links arms with mine and says, "It's best that you just play along."

Left with no choice, I climb into the back and settle in. I am somewhat familiar with Wilmington and figure I'll know where we're going after we start driving, but as luck would have it, the windows are covered.

"Let me guess, it's a secret?"

"Of course," she says. "Your boy is pulling out all the stops for a nice romantic dinner."

I want to be upset, but I can't. If he's putting in an effort like this, I'm going to enjoy it, even if I'd rather be at home waiting for him. We're not in the car for long when it's put into park and the back door is open.

"Close your eyes and don't peek," she says, taking my

hand and pulling me from the car. I do as she says, trying to be good for Ajay, but it's damn near killing me not to open them. She tells me when to step, when to turn and finally when to open my eyes.

We're in a room with no windows, but there's a mirror and a dress side-by-side. "Dhara," my voice breaks as I say her name. "What's going on?"

"Well, if I had to guess, I'd say someone is getting married today!"

I look at her, willing my tears to go away. "Explain please, before I have a breakdown."

She leads me over to the vanity and sits me down in front of the mirror. I look at myself, with my perfect make-up and my long hair done just the way I've dreamed. My hand covers my mouth as she hugs me from behind.

Dhara moves to my side and touches the dress hanging there. "For years, I've watched you mark dresses, hair designs and wedding ideas, knowing that if you were to ever get married again, you'd want your fairytale. Well, I'm here to say that your dreams are about to come true."

"How?"

"Ajay," she says. "He wanted to give you something new to start your life together over with. We've been planning this for weeks and let me tell you, Josie Westbury — that's Liam's wife in case you didn't know — has some *serious* pull when it comes to weddings. Ajay asked Mrs. Harrison, your mom and me to pull this together."

As if on cue, the door opens and my dad, dressed in a tuxedo, steps in. My mom follows and Evelyn is behind her, dressed in a matching gown. "Oh my," I say as tears start to fall. "Ajay did all of this?"

Dhara and my mom nod. "We helped, but it was his

idea. He wanted you to have your fairytale wedding, something he couldn't give you before."

"May I come in?" Katelyn asks as she peaks her head in.

"Of course," I tell her. I stand and give everyone in the room a hug. "I don't know what to say."

"You have to say, 'I do', Mommy."

I kneel and look at my daughter. "I think I can do that."

## 34

## AJAY

Quinn stands in the mirror, adjusting his bow tie. There's a smirk on his face, one I can't decipher, as he looks back and forth between his sister and me. To outsiders we're nothing more than a band, a group of people who get together and perform. But to me, we're family. They're my family. Keane and his daughter, Chandler, Dana, Hendrix, Elle, and Quinn... we're unconventional but it works for us.

Elle looks me in the eyes and smiles softly. I haven't asked her what she's thinking or even what her thoughts are about Whiskey and me, but I've seen her with Evelyn and she's a natural. Quinn and Elle's entire family have taken me in and welcomed my girls with open arms; it's like we've always been this close-knit group, like they've been my family from the beginning. It's taken me a long time to accept that blood doesn't make a family. Love is all you need.

The door opens and Harrison and Katelyn walk in. One look at the woman who has become a mother to me and my heart lurches. She dabs at her eyes and comes over to me and Elle but pushes her daughter out of the way. "I'm so proud of you," she says brushing her hands over my shoulders. "This is going to be the most perfect day."

"I hope so. I'm waiting to hear from Dhara to make sure everything is okay."

"It is," she tells me. "I've seen her and Evelyn, and oh my... Oh Ajay, they're just so beautiful."

My throat tightens. "She's here?" I don't know why but there's a part of me that thought she wouldn't come, that being with me wasn't what she wanted. I know what I'm feeling is relief, but it's more than that and it's hard to describe.

Katelyn nods. "And dressed. The church is filling up and Chandler looks so cute handing out the programs. The quartet is already playing, and the flowers are lovely. I've never seen whiskey colored roses until today. I don't know how Josie finds these impossible colors."

"You did an amazing job, Mom." Quinn kisses her on the cheek. "Maybe you and Aunt Josie should go into the wedding planning business."

She shakes her head. "I only plan weddings for my kids, that's it. Two down, two to go," she eyes Quinn and Elle. Elle holds her hand up, showing off her ring.

"I'm one step closer than Quinn."

"Hey," he says. "We haven't been together that long. You and Ben, Noah and Peyton, and Ajay and Jamie have known each other for years. Years!" he throws his hands up in the air and we all laugh.

"Well, at least Ajay is making me a grandma."

Elle and Quinn's eyes go wide and there seems to be an intense standoff between the James's. I want to step away but am intrigued with what's going on. Harrison stands next to me, watching the three of them battle it out via staring contest. Katelyn raises her eyebrow, challenging her children.

"I'm not married yet," Elle stammers.

Katelyn tilts her head and looks at Quinn. He tugs on the collar of his shirt and asks, "Is it hot in here?"

"Nope," I say. "It's a cool sixty-five."

"Feels like it's eighty," Quinn says as Harrison laughs in the background.

"Feels like you're dodging the question," Katelyn says.

"I don't believe one was asked, Mom," Quinn fires back. "Besides, shouldn't you be having this conversation with Peyton and Noah? They're at least married."

"Do you think you need to be married to have children?" she asks them.

Quinn shakes his head. "No, ma'am," he says quietly. "But her parents would appreciate the gesture and I want to respect their wishes."

Katelyn steps forward and sets her hand on Quinn's cheek. "You're such a good boy, Quinn." He leans into her hand and tells her thank you. She goes to Elle, who has a sudden fascination with her fingernails. "And you?"

"Mom," Elle says sternly.

Katelyn laughs. "I'm only messing with you both. I know when you're ready, it'll happen but until then, I'll spoil Evelyn."

"I think she'll like that," I add.

She turns and looks at Harrison. "You've been awfully quiet while I've given them grief."

He shrugs. "I'm just damn happy that my family is happy."

"We are happy, aren't we?"

The group of us nod and Katelyn tells us that we need to finish getting ready. Quinn's my best man. The decision to ask Quinn over Harrison wasn't easy. They've been there for me in different ways and I'm close to both of them. But having Quinn right next to me feels right.

Keane, Hendrix, and Dana come in. The guys are in black suits and Dana is in a knee length dress, all chosen by Elle to match the bridal party. When Dhara asked me what colors I wanted, I blurted out Whiskey, meaning that she should decide, but that would be near impossible if I were to keep this wedding a secret. Dhara explained that Pinterest would save our asses, whatever that meant, and got to work picking out the attire for everyone. All I know is that Dhara and Josie worked magic, and that I'm going to owe them both until the day I die. Dhara's words, not mine.

"It's time," Keane says. "Mrs. James, if you'll allow me to do the honors?" He holds out his arm and Katelyn goes to him, but not before stopping at me first.

"Do you have your vows?" she asks.

"Memorized," I tell her, pointing to my head.

She adjusts my lapel and straightens my boutonniere. "And the ring?"

"In my pocket, Mom," Quinn adds.

"And Saul took care of your divorce, making sure it was withdrawn?"

I nod. "Yes. Elle's sneaky way of having Whiskey sign a non-disclosure agreement worked perfectly."

Katelyn smiles. "While I wouldn't usually condone that tactic, in this situation it was perfect." I wink at Elle, who grins back. She's the best manager a guy like me could ask for.

"Okay, I guess we're all ready then! In a few minutes I'm officially going to have another daughter and be a grandma. I'm not sure if this day could be any more perfect."

Me neither, but I'm not about to count my chickens before they hatch or is it count my eggs? Either way, I'm not counting on anything until I slip a ring onto Whiskey's finger and marry her in front of our friends and family.

We follow Keane out of the room and when I step into the church, I'm taken aback. The pews are filled with people I've known for years, people who shouldn't give a rat's ass about me, but they do... or they at least care for Whiskey and Evelyn.

"I can't believe Elle pulled this off, getting everyone here without alerting Whiskey," I say to Quinn.

"When Elle puts her mind to something, anything is possible. My sister is a force to be reckoned with when she wants something."

No truer words have ever been spoken when referring to Elle James. I know she moved mountains to get her brother to join Sinful Distraction. We would've been good without him, but having him makes us incredible. And all of her efforts gave me a best friend.

The music shifts and people turn toward the double doors. Once they open, Dhara walks toward the alter, a huge smile on her face as her eyes are laser focused on Fletcher. If they're not together soon, Whiskey is going to lock them in a room. It's all she talks about — how they love each other but are too dumb to realize it themselves.

My eyes are on the doorway when Evelyn steps through. I quickly glance at Katelyn, who is dabbing her eyes, but go back to watching the little girl that I'm going to raise as my own. Her hair is pinned up, making her curls bounce as she walks toward us. When she reaches me, I kneel so that we're eye level.

"Aren't you the prettiest girl in the room?"

She shakes her head and looks over her shoulder. "Mommy is, just wait until you see her," she whispers.

The music switches and the vibe in the church changes. Everyone stands and I'm forced to move from where I'm standing so I can see my bride coming down the aisle.

"Damn," I say aloud as Whiskey makes her way toward me. Her dress is tight around her chest, poofy at her waist, and according to Dhara and Elle, this is her dream dress. I don't know anything about fashion or wedding dresses, but I do know that Whiskey looks fucking hot, beautiful, and drop dead gorgeous in it... and I can't wait to take it off her later.

As she gets to me, I'm tongue-tied and my palms are sweating. I want to touch her, kiss her, and tell her how much I love her. I want to pick her up and carry her out of here to an empty room and make love to her. Mostly importantly, I want to profess my love and desire to be her husband in front of everyone so that there's no question in anyone's mind that this is where I belong... with her. I can't take my eyes of hers. We stare at each other, both of us smiling, dreaming about our future. She may already be my wife, but this was how our wedding should've happened the first time.

The preacher clears his throat, and everyone sits as my knees shake. They're knocking together as if playing their own song.

"We are gathered here today to witness the marriage of Jameson Foster and Ajay Ballard. Who gives this woman to this man?"

I look at the Sheriff and pray that he's in a giving mood today. "Her mother and I do, happily," he says as he kisses Whiskey on her cheek. He then places her hand in mine and helps guide her up the stairs to where I'm standing.

"I can't believe you did this, Ajay."

"Do you like it?" I look around, seeing everything more vividly now that she's here.

"I love it and I love you."

"I love you too," I lean forward to kiss her, but Quinn pulls on my tuxedo. "Not yet," he whispers loudly enough for his parents to hear, who start to giggle along with everyone who saw me try to sneak one. I smile and shrug.

The preacher talks about our love story, from when we met to how we found each other again. He tells about our lives and how they blend together and what our future holds, and how our parents can't wait for the pitter patter of baby feet. I glance at Katelyn, suspecting she might have said something. She shrugs as if to say it wasn't her, but I know better. When he tells us it's time for our vows, Whiskey hands her bouquet to Dhara and grips my hand.

"Ajay, all my life you've been the guy who helps me up after I've fallen, who holds my hand in the dark, who makes sure I get the last bite of ice cream. Even though we took a detour in our lives, I know we were meant to, that we had to pass that test before we could find each other again. Our love story may not be perfect, but it's ours and no one can take that away from us. I can't wait to restart our lives, to raise our children, and to live happily ever after."

My eyes go wide at her choice of words. I want to ask her if she's pregnant but figure this isn't the time nor place to blurt something like that out. Instead, I clear my throat and try my hardest not to picture her with a growing belly.

"Ja..." I stop and shake my head. "I'm sorry, I can't say your name because to me you'll always be my Whiskey Girl." Everyone around us laughs. "Whiskey, from the day I met you, I knew you were always going to be in my life. You're the one person who saw me for me and not where I was from. You never cared that I didn't have the same things as you, and it never escaped me that you always had enough of everything to share. You've seen me at my worst, and baby, I'm here to say that my best is yet to come because without you, I'm only a shell of who I can be. You're my partner and my wife, and as I stand in front of our friends and family, I swear to you that I will always be the man that deserves to be loved by you. I love you, Whiskey, and I love Evelyn, and I can't wait to build a life with my girls."

Whiskey nods and a single tear falls down her cheek. I let go of her hand and wipe it away with my thumb.

"Jameson Foster, do you take Ajay to be your lawfully wedded husband? To have and to hold, until death do you part?"

"I do," she says with the biggest and brightest smile I've ever seen from her. Yeah, this day is so much better than last time.

"Do you, Ajay, take Ja, er, Whiskey..." Everyone laughs, but I must hand it to this man as he knows what to call her, "...to be your lawfully wedded wife? To have and to hold, until death do you part?"

"Fuck yeah, I do."

"Ajay said a word," Evelyn says loudly. I lean to the side and see her watching me. I beckon her to come to me and she does.

"Ajay, what are you doing?" Whiskey asks, but I ignore her question.

When Evelyn is standing next to her mom, I drop to my knee and pull a necklace out of my pocket. "I know your mom and I get rings and you're probably wondering what you get, right?"

She nods as I fumble with the necklace I had made for her. Katelyn comes over and finishes the task for me.

"Evelyn, I'm wondering if you'll accept me as your dad?"

Evelyn fiddles with the heart, which is etched with our names and today's date. She looks at her grandparents, her mom and finally at me. She shrugs. "Can I call you dad?"

"Of course," I tell her. "Or Ajay, whatever you want."

"I don't have a daddy," she says quietly.

Tears form in my eyes and search for the right words. "You do now."

Evelyn springs forward and wraps her arms around my shoulders. "I love you, Evelyn," I tell her in her ear before letting her go. I stand, but keep my hand on her shoulder, unwilling to let her go. When I look at Whiskey, she's dabbing at her face and trying to smile at me.

The preacher breaks our moment by asking for our rings. Quinn hands them over, two new ones for her and one for me. I can't wait for her to slip the band on my finger. I'm going to wear it proudly and never take it off.

"Repeat after me," the preacher says as he hands Whiskey's wedding band and engagement ring to me. So what if we're doing things backwards? The point is, we're doing them our way.

Whiskey holds her hand out and I take it in mine. I repeat what the preacher says as I slip the set onto her finger. She does the same for me and we lock hands, waiting for the words that tell me she's mine.

"Hey, Daddy," Evelyn says as she tugs on my jacket. "I think you're supposed to kiss Mommy now."

I can't help but laugh as the most unthinkable words come tumbling out of my mouth. "Damn straight I am."

It's only when the preacher announces us as Mr. and Mrs. Ballard that I finally pull my lips away from my wife, and even then, it's only for a minute.

EPILOGUE

*M*oving across country sucks. In hindsight, we should've left Evelyn with my parents until we were unpacked and settled in, but no, Ajay had the bright idea of bringing her with us. What should've been a five-day trip ended up being almost ten because we stopped at every tourist spot known to man along the way. Not a good idea, at least from where I was concerned. Honestly, I had this grand idea that Ajay and I would sow our oats in every State, like make it a game or something. A random pitstop in some unknown town, a romp in the trees along the highway, a backseat fuck in the middle of the night. Not that we'd tell people 'Oh, yeah we screwed like rabbits in Oklahoma', but that's what I thought we were going to do. I get that Ajay was new to this whole parenting thing and he wanted Evelyn to love him, but I had a serious lady boner for my husband and wanted to screw his brains out every chance I could get.

However, I wouldn't trade those two weeks for anything because I was with Ajay and Evelyn, and every single photo

I have is filled with smiles. So what, if our honeymoon was spent with a five year old sleeping between us and the only privacy we had was in the middle of the night, in a cramped bathroom, with me screaming into a towel? We were together and that's the important part. Despite the storms we drove through, heat wave we endured and the nasty fast food we ate, Ajay made our trip perfect.

Now that we're settling in and enjoying California, Evelyn and I are finding a happy medium in our routine. During the day, Chandler, Evelyn and I drive my fully decked out golf cart over to the pool. I never thought I'd be the type of woman who drives a golf cart but let me tell you something: It's the best, and I'm not the only one in the neighborhood who has one. Ajay teases me and the other ladies though, saying we need to have a drag race to determine the leader of the pack. Personally, I think he's jealous.

I also never pictured myself has a subdivision mom, but that's what I am. I attend the condo association meetings, I help with our community events, and I walk with the other stay at home wives in the early morning. But the best part is having a pool. The girls love it and are both taking swimming lessons. For me, being four months pregnant, it helps keep me from overheating. I don't know how I did it with Evelyn and the east coast humidity, but this California sun is a killer. I don't know how I'm going to make it another five months because right now I feel like a beached whale.

Someone whistles and I look over at the fence where I see Ajay coming through, looking hot as fuck with his sunglasses on. He bends down and gives me a scorching kiss, almost falling into the pool with me. He left early this morning with Keane to beat the traffic into the city.

"How's work?" I ask, as if his job is a normal nine to five.

Sometimes I wish it were, but then watching him on stage, banging on those drums, and knowing that he's coming home with me after the show makes the long hours so worth it. I'm also very thankful for Katelyn and her eagerness to be a grandmother because she always volunteers to take Evelyn and Chandler, giving Keane a night off and allowing Ajay and I to pretend like we're still on our honeymoon.

"Good," he says. He slips off his shoes and socks and sit down on the edge of the pool, his legs in the water. I stand between them and put my wet hands up the back of his shirt. He shivers but laughs it off. "The new album is almost done."

"Does it have a release date yet?"

He shakes his head. "No, Elle's working on it. Doesn't have a title either."

"Know what else doesn't have a name?"

"Our son," he says, placing his hand on my ever-growing mid-section.

We found out about two weeks ago that we were having a boy. We wanted to have one of those gender reveal parties, but we didn't tell the technician not to tell us in time and she pointed out that the baby growing inside of me had a penis. My husband — in his oh so classy way — commented with, "yeah, he does."

"How is my boy?" he asks.

"Giving me butterflies. I can't wait for you to feel him kick."

"It should be soon, right? That's what the book said."

I nod, loving the fact that he's taken a hands-on approach to becoming a Dad. My fear though, is that their next tour will start and he'll miss the delivery.

"I'll be there," he says, stroking my cheek.

"How did you know what I was thinking?"

"Because I know you, Whiskey. But I promise you, I won't miss the birth of our son. I'll be there to hold your hand. I'm not missing this." I lean into him, not caring that I may be getting him wet, and if he has an issue with it, he's not saying.

As soon as the girls are done with their lesson, they both come over. Ajay stands and prepares for Evelyn to launch herself into his arms. "Daddy, I can do the breasted stroke," she says, causing us to laugh.

"Breast stroke," he corrects her in his most serious tone. "Say it with me." They repeat the word a few times before she finally has it right. Ajay sets her down and helps me out of the pool. He walks the three of us to the lot where the line of golf carts is, shaking his head and laughing. "I feel old."

"Hush, the girls love it and it's so much easier to drive this around the subdivision." He gets in the back with Evelyn while Chandler sits next to me. She's fiddling with the radio as Evelyn shows Ajay that she can ride without holding on. The whole drive home I'm laughing, knowing Ajay is probably having some sort of fit back there.

At home, Chandler tells me that she'll see me in the morning and darts across our yard to her house while Ajay, Evelyn and I head inside ours.

"Fuck, it's cold in here."

"Daddy, you owe me a quarter."

Ajay digs into his pocket and hands her the money for her swear jar. He tries hard but is likely putting enough away to fund her college education. It's just a good thing no one is counting when we're alone or he might end up broke.

"Sorry," I tell him. "I was hot earlier."

"Maybe we can keep the air conditioner at sixty-five and not fifty," he says as he adjusts the dial to turn the AC back to normal.

"Noted. I'm going to go take a shower."

I leave him and Evelyn downstairs and head to the second floor. The room that was Ajay's band room is slowly being converted to a nursery. The walls are now a light blue and there's a black crib in there, a gift from Harrison and Katelyn. I stand in the doorway and look at what's becoming our son's room.

"I thought you were taking a shower," Ajay whispers into my ear as he presses against me. I lean back, molding into him.

"Just looking."

His hands caress my stomach. He's been waiting to feel his son kick since I told him he's started. I wish I could tell him when it will happen because soon doesn't seem to cut it anymore.

"He needs a name."

"I know, we'll make a list soon. Where's Evelyn?"

"Downstairs, wrapped in her blanket and watching cartoons."

"Mhm..."

"Does that mean what I think it does, Mrs. Ballard?"

"Like I said, I'm going to take a shower. Maybe you care to join me."

"Lead me to salvation, Whiskey."

I turn and look at my husband, thankful that I had the keen sense to listen to my heart when my thoughts were telling me to run. There isn't any other place I'd rather be than right here, in his arms, loving him for the rest of my life.

*The End!*

&

WANT TO TALK ABOUT BOOKS, movies, and have meme wars? Join us on Facebook in The Beaumont Daily

Continue reading for preview of SHATTERED STARS by Shari J. Ryan.

# SHATTERED STARS BY SHARI J. RYAN

*D*r. Sheila scribbles words onto a piece of paper, halting our conversation to concentrate. I'm struggling to see what she's writing, but my train of thought stumbles when a knock raps against the chestnut wooden door.

"Come in," Dr. Sheila calls out, still holding her gaze on the fresh piece of white paper.

"Your twelve o'clock is here," a woman speaks from the corridor. I glance down at my watch, noticing the time is ten past twelve. I didn't think our session had gone so late.

The visible space between the door isn't wide enough to catch who is speaking, but I suspect it's the young receptionist from the front desk.

"Thank you. We're wrapping up now," Dr. Sheila responds. A hiss embraces the conclusion of her remark, emphasizing an irritation. I wonder if Dr. Sheila doesn't have a high tolerance for assistants, or if the woman isn't doing her job well.

"I didn't realize the time was past twelve," I offer as an apology even though Dr. Sheila was the one speaking most.

This is only the first time I've met Dr. Sheila, so I'm not sure I have her figured out just yet. She seems nice enough, but I have the sense she's all work and not much play. However, if I hadn't already spoken to her, I might guess she's a stick in the mud by the sheen bouncing off her glossy hair, held in with a tight knot on the top of her head. Plus, her frameless glasses, and neutral pallet of a complexion don't offer her a fun and friendly appearance. I suppose I shouldn't be one to judge since it's her job to appear perfect, like nothing in her life would give her cause to be in my seat versus hers. I know it's a myth, though because even doctors need psychiatric help sometimes.

"It's all right. We can check in next month around this time, but if you encounter any side-effects or new symptoms before then, please call."

Dr. Sheila tears the paper from the stack and places it down on the desk in front of me. "Thank you," I reply, reaching for the prescription.

The brief moments of our exchange feel worthless, like I'm just another patient and this is just her job. I want to tell her how lucky she is to leave behind all these problems at the end of the night. How she can forget about everyone's troubles. However, despite Dr. Sheila's cold front, I wonder if she shuts her day out that way. Although, it seems like it at this moment since she can't seem to make eye contact.

I slip the paper into my bag and show myself out, striding as if in a trance. I don't know if I understand the irony of someone flushing narcotics through my body without hope of finding a solution. I'm not sure the pause button has the same effect on life as it does when watching a video or listening to a song. The inevitable is still there and part of me wonders if it will be easier once I reach that dark serenity.

The clouds are overbearing today, casting a chill in the late summer warmth. I locate the black Grand Cherokee with the fog lights highlighting the thick air. Mr. H perks up when he spots me walking toward the car and hops out to greet me as if I have a broken leg.

"What did she say?" he asks, hope filling his eyes just as it has every time I meet with a new doctor. I wish he wouldn't sound so excited to find out what happened. I've trained myself to ignore his optimism because I've worked hard to adjust my state of mind and to accept what is, knowing there is no good solution.

I reach into my purse and pull out the prescription she gave me. "Here," I offer with a sigh, handing it to him. "This is the solution given by the 'infamous' Dr. Sheila."

Mr. H glances down at the chicken scratch and shakes his head. "What is so difficult about alternative medicine? I thought that was Dr. Sheila's specialty? Did you press her for more advice?" I get it. He's distraught. It's because he feels hope.

It's not that I don't have hope, I'm just a realist. I'd rather not lie to myself.

"There are no other options," I repeat Dr. Sheila's words, verbatim.

"Yeah, well, I would have had choice words for her in response," he says.

"That's why I asked you to stay in the Jeep," I explain him with a lifted eyebrow and a slight arch to my lip.

"No more, Dani. I'm coming into these appointments with you. Maybe you're ready to accept all this, but I'm not. I will fight for you!"

"There's nothing to fight for," I argue, heading for the passenger side of the Jeep.

Mr. H snags my arm as I walk past him and he pulls me

into his chest, clasping my head against his ribcage. "Do you hear this sound?"

His heart is racing. It's pounding. "Yes."

"That's because of you. It's always been because of you and I won't let anything come between us."

"This is why I'm with you, Mr. H. This is why I fell in love with you." He has an uncontrollable need to love, and I've needed to be the recipient. It has saved me so many times, and I've wanted to believe it might be the one thing that always saves me.

"Don't call me Mr. H right now. It's not funny anymore."

"It's funny to me, so let me have my funny right now."

What isn't funny ... is that no amount of love in the world can save me from losing my mind.


Visit Shari J. Ryan for more!

275

# ACKNOWLEDGMENTS

Authors are always asked what our favorite book is or who are favorite characters are. For most, it's like choosing you one child over the other, a near impossible task. However, when I created Ajay and Whiskey, I had no idea where they would end up, until I started writing Chasing My Forever. Ajay was perfect for the Beaumont Series, an addition edition for Katelyn and Harrison, and a much needed friend for Quinn... you know since Noah's playing football (and hopefully trying to make Liam a grandfather). My heart ached for Ajay though. He was a lost boy, searching for a place to belong, and he found that with the James' and Sinful Distraction. While the original group from Beaumont will always be my number one, Ajay and Whiskey rose pretty high in the ranks of favorites!

I want to thank my agent, Marisa, for working tirelessly to make sure everyone across the globe has access to my novels. My team: Yvette, Traci, Ellie & Emma for making my words and thoughts more eloquent.

And to the readers: Without you, I wouldn't have anyone to tell stories to.

Huge shout-out to all the Beaumont Babes – you're pretty awesome!

## ABOUT HEIDI MCLAUGHLIN

Heidi McLaughlin is a New York Times, Wall Street Journal, and USA Today Bestselling author of The Beaumont Series, The Boys of Summer, and The Archers.

Originally, from the Pacific Northwest, she now lives in picturesque Vermont, with her husband, two daughters, and their three dogs.

In 2012, Heidi turned her passion for reading into a full-fledged literary career, writing over twenty novels, including the acclaimed Forever My Girl.

When writing isn't occupying her time, you can find her sitting courtside at either of her daughters' basketball games.

Heidi's first novel, Forever My Girl, has been adapted into a motion picture with LD Entertainment and Roadside Attractions, starring Alex Roe and Jessica Rothe, and opened in theaters on January 19, 2018.

*Don't miss more books by Heidi McLaughlin! Sign up for her newsletter, or join the fun in her fan group!*

*Connect with Heidi!*
www.heidimclaughlin.com

ALSO BY HEIDI MCLAUGHLIN

## THE BEAUMONT SERIES

Forever My Girl – Beaumont Series #1

My Everything – Beaumont Series #1.5

My Unexpected Forever – Beaumont Series #2

Finding My Forever – Beaumont Series #3

Finding My Way – Beaumont Series #4

12 Days of Forever – Beaumont Series #4.5

My Kind of Forever – Beaumont Series #5

Forever Our Boys - Beaumont Series #5.5

The Beaumont Boxed Set - #1

## THE BEAUMONT SERIES: NEXT GENERATION

Holding Onto Forever

My Unexpected Love

Chasing My Forever

Peyton & Noah

Fighting For Our Forever

## THE ARCHER BROTHERS

Here with Me

Choose Me

Save Me

See Me - Fall, 2019

LOST IN YOU SERIES

Lost in You

Lost in Us

THE BOYS OF SUMMER

Third Base

Home Run

Grand Slam

Hawk - Fall, 2019

THE REALITY DUET

Blind Reality

Twisted Reality

SOCIETY X

Dark Room

Viewing Room

Play Room

THE CLUTCH SERIES

Roman

STANDALONE NOVELS

Stripped Bare

Blow

Sexcation

Santa's Secret

Christmas With You

Made in the USA
Columbia, SC
03 August 2019